DAUGHTERS
OF A
DEAD
EMPIRE

DAUGHTERS OF A DEAD EMPIRE

CAROLYN TARA O'NEIL

ROARING BROOK PRESS
NEW YORK

Published by Roaring Brook Press
Roaring Brook Press is a division of Holtzbrinck Publishing Holdings
Limited Partnership
120 Broadway, New York, NY 10271 • fiercereads.com

Library of Congress Cataloging-in-Publication Data

Names: O'Neil, Carolyn Tara, author.
Title: Daughters of a dead empire / Carolyn Tara O'Neil.
Description: First edition. | New York : Roaring Brook Press, 2021. | Includes
bibliographical references. | Audience: Ages 14–18. | Audience: Grades 10–12. |
Summary: Set during the height of the Russian Revolution and told in
alternating voices, sixteen-year-old Evgenia—a peasant and proud member of
the Bolshevik party—agrees to help a seventeen-year-old bourgeois girl traverse
the war-torn countryside in search of safety, but Anna is harboring a secret that
could cost them their lives. Includes historical note and author's note.
Identifiers: LCCN 2021019720 | ISBN 978-1-250-75553-7 (hardcover)
Subjects: CYAC: Survival—Fiction. | Friendship—Fiction. |
Social classes—Fiction. | Communism—Fiction. | Anastasia, Grand Duchess,
daughter of Nicholas II, Emperor of Russia, 1901-1918—Fiction. |
Soviet Union. Red Army—Fiction. | Soviet Union—History—Revolution,
1917–1921—Fiction. | LCGFT: Novels. | Historical fiction.
Classification: LCC PZ7.1.O6445 Dau 2021 | DDC [Fic]—dc23
LC record available at https://lccn.loc.gov/2021019720

Our books may be purchased in bulk for promotional, educational, or business
use. Please contact your local bookseller or the Macmillan Corporate and
Premium Sales Department at (800) 221-7945 ext. 5442 or by email at
MacmillanSpecialMarkets@macmillan.com.

First edition, 2022 • Book design by Aurora Parlagreco
Printed in the United States of America

1   3   5   7   9   10   8   6   4   2

For Mom, who heard every thought I had about this book
and took each one seriously
And for Dad, who always knew I'd do this

CONTENTS

HISTORICAL NOTE

In 1917 the Russian people overthrew their tsar.

People were angry after years of losses in World War I. Millions of soldiers had died. There were severe food shortages. And many Russians wanted a representative government. They wanted to elect leaders who cared about them. They wanted freedoms of speech and assembly.

Protests began in Petrograd[1] and soon turned into riots that spread across the country. When the army joined the revolt, it was all over. **Tsar Nikolai Alexandrovich Romanov** stepped down after only eight days of protests. The new government put him and his family under house arrest.

That was called the *February Revolution.*

Then came the *October Revolution.* An extremist communist party, the **Bolsheviks**, seized power from the new government. They chased off all the moderate, socialist, and conservative parties that had been governing together.

The Bolsheviks withdrew the **Red Army** from WWI in 1918. This infuriated moderates and tsarists, who joined forces and raised the **White Army** to take back control of Russia. They also allied with the **Czechoslovak Legion**, a foreign army stuck on Russian soil that wanted only to return home but was blocked by hostile Bolsheviks.

And so the Russian Civil War began.

---

1 *Petrograd is now known by its original name, Saint Petersburg.*

PRONUNCIATION GUIDE

In Russia people go by three names:

first name + patronymic (father's name) + last name

In polite company you refer to someone using their first name + patronymic. However, among friends and family, people often use nicknames instead. Here are the names you will encounter in this story.

MAIN CHARACTERS

Evgenia Ivanovna Koltsova. Pronounced *yev-geh-nee-ya*.
Nickname: **Zhenya**. Pronounced *zhen-ya*. *Zh* is soft, like the *s* in the word *vision*.

Anna. Pronounced *ah-na*.
Nickname: **Anya**. Pronounced *on-ya*.
Nickname: **shvibzik**. Pronounced *sh-vib-zick*.

KEY CHARACTERS

Konstantin Ivanovich Koltsov. Pronounced *con-stan-teen*.
Nickname: **Kostya**. Pronounced *coast-ya*.

Alena Vasilyevna Koltsova. Pronounced *al-yo-na*.

Jiri Valchar. Pronounced *zhee-ree*. *J* is soft, like the *s* in the word *vision*.

Yakov Mikhailovich Yurovsky. Pronounced *yoo-raw-v-ski*.

Nurka Olegovna Petrova. Pronounced *nyoor-ka*.

Foma Gavrilovich Petrov. Pronounced *foh-ma*.

Buyan. Pronounced *boo-yah-n*.

PART ONE
THE ROAD

1

ANNA

I SAW THE FIRE FIRST. It flickered in and out of sight between the leaves far ahead, somewhere beyond the forest. Fire could only mean one thing: *people*.

I rushed forward with a burst of new energy, though it took all my power to move. My feet dragged like anchors. Low spruce branches scratched at my hair and sleeves. I was exhausted and sore from running so long, but having finally found a sign of hope, I would not stop.

If I stopped I'd have to think about the painful, black hole yawning inside me. Or of the Bolshevik soldiers who must have noticed by now that I was missing. Or of the bodies I had left behind.

My jacket was stiff with bloodstains and riddled with jagged holes, gruesome souvenirs. I could hardly ask for help in such a state. I would terrify anyone who saw me.

I pawed at the buttons frantically until I could tear the jacket off and throw it away, leaving it a misshapen lump hidden in the brush. It was unrecognizable as the garment that Mama had chosen for me only two years ago.

"You're so careless," Mama tutted as she held the blue cloth up between us. "This is the third new suit you've needed this summer. Don't you know there's a war on?"

"Of course, Mama. Next time I fall off my bicycle, I will take care to land on my head so I don't damage my dress."

Mama wrinkled her nose at me, fighting a smile.

"Shvibzik." She shook her head. "When will you grow up?"

"Only when I have to."

She huffed and pressed the fabric against my chest, satisfied that it would flatter me, running her gentle hand over the cotton.

I left it in the dirt, as I had done with everything else I once cared about.

Then I emerged from the forest.

An overgrown field sprinkled with clovers spread out before me. It sloped upward to a little house; I could no longer see the fire, but its smoke rose dark and steady from the other side of the dwelling. As I stared, the sound of accordion music started up. It was a lively tune, as for a barynya, and soon the noise of clapping hands joined in.

I laughed, my hope spilling over into delirious relief, and plucked leaves and burrs from my hair as I ran up the hill. The sun had risen high. I moistened my cracked lips, trying to remember when I last had something to drink. I could already taste my next cup. I had been wandering these mountain outskirts of Ekaterinburg for so long that at times I had doubted I would ever find my way out. But I had persisted, because as Papa liked to say, you could always find a solution if you kept working at it.

The house was no more than a hut, small and ramshackle, made of dark wooden logs. Its shutters hung crookedly. As I passed I saw that the entire side of the house was dotted with bullet holes.

I looked away.

Everything on the far side of the house was brightness and joy.

The yard held a couple dozen people, peasants, dancing and laughing, showing no sign that they were in the middle of a war. Women in colorful dresses and scarves spun one another around the clearing as a few elderly men played the accordion or clapped along. Little half-naked children chased one another in play, darting around swinging legs and hiding behind spectators. There were only a few other houses in sight, all as impoverished as this one.

At the edge of the yard, a few people had gathered around a rickety-looking wagon to examine clay pots and bolts of cloth for sale.

The fire was small, set next to a little outbuilding a good distance from the celebration. A large, surprisingly young man was busy tossing heaps of filthy, bloodstained rags into it. The fire dimmed momentarily, the smoke thickening, before it perked up brighter and more energetic than before. A few chickens that had been pecking at the grass nearby flapped and scurried away.

"Fine clay pots! Woven cloths and sarafans in many patterns!"

The vendor with the wagon was a young woman around my age. She had a strong, booming voice. Our eyes met as she surveyed the field in search of more customers. Hers narrowed, dark and hostile, before moving on. I must have looked like a beggar to her. I stepped backward, my dread rising, and stumbled into someone.

"Get off me!" The villager shoved me away.

I tripped over my own feet and fell to the dirt. My hands skidded against the rough, dry grass, and my skin broke open, red blood blooming on my palms with a sharp sting.

"*Kulak!*" she hissed.

My face burned. I climbed to my feet. The music slowed for a moment; the dancers looked around in confusion before picking up again as they seemed to decide, as one, to ignore me. The few people nearest to me moved away, avoiding me like some plague carrier.

"Take some syrniki, child. Here, zaika." An older woman, her shoulders hunched and gray hair tucked under a plain flowered scarf, was making her way through the crowd and handing out food. She bore a broad, flat, covered basket before her, and every so often lifted the lid to reveal the golden sweets.

My mouth watered, and I swallowed, grateful for the moisture. I drifted toward her. The last time I had eaten was—it could not have been more than a day or two earlier, but I did not quite remember. My mind shuddered away from memories of the Ipatiev house. All I knew was that I was starving.

"Excuse me, please," I said.

The old woman scowled. She studied me, her eyes alighting on the stains and tears in my skirt, my bleeding hands, my filthy, uncovered hair.

"One kopeck," she said.

"Please. I'm so hungry." My voice cracked on the word. I hated begging, but the smell of the warm syrniki dough enticed me. "Just one, please. I have nothing."

She looked at my blouse and skirt again.

"Looks like you used to have plenty. Now you know how it feels, eh, pomeschitsa?"

Now I knew how it *felt*? My entire family was gone, and she thought that because I once lived in a grand house and my skirt was made of finer cloth than hers, I deserved it? That *they* had deserved it?

Her cruelty landed like a blow. I was no one's landlord. I touched my chest, trying to ease my anger, to keep from saying something I would regret. Hand over my heart, just like Mama used to do when she tried to soothe me.

My fingers slid over a little rounded bump underneath the thin silk of my blouse.

Masha's necklace.

I shut my eyes. This icon had touched her skin, too. Here was a reminder that I was not entirely alone. Brother Grigori had blessed this necklace. Perhaps his protection had kept me alive.

And then I remembered—I had more than just this necklace. I had something else of value, too.

While fleeing through the forest, I had loosened my corset several times and came close to removing it entirely. But something held me back. And thank God it had. Hidden inside the lining of my corset were diamonds, emeralds, and sapphires—the last of my family's wealth.

I was no beggar. I carried my family's legacy with me. I *was* their legacy. And I would survive because they had not left me destitute or helpless. I had something to trade.

I looked after the syrniki woman once more, but despite my hunger, I could not waste the jewels on something so paltry. They would fetch thousands of rubles, enough to last me the rest of my life, once I made it to safety.

And I *would* make it to safety.

A woman walking with her daughter reluctantly pointed me in the direction of a well at the very edge of the field. Renewed with energy, I scooped one handful after another from the bucket, gulping down the fresh water, not stopping until I felt like a sopping sponge. I nearly cried with relief. My entire life, I'd never been far from a cool drink and a warm meal. As hard as things had been in the Ipatiev house, I'd never felt this pinching in my stomach, or the demanding scratch of my dry throat and tongue. Nothing had ever tasted as good as that first cup.

I took the time to wash my face and arms and smooth down my hair again. I didn't bother trying to wash the dried blood off my skirt or blouse; they were ruined for good. My thirst quenched for the moment and my stomach heavy from all the water, my thoughts began to work.

I had left Ekaterinburg behind. But even a day and a half of travel on foot could not have taken me far. This village was likely very close to Ekaterinburg, a virulently communist city. The peasants here might or might not be communists, but they all seemed to despise me on sight. I needed to get as far away as possible, as quickly as possible.

That meant a train. If they were still running. The nearest major station was Ekaterinburg itself, but I could not return there. I needed to locate a small transfer station on its route, or else head to the next nearest city. The north, from what little news had reached us in the Ipatiev house, I knew to be under Bolshevik control. But Chelyabinsk was to the south—and General Leonov, a friend of my family's, had control of that city with his White Army.

My cousin Alexander was stationed with him.

Chelyabinsk was only a few hours from Ekaterinburg by train. Help was closer than I thought.

I tilted my head back and let the warm sun bathe me. The laughter of the villagers, the lilting accordion music, and the rough singing voices washed over me. The earthy smell of the bonfire tickled my nose. I had a goal in mind, and for the moment, at least, peace.

Then the words of their song began to sound clearly:

> *Our Russian tsar called Nick*
> *We dragged off the throne by his prick*

I wandered closer to the crowd. An elderly man with a white beard and felt cap played the accordion, his wrinkled face lit with a grin. Next to him was a younger man, the youngest I'd yet seen in the village, standing on a wooden leg. With a crutch beneath his arm, he clapped in time to the chastushka and led the singing with his strong baritone as the dancing villagers sang along.

To all the people, the tsaritsa said:
"As for a republic, go fuck yourselves instead"

Someone seized my shoulder and shook me.

"Sing along!" he cried drunkenly. This was a burly man younger than my own father. He looked fit enough to be off fighting and smelled powerfully of beer. "It's a day of celebration!"

He forced a leaflet into my hands. I noticed that the small yard was littered with them.

July 18, 1918: In the last few days, Ekaterinburg was seriously threatened by the White and Czechoslovak armies. At the same time, a counterrevolutionary plot to rescue the imprisoned ex-tsar, Nikolai Romanov, was exposed. In view of this, the Ekaterinburg Regional Soviet resolved to shoot the ex-tsar, and this was carried out on the sixteenth of July. The Executive Committee in Moscow recognized that the Regional Soviet's decision was correct.

They were all communists.

"Traitors." The word ground out of me.

"What's that?"

"Traitors! You're all traitors," I spat. "And you're destroying our country. Stop that disgusting song!"

Something had burst inside me, so explosively that I felt like a ball of fire. I had not stopped to wonder why these peasants had all gathered. Now I understood that it was a party. They were cheering the death of our empire, of all that had made Russia great.

I could not stop yelling, even as the music ceased and everyone stared at me, my hatred mirrored in their faces. I didn't stop until the burly man took hold of me and hauled me against his chest.

"We've got a bourgeois traitor here," he called out over my head. "She doesn't like our song! What'll we do about it?"

His dirty arm squeezed me hard, and his sweaty stench stung my nostrils. I tried to break free, but that only made him hold tighter.

"Show her what we do to pomeshchiki!" someone shouted.

"Teach her who's in charge!"

More peasants gathered around us, no longer keeping their distance but pressing close, pointing at me, spitting. I had nowhere to run. I had fled the Bolsheviks only to find myself surrounded by them here, closing in on me, murder in their eyes.

I screamed.

"Let me go!"

The wooden-legged man staggered over, balancing on his rugged crutch. His eyes were glassy, his cheeks flushed, evidently as drunk as the brute still gripping my arms. He reached out and grabbed my face, crushing my jaw with rough, filthy fingers. He put his face close to mine.

"She wants to be let go," he growled. "Why don't we let her go over there?" He jutted his chin toward the bonfire.

My knees buckled. I slid, falling free of the man's arms; he was too slow to catch me. I scrambled up and started running, but both men grabbed me once more. They dragged me nearer to the fire.

Masha was screaming. Was that her voice, or mine?

"Burn her!" someone cheered.

The men held my arms and shoved me closer to the bonfire. The heat was like an open stove, lighting up my skin, melting my back and the rear of my legs into sweat.

"Bodies don't burn fast. We'll be out here all night."

"No!" I cried, lost between fear and memory. "Please let me go!"

"How's it feel, tsar lover? Still want us to shut up?"

Stumbling over the stones and tinder as they pushed me, I tripped into the fire. I screamed. The flame ate at my skirt, the fabric curling away in black pieces as the men holding me laughed. Then the heat hit, biting my legs, crawling up the fabric. I lashed out in panic.

The men released my wrists, and I windmilled away from the bonfire, slapping at the flame, spinning as the heat rose and the fire grew. It darted close to my face. I reared back and kept beating the cloth, making an unholy noise as the peasants around me looked on.

Then a fountain of water splashed over my legs. Most of the flames subsided at once. Another pair of hands appeared, joining me in beating out the last of the fire, until it was just our hands colliding over my legs and turning my skirt to black char.

I fell to my hands and knees and took in great gulps of air. My throat was raw from shouting.

"Bourgeois sympathizer!" The insult was hurled not at me, but at my rescuer. The crowd had forgotten me and turned to her. I raised my head to see the one person who had been willing to help me.

It was the girl with the wagon and the dark eyes. She wore a cheap kerchief on her head, a plain blue-and-white dress, and her feet were bare.

"Who asked you to interfere, Evgenia?" the accordionist snapped at her. "Don't think you'll be staying at our house tonight."

I stared at the girl, hoping that the expression on my face conveyed all the gratitude filling my heart. But she did not even look at me. She picked up her bucket and walked away, leaving me alone once more with the mob.

2

EVGENIA

NO ONE HAD ANY DAMN MONEY. After days of driving between villages to sell my neighbor's clay pots and other goods, I was only fifty kopecks richer than when I'd left home. Normally I'd call that a good return for a wagoning trip, but it would take at least two rubles to hire a doctor for my brother. That was four times what I'd made.

The Pavlovo villagers had crowded around my wagon like crows circling spilled oats. They were all looking for a good deal. And like me, they were all as rich as beggars. No one wanted to *pay* for anything. They just wanted to trade. It'd almost been worth the trip to hear the news of the tsar's execution, but I didn't have time to waste. My family needed me on the farm.

Then that stupid, bourgeois otrodye got herself set on fire.

Her timing couldn't have been worse. A White company had just passed through this village days ago. They'd torn up peoples' homes, burned crops, taken their food, chased the women, and left behind a mess of broken furniture and garbage that the people of Pavlovo now lit up in their bonfire. It didn't surprise me that they wanted to add that girl to the pile.

But I couldn't let them burn her. Even a landlord's brat didn't deserve that. I'd seen it happen before, and it wasn't something I ever wanted to watch again. The only problem was that in saving her, I'd put myself right in her place.

I scooped up my bucket and walked away quickly. My cheeks heated as people hollered insults at my back. *Svolochi.* I was a proud Bolshevik and Redder than any of them. Mama's second cousin, who'd just kicked me out of his house for the night, knew that perfectly well. But arguing with an angry crowd would put me in danger. It didn't matter what they thought. Helping one lost girl with a bleak face didn't make me any less of a revolutionary.

My wagon sat under a cluster of tall poplar trees at the edge of the yard. It was an old, solid dray made of tough birchwood, two cubits high with open sides and sturdy wheels. The bed had plenty of room for the goods that I traded and sold along my route—clay pots, scarves, linens, dishes, whatever I could find. And a little ways behind it stood my most prized possession.

"Time to go, Buyan," I said. I untied my horse's lead rope from the tree. "We've overstayed our welcome. Maybe we'll do better in Iset." He bobbed his head agreeably. Buyan wasn't an elegant horse. He was strong, stocky, and short like me. And just like me, when there was something important that needed doing, he got it done.

Except I'd screwed up this time. I hadn't made enough money. There was only one town left on my route, Iset, and my chances at raising a couple of rubles there were smaller than a fly's shit.

My brother had caught a bullet in his left leg while fighting with the Red Army. The army doctors sawed his leg off before the wound could kill him, and then they sent him home. Now Kostya was always in pain. Sometimes his leg would swell and turn red. Mama and I didn't know how to help him. Our village healer was a fool who thought chanting would make a festering wound heal faster. I wanted Kostya to see a real doctor. I wanted to get him medicine. But the only doctor closer than Ekaterinburg lived in Iset, and he wasn't likely to travel home with me without payment.

It didn't look like that would happen. Four days on the road, four days leaving Mama and Kostya to work the fields alone, and I had little to show for it.

I was the fool.

"Come *on*, Buyan. We don't have time for this, damn you." He pulled against me, unwilling to leave the shade. He was always slow to start, stubborn on a good day. And on days like this, with the sun shining hot enough to crack a rock, he could dig in his heels. I tugged harder, aware of the people behind me that could be stirred to violence again at any moment.

"There is something bothering his front hoof." The soft, hoarse voice came from behind me.

It was the bourgeois girl. She'd followed me from the crowd, where the music and dancing had started again. She looked even worse close up. There was dried blood on her neck and clothes, under a layer of dirt. Her lips were flaking, and her eyes were wide and wild. Her messy hair was cut short, like a boy's. She also talked funny. If she was a landlord's daughter, she wasn't from anywhere near here.

And if she thought we'd be friends just because I dumped some water on her, she was wrong.

"Nobody asked you," I said. The truth was, I was a little embarrassed she saw me fight with my own horse. Worse, she saw me lose.

"Please, allow me to assist," she said. She crouched next to Buyan's left foreleg, which he *was* favoring. Before I could stop her, she coaxed him to lift his hoof and picked out a stone stuck deep in the sole. She tossed the pebble aside. "See? I have a talent for dealing with animals." She looked proud of herself. Like she knew my own horse better than I did.

"Good for you," I said. I took Buyan's lead again and started for the wagon.

She followed me.

"Excuse me," she said.

I ignored her. I'd done enough for her already. If she wanted a handout, she could look for it somewhere else. No landlord had ever showed *my* family charity. People like this girl didn't care when peasants went hungry. They enjoyed their fancy homes and rich food while we couldn't even afford doctors.

"I beg your pardon," she tried again.

"Fuck off."

"I was only wondering," she said more firmly, "if I might be able to purchase a ride in your wagon."

That got my attention. I turned to face her.

Her dark blue skirt, what was left of it, was made of good cotton. Her blouse was so fine I didn't recognize the material.

She was definitely a rich landlord's daughter and had probably been chased off her land. Sometimes things got violent when wealthy families didn't want to leave. They'd bring out their guns, but then more villagers would come with rifles, pitchforks, and fire. She looked like she'd just come from that kind of battle.

These days the peasants always won. The government was on our side now, and the police didn't care.

"You have money?" I asked.

Her eyes focused, more alert, like a sleepy old man waking up from a nap.

"I helped your horse," she said.

"And I saved your life. Do you have money or not?"

"You did save me," she said, still not answering my question. "And I thank you for it. And if you leave me here with these communists, it will have been for nothing. They will throw me back into the fire the moment—"

I finished tying Buyan to the wagon and climbed on. The way she said *these communists* made it clear whose side she was on. She might be my age, but without the revolution she'd have grown up into another landlord who didn't care how we suffered. Now it was her turn to suffer. Maybe she'd learn something.

"No, wait!" she cried. "I *can* pay you. I do not have money, but I can offer you something valuable, if you would only stop and let me show you!"

"Then show me," I snapped. She wasn't carrying a bag, she wasn't wearing an apron with pockets, and her clothes were too ruined to trade. Still, I couldn't turn my back on the word *valuable*. Even communists hadn't gotten rid of money yet.

The girl glanced behind her at the villagers, then hurried to the other side of my wagon. She turned her back on me and unbuttoned her blouse. So that was her secret. Whatever she had was hidden under her clothes. I noticed a thin, fancy-looking gold chain around her neck, but she didn't remove it. Instead, she quickly dressed again and then turned. She stuck out her hand.

In her palm lay what looked like a small piece of glass, but it shone like it was full of stars. I'd seen bits of quartz from the mines where some of our men went to work but never anything like this. It was no wider than a fingernail, with clean, sharp lines and more edges than I could count. As she lifted it closer to me, it caught the sunlight and flashed rainbows on her fingers.

"Is that a jewel?"

"A diamond," she said, "and an extremely fine one, I assure you. Any jeweler will pay you good money for this, at least several hundred rubles, if not more. It is yours, in exchange for a ride to the nearest train station."

I looked around. Luckily no one was close enough to hear her.

"Put it away," I said.

Hundreds of rubles. I'd heard of diamonds before. Now I could see why rich people paid so much for them. It was beautiful. If I could really trade it for that much, then everything would change. I wouldn't just hire a doctor for Kostya. I could buy a new home for my family. We could even move to the city. We'd live in a house with glass windows and a chimney, on a paved road. I'd get a job in a factory, and Mama wouldn't have to work at all.

I shook myself. I wouldn't let dreams cloud my common sense. This otrodye was probably lying. If things ever changed for my family, it would be because communism lifted us all together. Not because of speculators like her.

After our revolution toppled the tsar a year ago, counter-revolutionaries like her raised the White Army to fight us. They wanted to bring back the monarchy so they could steal back their land. I had no reason to trust this girl.

But that shiny diamond was worth *something*. More than two rubles.

"Get on," I said.

She hurried up next to me, sitting so close our elbows bumped. Her knees stuck out past mine, just like Kostya's when he taught me to steer the wagon. Her long skirt wasn't just blackened and tattered, it also had dark spots and tears above the burn marks. Her fancy blouse was the same. She kept fidgeting in her seat like a guilty child.

She smelled of sweat and desperation. Mama always said you could never tell what a desperate person might do. I'd been wagoning for only a few months, and I almost never picked up strange passengers. I had to be careful.

"Give me the jewel," I said.

Her blue eyes narrowed. "I shall pay you when we arrive at the train station. You already know that I have it to offer you. Why should I hand it to you upfront?"

"Because I don't trust you. Or you're welcome to go ask one of the Pavlovo villagers to take you."

"Why should I trust *you*?"

"I'm helping you when no one else will. We won't reach

Ekaterinburg until after dark, and the roads aren't safe. The White Army is everywhere. I'm taking the risk—"

"Not Ekaterinburg," she interrupted. "I need to find a different train station. I cannot go back to that city."

"You said the nearest station." This was exactly why you couldn't believe pretty stories from strangers.

"Surely there is a way station, or somewhere else I might get on."

"Not closer than the city! I'm not taking you halfway to Nizhny Tagil—"

"What about to the south? I am trying to reach Chelyabinsk."

Of course she was. Chelyabinsk was controlled by the Whites.

Besides that, it would take days to reach. I could already feel the diamond slipping away. I should've known that something so fine wasn't for me. My family toiled and saved when we needed something, like all peasants. I was an idiot for thinking that riches would fall into my lap.

"Please," she said. "I cannot stay in this town, and I can tell that you want my diamond. We can think of a solution. Are you certain there is nowhere else I can board the train? No other way for me to reach Chelyabinsk besides returning to the city?"

Her steady words made me stop and think.

"There's a mail coach," I said. "It passes through Iset, the biggest town in this area. But no one there has the kind of money you're looking for. You would trade your diamonds at a loss. I'm guessing you have more stashed away in there, right?" I pointed my chin at her chest.

She stiffened.

"No. I showed you my only jewel. That is all I have."

"Then how did you plan to buy a train ticket?"

She didn't answer.

"That's what I thought. You give me the first jewel now and I'll help you sell another one in Iset. It won't fetch much, but I'm sure we can make enough to get you on the coach. And I'll take two more rubles in payment for making the sale. Deal?"

Her lips narrowed as she gritted her teeth, clearly annoyed. She didn't like it. But if she had any sense at all, she'd say yes.

I waited. Sometimes you had to give customers time to get used to an offer.

"Very well," she said tightly. She dropped the diamond into my hand. "I accept your deal."

3

ANNA

THE PEASANT GIRL WAS NAMED Evgenia Ivanovna Koltsova. She was sixteen years old, a year younger than me, but evidently mature enough to travel through the countryside alone—even as war raged. For days back in Ekaterinburg my family and I had listened to the distant sounds of artillery fire. The White Army was fighting its way closer every day, and until the very last, my parents were certain that they would rescue us.

The Ipatiev house was made of stone, cold even in summer, and perpetually dark—not due to its architecture, but because the Bolsheviks covered all the windows with wooden boards or whitewash. It was a two-story mansion, but they had confined the eleven of us to just three rooms. We were never permitted to leave, and the Red guards watched our every move.

"*As long as we stay together, shvibzik,*" Papa had said more than once, using my old nickname, "*we can survive whatever trials may come.*"

He had never been so wrong. Now I was alone, bouncing

painfully along this quiet dirt road, next to a girl who smelled of rancid sweat and hay and who was almost certainly a communist.

"Do you live very far from this town?" I asked.

She barely glanced at me, but frowned, as she did every time I spoke.

"This isn't a town," she said in her country accent.

We had driven some ways from the bonfire and passed a few more peasant houses, and were now traveling through farmland. Several of the fields were charred, destroyed by some recent calamity.

"It's barely a village. I'm from Mednyy. That's half a day's ride north of Iset, where we're going."

She said it with some pride, so I did not mention that I had never heard of Iset, let alone Mednyy. Now that she knew I had come from Ekaterinburg it was easier to let her think that I lived there and had at least some familiarity with this part of the country. In truth I was completely ignorant. My experience of this area was confined to one house, a yard, and a basement.

"Your parents allow you to drive all this way by yourself?" I asked her.

"We need the money."

"Do you not worry about getting caught up in the fighting?"

"Are *you* worried?" she asked crossly.

I thought about the Red soldiers who had driven my family's bodies out to the woods in the dark of night. Who had unquestionably realized, by now, that I was not among them.

Whom I had run from for a day and night, terrified that they would appear behind me.

"Yes," I admitted. "Doesn't your father worry about keeping you safe?"

Her face creased. Everything I said landed badly with her, as though she were determined to dislike me.

"He's dead. Thanks to pomeshchiki like you who forced us to work their land, took our livestock, and left us to starve."

I sucked in a sharp breath. It was people like her who had killed *my* father. They were angry, greedy communists who used guns as casually as drawing breath. They'd murdered my parents, who had been the kindest people in Russia.

I wanted to slap her, to shove her straight off the wagon, tell her exactly what was wrong with her and every other lazy rebel who stole what they had not earned and killed whoever got in their way. Instead, I gritted my teeth, closed my eyes, and prayed for mercy.

Help me through this, I prayed. *I only need her to reach the mail coach, and once I do I'll never have to hear her spiteful voice again. Please just help me bear this.* I pressed my hand over the bump under my shirt, feeling Masha's icon beneath the fabric. Gradually, my breathing steadied. I was able to open my eyes and look at Evgenia's sulky face without wanting to strike her.

She was nothing more than a misguided child. She was not worth the effort of hating.

"I am sorry for your loss," I said. And then—to my own surprise—I found myself adding, "My father died as well." Just saying the words sent a tremor through me. He was gone.

They were all truly gone. The past two days had been a

nightmare. Two days ago I had had parents who loved me, a brother who spoke of finding peace outside of Russia, and sisters who dreamed of marriage and travel and study and parties and good works—all of their dreams interrupted. Nothing was left now but absence and memory.

I touched my icon again.

Evgenia pretended not to hear.

"Iset's not much farther," she said a while later. "We're nearly there."

"We're nearly there."

The Bolshevik guards spoke quietly in the night. I blinked my sticky eyes open, adjusting to the darkness, and saw bodies all around me. Olga's arm was flung across my forehead. Alexei sprawled on top of me, crushing my lungs; blood from his torso seeped onto mine. Someone's nose pressed into the back of my neck. I had to pull my arm free and clamp my hand over my mouth to keep from screaming. I wanted to explode, to shatter into a hundred pieces, to disappear and not be trapped among the dead. I knew that I needed to move. If I did not flee, the Bolsheviks would discover me alive and kill me, too.

"Bodies don't burn fast. We'll be out here all night," Commander Yurovsky said. He was riding a horse ahead of the wagon that carried our bodies. His low growl sent ice skating down my skin. The last time I had heard his voice, he had been announcing our execution.

"Buyan needs a drink," Evgenia said, her slurring, country accent jolting me from my thoughts. I grasped my own arms, reminding myself that I was safe and the commander far behind me.

We had been driving for at least a couple of hours by then. For a while we traveled alongside farmland, but at some point the road dipped back into forest. Tall evergreens curved together overhead, casting speckled shadows on the ground as the day grew later.

"Of course," I said as she stopped the wagon. I dabbed my forehead with my sleeve, grateful for the shade and silence.

Evgenia fetched a full bucket of water from the wagon bed, then took a drink herself from a flask.

"Want some?" she asked, holding it up to me.

"Oh," I said. "Yes, thank you."

"Don't sound so surprised," she muttered, almost too quiet to hear. I eagerly downed the rest of the water, but could not make myself ignore her.

"You continually surprise me," I said.

"I do?"

"Yes," I said. I carefully climbed down and returned her flask. "Sometimes you are kind and generous, and other times you seem to hate me."

"I don't hate you. I don't even know you."

"No, you don't," I agreed, and was pleased to see how that caught her off guard. "Now if you will excuse me, I need to . . . relieve myself."

"Toilet's there." She jutted her thumb toward the trees.

I felt some misgiving at leaving her with both the wagon and diamond, but I had little alternative. Besides, she seemed busy enough with her horse, so I lifted the ragged hem of my skirt and made my way deep into the tree cover. In addition to train tickets, I would have to ask Evgenia for help finding something new to wear once we reached Iset. Even a peasant dress would be an improvement.

I found a low, bushy tree to hide behind and pulled at my petticoat and combinations. It was far from the first time I had ever gone about this outdoors, but I could not help imagining how my sisters would react if they saw me. Masha would giggle, and Tatiana would scold, and Olga would roll her eyes at all of us and point out that some indignities couldn't be avoided.

I was so caught up in the reverie that I missed the sound of approaching horses until the ground beneath me shook. They came to a stop in front of the wagon.

I froze. My heart must have stopped, because when it beat again it pounded into my throat. Horses almost certainly meant soldiers, and these had been moving quickly. I could no longer see Evgenia or the road through the trees. It was safer to stay hidden here, but I could not tell how many had come, nor if they were Red or White troops.

Then I heard his voice.

"Come forward."

He had found me.

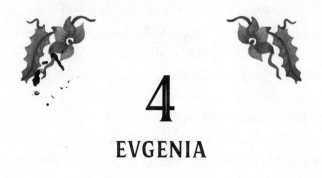

4

EVGENIA

I DIDN'T LIKE RUNNING INTO soldiers. As soon as I heard the galloping in the distance, I grabbed my knife from its slot under the wagon bench.

Four men on horseback came hard around the bend. They drew up short at the sight of my wagon, dashing my hopes that they would pass us by. Soldiers were unpredictable. I stuck to these smaller, older roads just to avoid them. But lone bands of soldiers wandering the countryside away from their battalions were much easier to predict. They always meant trouble.

The group trotted to a stop a few cubits ahead of me. All four men wore budenovki embroidered with red stars. So they were Reds, at least. A thick beam of sunlight shone down onto the man in front. It lit him up like a saint in an old religious painting. He wore the same khaki uniform as the rest of his men, but I spotted two red squares and a red star sewn onto his shirtsleeve. That meant he was a company commander.

"Come forward." He pointed to the ground in front of him.

I dropped the knife into my pocket before walking over to

them. The Whites were the ones you really had to be careful around. They tore up villages and robbed peasants, like they'd done to Pavlovo. They saw us as lazy, uneducated children who needed landlords to control us. As long as we kept quiet and farmed their land, they didn't care if we went hungry.

"Hello, comrade," I said.

The commander stared down at me coolly. Like he knew that if he told me to jump, or sit, or run in circles like a chicken, I'd do it.

Then he dismounted, and I wished I hadn't stashed my knife.

He was tall, with a sharp nose and aggressive eyes. He was older, maybe forty. Leather straps crisscrossed his chest, holding a long rifle on his back. His hand rested on the rifle strap casually. He stood very still. I could tell that if I said the wrong thing, he'd have that rifle pointed at my face faster than the flap of a warbler's wing.

Like a nervous recruit, I saluted him.

"At ease, comrade," he said with a smirk. It was mocking, but it was also a sign of good humor that made me feel easier. "Do you know this area well?"

"Yes, I take this road often."

"We're looking for an escaped prisoner," he said. "What's the nearest place someone might seek shelter around here?"

"There are a few," I said. "I just came from Pavlovo. It's up that way, a bit. Or you can go back the way you came to reach Iset. That's where I'm heading. It's the biggest town in the area."

"Very good." He started for his horse, then turned back to me. "Have you seen anything unusual? Any strangers?"

"There were a few visitors in Pavlovo," I said. "We heard

they executed the tsar, so we were all celebrating. But no one who looked like a prisoner." It was too bad, really. I would've liked to help catch a counterrevolutionary prisoner. My best friend, Dasha, would've been so jealous.

The commander smiled.

"It was long past time that the tsar paid for his crimes," he said. "We lost too many men to his wars."

"Yes," I said, thinking of my oldest brother. "We did."

"So you didn't see any strange bourgeois around? Male or female, we don't want the wrong people stirring up trouble."

My breath stuck in my throat. There was Anna, of course. She was bourgeois. But why would a Red commander care about the young, lost daughter of a landlord? He had better things to do, like catching escaped prisoners. Right? If I told him about Anna, and he asked to see her, he might search her and take her jewels. He might search *me*. Then I'd be left with nothing for my trouble.

"No," I said, my voice tight.

His eyes narrowed.

"Are you sure?"

I hesitated. Kostya would be ashamed of me if he knew that I'd lied to a Bolshevik commander.

But I'd rather he be ashamed and healthy than proud and sick.

"I'm sure, comrade," I said.

The commander looked me over from head to toe, like he was memorizing me. Like a book he was reading. My heart beat too fast, and my hands itched. I clenched them so he wouldn't see them shake.

He finally nodded. I let out a big breath as he climbed back on his horse, and he and his men galloped off.

I hugged Buyan quickly, trying to shake off my guilt. I didn't like lying. And lying to a Red Army commander was a new low for me.

But it was a harmless lie. And it would be worth it. For my family.

"Ey, Anna," I called. "Come out already. The soldiers have left."

She didn't answer. I headed into the woods to find her.

I almost stepped on her. She was crouched behind a tree with her skirts still up, not pissing anymore. She shook like a struck bell. Tears poured down her face. She looked like a rabbit about to have its throat slit.

"What the devil is wrong with you?" I asked, afraid to touch her.

Her eyes flew open. She stared at me like a madwoman.

"Has he gone?" she whispered.

Her white lace underthings were dark with moisture. She'd peed all over herself. Was she really this scared of soldiers? I cleared my throat uncomfortably.

"Yes, he's gone. What's the problem?"

"H-his name is Yurovsky," she said, still whispering. "He is evil." Her voice broke on the word.

I thought back to the way the commander had looked me up and down. If I were superstitious and believed in evil, I'd be worried.

"Stop crying," I said irritably. "How do you know him?"

Anna just shook her head, and I threw my hands out in

frustration. Anyway, I could guess from her reaction. Yurovsky must've been the one to chase her out of her home. Maybe he even killed her father. Now she was alone and terrified.

Was he looking for her?

"Can you get dressed?" I asked.

She didn't answer.

"*Chyort*," I cursed.

I wiped her damp legs with some leaves, then tried to fix her underthings but couldn't figure out how the fancy waste of cloth worked. In the end I just pulled down her skirts and helped her stand.

This was more than I'd bargained for in selling her a ride. I should've remembered that money never came easy. Part of me felt bad for her, anyway. Hoarding parents like hers deserved what they got, but it was a shame when children were orphaned in the process. Anna wasn't exactly a child, but she didn't have enough sense to be on her own. And she definitely wasn't a threat to anyone.

At least my actions quieted her. I led her to a nearby stream and cleaned some of the mess off her, then did what I could to neaten her hair so she looked a little less crazed.

Just a little, though.

5

ANNA

I SAT BESIDE EVGENIA IN the wagon and closed my eyes, letting her think I had fallen asleep. But I was lost in a void. Mama—Papa—thoughts of them flitted close and then shattered, too frightful to hold on to, leaving only the darkness. Commander Yurovsky's voice echoed through my mind. It hounded me, just as he stalked me in real life. He was hunting me.

> *Papa's body spasmed. At the same moment, a sharp pain stopped my heart.*
>
> *When I awoke later, the ground was trembling beneath me. We were no longer in the Ipatiev house. I lay in the back of a wagon and could only see straight up, past Olga's arm, to where the edges of pine trees pressed like daggers against the black sky.*

I had fainted when the soldiers shot us, and they assumed I had died. They piled my body in the wagon with the rest of my family. If I had regained consciousness any earlier, they would have spotted me—or any later, and I would have been burned, too. God had protected me. But why me and not them? Mama and Olga used to attend church every day. They were the ones who dragged the rest of us whenever we had been away too long; usually that meant every few days. Papa had been deeply devout, as well. Why did God reward their faith with violent death?

I had been the least worthy of my family. The least pious, the least kind, the least studious—the least important in every way. So why had God spared my life and taken theirs?

"This is Iset."

We had turned the corner into town. Iset certainly looked much larger than the village where Evgenia and I had met. The road continued along with houses lining either side not far ahead. The road was still unpaved and dusty, but at least we had found signs of life again. I saw people walking in the distance, young and old. Farther off, a faded white onion dome peeked over a hill.

The sun was beginning to set behind the mountains. My limbs still felt weak from our encounter with Commander Yurovsky. I kept glancing at the road behind us, worried that he might reappear. His rage at discovering my body missing must have been terrible. I had never witnessed him lose his temper, but the threat of it had always been there when we were his prisoners. And I knew how dedicated he was to the Bolshevik cause.

Once, in the Ipatiev house, the commander had joined us for tea, and he and Papa fell into a debate about the war.

Papa had listed out all the horrible deeds committed by the Bolsheviks—the betrayal of their political allies, their violent coup. He had finished by asking if such crimes did not reveal the ugly heart of the Bolshevik Party.

Commander Yurovsky had listened intently to Papa's words before giving his answer.

"Our cause," he had said, "is complete equality. It is freedom from poverty and an end to the rule of greed. If other countries follow our lead, even an end to war. I would give my life to that cause, Nikolai Alexandrovich. As much as I love them, I'd give my children's lives to it. The leaders of our party feel the same. *That* is our true nature."

Chills had run down my spine to hear him speak of his own family that way. From what the local servants said, the commander was a loving husband and father to three young children. Yet he would sacrifice them all to his fanaticism.

If he was hunting me, then nothing would stop him. I would not be safe until I was not merely in White Army territory but under the protection of leaders who knew my worth. Someone like General Leonov. He could keep me out of Commander Yurovsky's reach. As tranquil as Iset seemed, there was no safety for me here. I was only grateful that whatever Evgenia had said to the commander, it had sent him continuing in the wrong direction.

That thought aroused my curiosity.

"Evgenia, what did you say to Commander Yurovsky?"

"Oh, you can talk again."

"Please answer my question," I said, straining to keep my voice mild. The peasant girl was as irritable as a cat.

"I didn't say anything. He's looking for some prisoner and was asking his way to the next town. I told him about Iset, but I guess he'd already been here."

"Did you direct him somewhere else?"

"No, I just told you. He probably went on to Pavlovo."

I leaned away from her, astounded by her foolishness. As soon as he reached Pavlovo, the people there would tell the commander that Evgenia and I had left together. He would turn right around and come after us. As fast as his horses were, he could make it here before nightfall and comb the entire town looking for me. I would not be safe anywhere.

I wanted to snap at Evgenia for her stupidity, for not sending the commander off in a different direction. Then I realized—she didn't understand that *I* was the prisoner he sought.

"I see," I said.

"Listen, you can't walk around Iset like that." She pointed at my ruined skirt. "I have an extra sarafan you can wear. You can pay me for it when we sell your jewel."

"The day is already growing late," I said. "We mustn't waste time. We should—"

"Iset is blood Red. Believe me, if they realize you're a landlord's daughter, they won't want anything to do with you."

She pulled her horse to a stop and leaned over to dig around the boxes in the back of her wagon. I glanced up the empty road again. Complying would be quicker than arguing with her, and I needed the clothing, so I accepted the cheap, rough gown that she handed me and unfastened my skirt, jumping down to take shelter behind the wagon.

Underneath my petticoat, my combinations were undone. I paused, surprised—and then felt the skin on my neck and back heat. I had forgotten that I'd soiled them. Evgenia had not merely sent Commander Yurovsky on his way. She had helped me wash and gently led me back to the wagon, all the while speaking softly to me. She had not once scolded or shouted at me. She had been patient. Kind.

Because I had frozen at the sound of his voice. Helplessness had stolen over me like a fog, and I had not been able to move at all. What would I do if he found me again?

I needed Evgenia. I needed *someone* to protect me.

I drew the peasant garment on over my blouse. It was red, with simple white flowers, and it covered most of the stains on my shirt. The silk blouse and linen sarafan looked odd together but would certainly call less attention than my ruined skirt. I rolled the skirt and petticoat into a ball and dropped them into the field; the tall wheat hid them well. Piece by piece, I was leaving the remnants of my old life behind.

"That's better," Evgenia said when I climbed back on the wagon. She nodded in approval.

"Where exactly are we going?" I asked as we began moving again. "Is there a town supervisor or a mayor we can deal with?"

She scoffed.

"No. That coward fled last year. Iset has a soviet now. I've got a letter to deliver to the chairman, so we'll start at his house. Then we can go on to Vitaly Stravsky's. He's a member of the soviet, too, but more likely to buy something under the table."

So Iset was under communist rule, like Ekaterinburg.

Which meant that I would be in danger again even if Commander Yurovsky did not return this way.

"Why are *you* carrying a letter for him?"

"I'm part of a Bolshevik group in Mednyy," she said proudly. "We're trying to set up a soviet there, too. Since I have this wagon, and Buyan, I act as messenger."

I swallowed, my mouth drying. "You are a Bolshevik, then."

"Is that a problem?" She raised her brow.

"Of course not," I said at once, even as the hopes I had been clinging to shriveled inside me.

"In fact," I made myself say, "that is excellent. If you know the leader of the soviet here, then we can sell my diamond directly to him. Surely the most important man in town would make the best customer."

She furrowed her brow.

"Comrade Morozov won't want anything to do with this. Stravsky's the one who always did business in the city. He made a lot of money selling the local millet. He swears he's reformed, but my brother says he's still a capitalist at heart. He won't have any problem turning around your jewel for a profit."

"Then we must go directly to him and not tarry. We do not know when the mail coach will pass through town, do we? We cannot take the risk of missing it."

"Relax, Anna. There's only two roads through town. We won't miss it."

"But—"

"The Morozov house is on the way to Stravsky's. Look, it's just ahead," she said, pointing to a house in the distance. "I'll be in and out."

We were in Iset proper by then. The houses were small, single-story cabins spaced close together and bordered by simple plank fences. A few old women and small children wandered in and out. Some of them called out greetings to Evgenia as we passed. The women went about their chores, gardening or washing, while the children carried rags and buckets or chased naughty hens back into their yards. All of them, especially the children, were coated in a layer of dirt that made me feel less self-conscious in my stained blouse and ill-fitted sarafan.

Evgenia stopped us in front of one of these cabins. She bade me wait in the wagon before entering through the front gate. I sat in full view of the road and houses and grew more nervous with every breath.

A few small children walked up to gawk at me, asking me questions that I ignored with a smile, while women walked by and glared suspiciously.

"Are you lost?" one of them stopped to ask. She had a narrow face and carried a basket laden with cabbages. When I didn't answer at once, she placed it down and folded her arms. "Can you not speak?"

"I am not lost, thank you. I am waiting for my friend inside the house."

"What friend? I don't see anyone. Where are you from? Are you visiting someone?" She walked closer and examined my clothing with interest. Some of the little children began meandering back to eavesdrop.

I twisted my hands nervously. I was attracting too much attention, and it was all Evgenia's fault, as she was taking far longer than promised. This woman seemed friendly enough. But the fewer people who noticed me, the better.

"Yes, my friend will be out any minute now," I said.

"You sound like a city girl," the woman pressed. "Where are you from?"

The gate creaked open and shut heavily. Evgenia finally emerged. She recognized the nosy woman and exchanged polite pleasantries with her, then outright told her that I was a traveler she'd picked up on the road.

From my seat in the wagon, I gently nudged her in the back with my foot.

Somewhat gently.

She whirled on me.

"Watch it," she snapped.

"We must get going," I reminded her.

Evgenia curled her lip, bid the woman goodbye, and joined me in the wagon to take up the reins once more.

"You took forever," I added. "You said you would be in and out."

"I wasn't that long."

"That woman asked so many questions—"

"Why shouldn't she? Are you hiding something?" she demanded. She gave me a long look when I didn't answer. "Where'd you get those jewels, anyway? Are you supposed to have them?"

I was used to her maligning my character by then, but this was something new.

"Did something happen when you were visiting the chairman?"

"Nothing happened," she muttered. "I just remembered myself. You and I are meant to be equals now, but you're hoarding jewels. And I'm helping you." She shook her head.

"These jewels," I said tightly, clenching my teeth, "are all that I have left of my family. And selling them is the only way I will reach my friends in Chelyabinsk. If you abandon me now, you will have come all this way for nothing. Is that what you want?"

She scowled, as usual, but gave in. We drove the rest of the way in silence. Farther into town, nearer to the church, the houses began to spread out more. These homes looked sturdier, with wooden roofs instead of thatch, and in better repair. They bordered more forest instead of farmland.

Vitaly Stravsky's house surprised me. It was two stories tall, painted white, with glass panes in the windows. True, it was in some disrepair, as a few shingles had fallen off, and the yard was overgrown and weedy. But compared to every other house I had seen since leaving Ekaterinburg, this was the only one that appeared decent. Perhaps the merchant would be of even more help than I had expected.

One of the windows on the side of the house was open. As Evgenia stopped the wagon and the noise of the wheels and rickety joints faded, we heard music coming from the house. It was a violin suite, part of a composition I could not quite place. Tatiana would have been able to identify it at once. The song was melancholy, and slow, and I smiled, because if this Stravsky took the time to collect and appreciate modern music, then he couldn't be a heartless, full-blooded communist. Evgenia's suspicions that he was not entirely reformed must be correct—which boded well for me.

I climbed off the wagon, only to notice that Evgenia had

not moved. Her mouth had fallen open. She stared at the house, stunned into silence by the music.

"Evgenia?" I prompted.

She shook herself and gave a little laugh.

"He has a phonograph," she said. "That's recorded music!"

I did not know quite what to say.

"Yes," I agreed.

"Oh," she said, seeming to realize that I was not as impressed. "Well, he's obviously home. Let me settle Buyan over there so no one bothers him, and we can go inside." She parked the wagon behind a nearby barn and rejoined me in front of the house. "Look, I want you to stay quiet when we go in. You talk funny."

I blinked. *She* spoke like a country grandmother. But the nosy Iset woman had thought me a city-dweller, too, so apparently my accent betrayed me.

"I can change how I speak."

"Don't be stupid. Where are you from, anyway? I know it can't be Ekaterinburg."

"We do not have time for this," I said, waving her off in annoyance. I pulled the second diamond out of my pocket and dropped it into her hand, as we had agreed. "Let us go inside already. I will act deaf and mute if it makes you happy."

"Perfect," she said, and then laughed at the face I made. "I think we'll get along much better this way."

She knocked on the front door before I could respond.

6

EVGENIA

I DIDN'T LIKE MAKING DEALS inside someone else's house.

I didn't like having a spoiled otrodye for company while I did.

Seeing Comrade Morozov had reminded me that I didn't like making illegal deals, either. If the Red Army had killed Anna's family, then her property wasn't hers anymore. She shouldn't have any jewels. I should have turned her in.

Morozov and his wife, Katia, had been so nice when I visited. They'd told me about the last Iset soviet meeting, where Katia was voted in as the first committee chairwoman. They let the women of Iset vote in the election. And they let other communists join and vote, too, not just Bolsheviks. The soviet was getting bigger and more diverse. We hadn't even won the war yet, and communism was already making us equal.

I'd left the diamond on their doorstep, wrapped in a handkerchief.

I couldn't keep it. My dreams had been selfish. And anyway,

Kostya would never accept money that came from speculation. He'd be right. Why should we get a rich new life in Ekaterinburg when the rest of our town was still poor?

The Morozovs would turn the jewel over to the soviet, I was sure. And I'd still get the few rubles I needed once I sold Anna's other diamond to Stravsky. That would be it. I'd send Anna off to join her White friends, find the doctor, and then forget I ever met the strange bourgeois girl.

"Come in!" Stravsky's grating voice called from inside the house.

I led Anna in. My skin started buzzing, like it always did before a tricky negotiation. I was about to ask for more money than I'd ever seen in my life. Usually I traded in the open, with plenty of people around. There was less likely to be trouble that way. I didn't make black market deals, either. The things I normally traded were small, like my neighbor's clay pots or nice cloths Kostya brought back from the city. No one cared if I made a few extra rubles that way.

A jewel was different.

Kostya had complained enough times about how corrupt Stravsky was, so I knew he'd be interested in buying. But he'd try to send me off with just a few kopecks. I'd have to stand my ground. I patted my apron pocket where I'd hidden my knife.

The front hall was gray and shadowy. It had wooden floors, hanging lamps, and cobwebs in all the corners. The house smelled like a scummy pond on a hot day. Stravsky had lived here by himself since his wife died years ago. They never had children, so I didn't know why he needed such a big house all to himself, but that was the way of wealthy merchants. The house had a whole room just for eating, with a long table and chairs. We passed another room with nothing but cushioned chairs in it, where I guessed he sat with visitors. I followed the sound of the music to the rear of the house.

The room we entered was small. Low ceilings and dirty windows made it dark and cramped. A faded white desk sat in the middle of the floor. Other than the phonograph in the corner, everything was covered in papers and dust.

Stravsky sat behind the desk. He shut off the phonograph. The sudden silence felt like a loss.

I'd never heard music so pretty.

"Who are you?" he demanded.

"Evgenia Ivanovna Koltsova, comrade," I said. "Of Mednyy."

Stravsky wasn't much to look at. He had stringy gray hair, fat lips, and eyes that bugged out like a frog's behind his glasses. He was as tall and bony as a skeleton. I'd met him a couple of times before, and when I mentioned my hometown, his eyes lifted with recognition.

"You're the girl wagoner, aren't you? Konstantin Ivanovich's sister?" he asked.

I tried to ignore the spray of spittle that hit my face as he spoke.

"Yes, I am."

"How is he?" he asked.

Some of my nerves eased. At least he had the decency to ask after Kostya, who'd gone to many Bolshevik meetings in Iset before joining the army.

"He's back home with an injury," I said. "They sent him home two weeks ago."

"Sorry to hear that," Stravsky said. "Why are you here? And who is this?" He narrowed his eyes at Anna.

"I found this girl on the road," I said carefully. "She's dumb, but she paid me something in exchange for a ride. I thought you might be interested."

Stravsky finally met my eyes. He licked his lips.

"What is it?"

I held out Anna's second jewel in my hand.

His eyes grew even bigger. He walked around the desk for a closer look, and I forced myself not to flinch away from him.

"Is that a diamond?"

"Yes. I think the girl comes from money." I plucked at the fine cloth of Anna's shirt. She said nothing, playing her part well.

"Who is she?" he asked.

"She doesn't talk, so I don't know. But she had a train ticket to Chelyabinsk in her pocket. I figured I'd put her on the mail coach. We need money for the ticket, and for my payment."

He kept staring at the diamond.

"That coach stopped running a while ago," he said. "You know the driver was Jewish, yes? The Whites killed all the Jews south of the city. The mail hasn't been running since."

I glanced in alarm at Anna. She looked paler, and her eyes upset, but she kept her silence, thankfully.

"Then I'll find her some other way south. But she needs money. What do you think of this jewel? I've been told it's worth hundreds of rubles. You could sell it easily in Ekaterinburg. I'll give it to you for much less."

"Told by who?"

Chyort.

"By someone who would know," I said awkwardly. I couldn't tell him that Anna'd spoken to me after lying about her being mute.

"How do I know you didn't steal it?"

"Who would I have stolen it from? I got it from her. She doesn't mind."

He studied Anna, who stared convincingly at a spot on the floor.

"Yes, she looks like she comes from upper-class stock," he said. He didn't comment on the scratches on her skin or the stains on her shirt. "Let me see it again."

I twirled the diamond in front of him. It caught the dim light beautifully, like moonlight on snow.

"You can see how valuable it is, can't you?" I asked. "You're the only man in town who could appreciate something of this quality. You can have it for fifty rubles."

He snorted.

"If I'm the only man in town you can sell this to, why would I pay so much?"

"Well, I'm not going to *give* it away," I said evenly. "I'll bring it to Ekaterinburg if I have to. But, Comrade Stravsky, fifty rubles is not much. And I need the money for Kostya. He needs a doctor. You'll be helping him by helping yourself."

He kept looking at it. I waited for him to offer a lower price, for our back-and-forth to begin.

"I'll give you your rubles," he said.

I nodded and tried to keep in my grin.

"*If* it's real," he said. "Let me examine it."

I reluctantly handed it to him. He held the diamond up to his big glasses for a long moment. Then he closed his fist around it. "You've obviously stolen this. Get out of my house before I report you."

My insides turned hot with anger.

"No," I said. I reached in my pocket. "You can pay me fifty rubles or give it back. It's ours."

He laughed nastily.

"You're a rude, unnatural girl who should be home and not roaming the countryside like a common whore," he said with an unnerving smile. "If you don't leave immediately, I'll have you arrested for stealing. This is *my* town. You're nothing but a child from a backwater village. Get out of my sight."

I gritted my teeth. In four months as a wagoner I'd dealt with meaner and smarter people than Stravsky. None as powerful, but I had never let anyone steal from me. I wasn't about to start.

I pulled the knife from my pocket. His buggy eyes widened.

"You can pay me or give it back," I repeated, holding the knife low between us. "If not, I'll make you sorry. And then I'll go to Comrade Morozov and tell everyone you robbed this girl and kept her jewel. What will people think?"

"Get out of my house," he snarled.

I lifted the knife, but before I could scare him with it, Anna grabbed my elbow and yanked hard. I fell back a step.

"I have more," she whispered in my ear. "This is not worth getting arrested."

I jerked my arm free. She didn't know anything about it.

I wasn't about to let this *svoloch* steal from me. With a bosom full of diamonds, everything Anna had ever wanted was hers at the snap of a finger. She'd never had to fight for anything. She wasn't going to stop me.

"Give it back," I said to Stravsky, "or pay me a fair price. Those are your choices, comrade."

He curled his lip.

"Morozov won't take your word over mine. Don't make me throw you out of here myself."

He stepped forward, and I reacted without thinking. I punched him with my free hand, hard, right in the face.

Stravsky's head flew to the side. He dropped the jewel, but I was slow to grab it, too busy flinching from the pain that shot up my hand. We both recovered and went for the jewel at the same time. He shoved me, hard, making me lose my footing and stumble into Anna, who fell into the doorframe. Stravsky was just about to pick up the diamond when I hurled myself forward and slammed into his chest. We crashed into the desk. His head smacked the solid wood with an awful sound, and he yelled and reached back, cradling his skull.

I didn't wait to see if he'd bleed. I scooped up the diamond quickly, then turned and shoved Anna ahead of me out the door.

"You fucking *suka*!" Stravsky shouted after us. "Come back here!"

7

ANNA

"SVOLOCH!" EVGENIA KICKED THE EXTERIOR of the barn, then began pacing back and forth beside her wagon, steaming with anger. Buyan sidestepped her nervously. We had run here and hidden until we were certain that Stravsky wasn't following. He might have been too old to give chase, but given his position he could easily send the police after us. He would certainly blacken Evgenia's name and make it difficult for her to do any business in town.

We had to find someone else to sell to. Yet once we did, where would I go? The mail coach I had planned to ride south no longer operated. I was trapped in this Bolshevik town. I needed a new plan.

I could not think straight while Evgenia's rage rose like a slowly exploding bomb. She had rested all our hopes on a scoundrel. Then she, who I'd once taken for my rescuing angel, had threatened him with a *knife*. For one terrible moment I'd expected to witness another murder and end up imprisoned again. She was unpredictable.

"Would you please calm yourself?" I asked. "If someone overhears your tantrum, you will land us in trouble all over again."

"Me?" she shouted. "This is your fault. I saved you for nothing! Now I have no money, *and* I'll be in trouble with the soviet."

"You needn't have punched him. I told you to—" I cut myself short. As much as I wanted to point out all the ways *she* had brought this situation upon us, arguing with her would only delay us. "We must assess our remaining options and work out a practical way forward. A strategy," I said, thinking of all the times Papa had agonized over military movements. "A plan of attack."

"'Remaining options'?" She sneered. "I guess you mean more diamonds. How many of those damn things are you carrying anyway? I still don't know where you come from or how you got them. I should just leave you here. You and Stravsky deserve each other. *Chyort poberi!*"

I breathed in slowly through my nose, trying to block out my irritation with Evgenia and my panic over learning that the mail coach was gone. Commander Yurovsky was still out there. Either I found another way to get on a train heading south, or walked for days along dangerous roads, or else convinced someone to drive me. Someone like Evgenia.

She'd told Stravsky that she needed money to hire a doctor for her brother. If that was true, then I could offer her enough to build her own *hospital*. I had to change her mind about bringing me all the way to Chelyabinsk.

"Evgenia."

She stopped pacing and glared at me.

"What?"

"Do you truly want to help your brother?"

"Yes," she bit off. "I want a doctor to look at him. He lost his leg in the war."

"Oh." My heart sank as I remembered row after row of bandaged, moaning soldiers lying on cheap cots. Masha and I used to visit war hospitals before we were sent to Ekaterinburg. We sang to the soldiers, entertained them with silly jokes, and sometimes, held them as they died. "In the . . . the war against Germany? Or—"

"Against the *Whites*, Anna. Because he's a *Bolshevik* soldier. Because my family are *Bolsheviks*. Because—"

"Yes, yes, I understand," I said quickly. The conflict with Germany had ended earlier that year, when the Bolsheviks pulled Russia out of the great global war. Mama and Papa had been heartbroken to learn the news. Our allies in England, France, the United States, and elsewhere fought on, despite Russia's shameful surrender.

Yet I should have guessed that any brother of Evgenia's would fight for the Red Army, not the old Imperial one.

"I only meant to say that we must not give up. Can we find someone else to sell the jewels to? Stravsky is no better than a small-town nobody. Do not waste time fretting over him. As long as we move faster than him, we can still succeed."

"That *small-town nobody* is the richest man around for a hundred versts." She scowled. "We ran all the pomeshchiki out of Mednyy and Iset. I don't know where you think we are. If he's not willing to pay, we're done." She shook her head.

"We will sell the next jewel for kopecks, if we must!" I

said. "We do not need much money—only enough. Forget about that horrible little man and all his talk of how 'this is *my* town.'" I held my rounded fingers up like glasses and widened my eyes to look like Stravsky. I mimicked his nasally voice and puffed out my chest.

Evgenia's mouth fell open. She closed it quickly, but the corners of her lips kept flicking upward as she fought a smile.

"I didn't know you could joke," she said. She finally started to look calm again.

Before I could suggest we get moving, a rumbling noise in the distance caught my attention. At first I had the wild thought that it was thunder and that we needed to find shelter. But then anxiety rose in Evgenia's face like a shadow, mirroring my own dread. In unspoken agreement, we hurried to the edge of the barn and peeked around it.

A flurry of tawny warhorses galloped around the bend and bore down the road toward us. Inevitably, undeniably, it was him.

The soldiers dismounted at Stravsky's house and tied their horses to the fence, before barging inside with scarcely a knock.

"We must leave," I whispered.

Evgenia turned on me, her face contorted with confusion.

"Why would he come back this way? Is he after *you*?"

I shook my head.

"He is," she insisted, glaring at me. "Are you the prisoner he's after? What did you do?" She looked me up and down. "What *could* you do?"

"Please," I said, barely voicing the words. "He cannot see us. We are both in danger."

"*I'm* not."

"You are. You helped me," I reminded her. "And you attacked a member of the soviet. He won't believe you."

Fear washed across her face for only a second, before disgust quickly replaced it.

"It's the jewels, isn't it? You're not supposed to have them. They're worth as much as you said, and now he's trying to get them back. I *knew* I should've turned you in."

"No," I growled, desperate. "You don't understand. It isn't the jewels. He murdered my sisters, my parents, my little brother. He is determined to finish what he started. We did nothing wrong. He's mad."

"I don't believe you."

"You *must*," I said more forcefully. I made myself stand tall, like Mama did when she faced down a combative government minister. We could not linger here. "I swear to God I am telling you the truth. We must leave. Please, Evgenia, trust me."

"No. I think if I go offer him your jewels, this'll end. So you can hand them over now, or you can keep running. But I'm not helping you anymore."

"I am telling you, even the thought of it—"

"It was your choice to hoard them, Anna. Not mine." She turned her back on me. And then she walked straight toward Stravsky's house.

She would get us both killed. I watched in shock, unable to move, until she disappeared around the far side of the house. Even then I waited, certain she would return. I could not believe that she had truly left. That she was this obtuse.

Run.

I heard my sister Tatiana's firm voice, an echo of a memory. Tatiana had always been the sensible one. She'd always known what to do. *Do not just stand there. Run.*

I reared away from the side of the barn and started to run past Evgenia's horse, still attached to her wagon.

I hesitated.

You cannot steal from a dead girl.

My fingers fumbled along the shaft and ties affixing Buyan to the wagon, untangling the straps as I worked out how to unhitch him. He would carry me to the next town, the next kind soul, as far from Yurovsky as I could make him go. Evgenia would have no more use for him once Commander Yurovsky finished with her.

I hoped God showed her mercy. But I had come too far to risk being found now.

8

EVGENIA

YUROVSKY WAS ON MY SIDE. He didn't seem evil when I spoke to him. Anna, on the other hand, was rich, and on the run, and hiding jewels. I had no reason to trust a half-mad bourgeois fugitive. The choice between her and a Bolshevik commander should've been easy.

But it wasn't. I kept picturing Anna shaking and pissing herself in the woods. It made me uneasy. Dasha liked to say that *fools and madmen speak the truth.* And Anna was both of those things. So instead of knocking on the front door again, I rounded Stravsky's house and found his open study window.

He'd turned a light on. The window glowed in the purple dusk. It was too high up for me to see in, but the wooden siding underneath had a few knots and holes. I grabbed the rough windowsill and stuck my toes into a gap between two planks, then heaved myself up to peek inside.

They stood right in front of the window, their backs to my face. Stravsky, Commander Yurovsky, and another soldier had crowded around the desk. They were reading something.

Yurovsky's two other men stood in the doorway, facing each other and talking quietly. None of them saw me.

". . . threat to the Ekaterinburg Soviet," Yurovsky was saying. "We can't let her information get out."

"I only wish I'd been notified sooner. I would've arrested them both on the spot."

"Now you know. If she reaches the Whites and tells them anything, we're in trouble. She has to die. And so does that girl who's helping her—I'm guessing she's heard the whole story by now. Any idea where they're going?"

Yurovsky meant *me*, the damn *svoloch*. So much for being on the same side. I crouched down lower to keep my head out of sight.

"Your girl is trying to go south," Stravsky said. He didn't say a word about me being a Bolshevik or the sister of a Red Army captain. "That Koltsova girl might take her. She's from Mednyy, here"—he pointed at the desk, maybe at a map—"just a few hours' ride away. They may go there first."

"Commander," one of the other soldiers said. "Mednyy is now occupied, isn't it?"

"Damn it!" Yurovsky slammed his hand on the tabletop, the sound like a gunshot.

My skin jumped. My foot slipped lower on the knot, and I scrambled to catch my balance.

"Then that's exactly where they're headed."

"Occupied?" Stravsky asked.

That word was nagging me, too.

"The Whites are gathering to join the Czechoslovaks," the soldier explained. "We learned that a company of Whites

settled in Mednyy to await orders. We won't be able to enter
the town."

My sweaty palm slipped from the wood. I floundered to
catch myself and slapped my arm onto the sill without thinking. The men turned at the noise. Yurovsky's dark eyes met
mine, narrowed, and while the other men exclaimed in shock,
he leapt at me like a dog pouncing on a rat.

I threw myself off the windowsill. I skidded down the wall
and landed hard, on my back, all the air flying out of me. Above
me Yurovsky was trying to force the window open further so he
could climb out. But it was old and painted over and wouldn't
budge. His face, the one I'd thought was normal, turned ugly
with frustration.

"She's outside the house—get her!"

I wasn't about to wait and see what they'd do. He thought
I knew something I didn't, and he wanted to kill me for it. He
didn't look to be in a listening mood. I jumped up and ran for
my wagon. Behind me, the soldier's footsteps pounded noisily
over Stravsky's wooden floors. I glanced over my shoulder just
as the men burst from the front door.

I'd never been a fast runner. But I found myself soaring over
the tall grass like a deer, my feet hardly touching the ground,
my heart in my throat.

I couldn't die in Iset. The Whites were in Mednyy. I had
to make it home.

I hopped the fence between Stravsky's property and the
next, and as I circled the barn, I realized that I wouldn't have
time to unhitch Buyan. If I had any chance of escaping them
and getting home to Mama and Kostya, then I had to go on

foot and lose them in the woods. I knew this area better than they did. I knew where Anna and I could hide.

When I rounded the last corner, I stumbled at the sight of my bare wagon leaning in the dirt. Buyan was gone. And so was Anna. Had she left? Had someone else caught her?

"Evgenia!"

She was there, across the next field, halfway to the road. Riding Buyan. Maybe she'd expected trouble. She waved her free arm and turned Buyan in my direction. I ran toward them.

I practically jumped onto Buyan's back. Anna caught my arm and tried to pull me up, while Buyan fidgeted beneath us. I managed to swing my leg over, then wrapped my arms around Anna's waist, tugged my sarafan above my knees like she had, and held on tight. She kicked Buyan's side firmly.

"No, go into the woods!" I panted over her shoulder. "We can't outrun them on the road."

Anna nodded and brought Buyan around. She leaned forward, digging her heel in again, and Buyan began to gallop toward the trees, faster than I thought my old horse could move. My ass lifted and landed on his back roughly. My legs kept sliding as I tried to catch my balance. Anna seemed to be riding easier, and I did my best to copy her stance, hugging my knees in tighter.

Then came the gunshot.

Anna and I both flinched. The bullet hit a tree ahead of us, sending up a spray of bark like sparks. By then we'd cleared the barn. I looked over my shoulder to see how close the soldiers were and was surprised to see them running in the other direction. They were going for their horses. Only Yurovsky continued toward us now. He lifted his rifle, stopped to take aim, and fired again.

The bullet whizzed right by us, hissing like a hornet.

"Faster!" I shouted at Anna and Buyan.

Yurovsky fired again, and we plunged past the tree line.

The woods were sparse enough for us to ride through, but not open enough for a full gallop. Branches and leaves batted at our faces, forcing us to duck and dodge them as we plowed past the low brush. Anna got the worst of it. Buyan did, too, and he kept trying to slow down. He didn't understand why we pushed him on. But Anna didn't give him a moment's break.

"There's a path that way." I pointed. Anna started us in that direction.

The soldiers' fast horses wouldn't help them as much in the woods. But we were leaving a trail as plain as a signpost. They'd catch up soon.

Had Lev, my oldest brother, felt like this before he died? Did enemy soldiers run him down, too, chasing him to his death on the battlefield? Maybe he'd felt this same rattling fear. Maybe his last thought was of our family.

I wasn't going to die. We just needed a place to hide. I had to get home to Mama and Kostya. The Whites would kill Kostya if they found out he'd been a Red soldier. I'd left my family behind, and the only way to make up for it was to get back there and protect them. Anna could join the White forces for all I cared.

"There's a place ahead where we can take cover," I told Anna.

"You want to hide?" she said, her voice panicked. "Should we not continue riding? It is nearly dark."

"They won't stop looking for us. We need to lose them, somewhere Buyan can hide, too. Speaking of," I added, thinking again on how I'd found her, and how we'd left my wagon, with all my belongings, my neighbor's clay pots, and my money, behind. "Were you stealing my horse back there?"

"Of course not!" She sounded offended. "I was readying him so we could wait for you by the road. I knew that there would be danger, and I hoped you would reconsider and return."

I grunted, not sure I believed her. But she had saved me, so I let it go.

I pointed Anna onto a trail that was barely wide enough for Buyan to walk down. It led to thicker brush and lower, bushier trees. Buyan whinnied unhappily a few times, and he had to pick his steps with more care. He stepped over shrubs and old, rotted trees while we pushed aside branches. I couldn't hear Yurovsky's men behind us anymore. That had to be a good thing. My heart started beating at a normal pace again, though my skin still buzzed nervously.

We came out of the path's end at the devil's wall. It rose straight up before us, full of shadows. We called it the devil's wall because it was so huge and unnatural-looking that only the devil could've dreamed it up. The dark, rocky cliff face was fifty cubits high and made of black and gray stone. My brothers and I used to play hide-and-seek there as kids. I knew all its corners and secrets, but Anna looked at it distrustfully.

I led us to the south side, where the wall sloped downward

along the mountainside. Boulders jutted up here and there down the hill until the trees took over into grassy forest again. From the top of the wall you could see the whole valley.

"We get off here," I told Anna.

"Yurovsky and his men may still be after us."

"I'm sure they are," I said, sliding from Buyan's back. Anna followed me, her eyes wide as she took everything in. I walked Buyan into a small cave at the foot of the wall. It was just high enough for him to stand with his head bent. It wouldn't be comfortable, and it was less safe than where we'd hide, but it was my best chance to keep him. Otherwise I'd have to set him free and leave him to wander the woods alone.

I tied the reins to a jagged rock and then petted his head.

"Be good, and stay here," I said. "You hear me? I'll be back for you. Just stay here."

"Evgenia," Anna whined.

I knew I was taking too long. I gave Buyan a fast hug, then hurried back out of the cave. There was still no sign of Yurovsky or his men.

"We have to climb. Can you do that? Can you follow me?"

"Of course," she said.

I grabbed hold of the familiar stone. It'd been years since I'd last climbed the wall, but I'd done it so many times that I didn't even need to think about where my hands went. My fingers slipped into grooves in the rock, and I climbed from one jutting slab of rock to another, higher and higher. Halfway up I spotted what I was looking for. Two slabs of rock curved together around a small opening, covering the hole so that it looked like solid wall. In this dim light, it would be invisible from every direction.

I lowered myself in feetfirst, and then backed against the side to make room for Anna. She slid down against me, barely squeezing in. My hips were wider than they'd been last time, and it was a tighter fit than with my brothers. But we managed it. The hole was deep enough that if we crouched a little, our heads were covered, too. I guided Anna to do so, and then we waited.

It didn't take them long. Yurovsky and his men rode up not long after.

"They could be hiding here. Search the area," Yurovsky ordered.

Anna's breath landed against my cheek as we crouched side by side. Her breaths grew shorter and faster, and I felt my own back break out into sweat.

We listened to the men dismount and stomp around the ground near the wall. I took long breaths to try and calm my pounding heart. I put my hand out against the cool rock, and my fingers brushed against thin, sharp lines in the granite.

I'd forgotten about this carving. Kostya had etched our initials into the stone here: *KEL*. My fingers traced the letters, each one the first letter of our names: Konstantin, Evgenia, Lev. There were just two of us left now. I squeezed my eyes shut and thought about my family. I'd soon see Kostya, and Mama, too. I had to. Mama wouldn't lose yet another child. I wouldn't do that to her.

"They may have climbed up."

"Check, then," Yurovsky growled. The men had run all

around the wall at the base. They hadn't found Buyan. Now we heard the men climbing on either side of the wall. One was much faster than the other, and he reached the top first. His boots slapped against the stone, not five cubits above us, as he ran from one end of the wall to the other. Anna grabbed my arm and dug her fingers into my skin tight.

"They're not here." It was Yurovsky. He'd climbed the cliff face himself.

If he looked down and searched hard enough, he might see us. I resisted looking up. My dark hair would be less visible than my face, and any movement might catch his attention. I held my breath and clenched my fists, trying to stay perfectly still.

"Forget it, Kuzmich. We keep going." Yurovsky began climbing down the other side.

I relaxed my fists, letting go of my knife. I hadn't even realized I'd grabbed it. Anna let out her breath in a big gust against my cheek, and eased her hands from my arm.

Yurovsky and his men rode past the wall and deeper into the woods, toward Mednyy. We'd fooled them.

We waited for the sound of the soldiers to fade, while I thought about what to do next. I'd just helped a criminal escape. Was I a traitor? Yurovsky had said Anna had information that could help the Whites. If I brought her with me, and she knew something important, I could hurt the cause.

Or we could part ways here. She and her diamonds could make their own way. Was that the right thing to do?

If Batya were still alive, he would've wanted me to help Anna. He never liked the Bolsheviks. He and Mama wanted peaceful change. But my father died before any change came at all. When we went hungry that year, the landlords still banned us from hunting, so we tried to forage for food. When the snow came, we made do with scraps. When there were no scraps left, Mama made soup from tree bark.

Batya went without. "*I eat last,*" he'd say. "*It's my responsibility to keep this family fed.*" We all grew thin, but he fared worst. He got weak. When Mama cooked up a half-rotted grouse she found in the woods, we all fell sick. Batya never got better.

The revolution came a year later. The Bolsheviks ordered that all the land being worked by the peasants belonged to the peasants. They set up soviets wherever they could, including in Iset and Ekaterinburg. And they waged war against the Whites, who wanted to put a Romanov back on the throne and put the tsar's crony landlords back in power. The Whites didn't care if we starved. The Bolsheviks would make sure it never happened again.

Batya's kindness hadn't saved him, but I was still his daughter. I couldn't shame his memory. I'd hand Anna over to her White friends, and then I'd go back to being a good Bolshevik. Everything would make sense again once I was home, back with my family, and rid of Anna.

9

ANNA

I COULD NOT TELL HOW long we waited in that tight, grimy gap in the rock wall. It was agony. The commander came so close to us that I feared he would hear me breathing; I held my breath so long that spots appeared before my eyes. Then he left, and we were safe—thanks to Evgenia. I had somehow found a girl who, despite her occasional foolishness, was braver and quicker-thinking than an Imperial officer.

"That's long enough," Evgenia said at length. "He's gone." She climbed out before extending a hand to help me, and we carefully descended to find her horse in the little hollow where we had left him.

"Where will we go from here?" I asked, my jaw aching. Every part of my body had tensed while we crouched in the wall. "Should we head back to the main road?" I circled in place, unable to figure out which direction that would be. Evgenia clearly knew these woods well, but we could not risk catching up with Commander Yurovsky.

She sighed. "I'm going home."

"What do you mean? To your hometown? The commander will head straight there once that Stravsky man tells him where you live. You—"

"The Whites took over Mednyy. I heard Yurovsky say it. I have to go back and make sure my family's all right." She stroked her horse's flank, averting her gaze.

Her family was Bolshevik, and her brother had been a Red soldier. I swallowed.

"Would returning even help? Are you sure there is anything you can do for them?"

"I have to try."

Night was falling in the forest. A chilly wind nipped at my bare neck and seeped through my thin blouse. I felt as though I had fallen into a hopeless, cold, dark pit. All around me, beyond the circle of our little trio, the world was angry and waiting to pounce. Where would death strike next? Its scythe might sweep me down with Commander Yurovsky's gun. It might take Evgenia, who had only wanted to care for her family. Or it might take her mother and brother. I knew, with a dreadful certainty, that it would strike again.

I reached inside my shirt and clasped the icon necklace so hard that the gold filigree left traces in my palm. *Oh, Angel of Christ, let us live in peace.*

"You should come with me."

I opened my eyes. Evgenia was watching me, and she followed the movement of my hand as it lowered.

"To Mednyy?"

"Yurovsky and his men won't be able to get into town with the Whites there. Maybe they'll be able to help you."

It would be temporary protection, at best. Any White soldiers here, in communist territory, had to be on their way to join the fighting in Ekaterinburg. Yet I could hardly return to Iset. And there would be officers leading the company—perhaps high-ranking officers who had ways to contact General Leonov in Chelyabinsk. Many officers were holdovers from the old Imperial army, loyalists horrified by the violent revolution. Perhaps one would take pity on me.

"All right," I said.

Evgenia led us away from the colossal cliff that she had appropriately called the devil's wall. We walked along an old loggers' path heading north, pulling Buyan behind us, making slow and clumsy progress in the scant light that remained.

"What happened when you returned to Stravsky's home?" I asked her. "You'd threatened to turn me in. What changed your mind?"

She considered for a minute before answering.

"He said he was going to kill both of us. He doesn't know anything about me, but he was ready to kill me just because he saw us together. I don't think he'd even care that I'm a Bolshevik."

"That is what Commander Yurovsky does," I said. "He kills without hesitation." The memory of him coldly reading out my family's order of execution washed over me. He had shot my innocent sisters, my thirteen-year-old brother, all of us—even though all we wanted was to live out our lives in peace.

"He didn't mention the diamonds, either. I guess you didn't steal them," she said lightly, as though joking.

I pursed my lips.

"He did say you know some information that can help the White Army win. Is that true?"

"Is *that* what he calls it?" I said, disgusted. "Information? I watched him murder—" My voice broke. I clapped my hand over my mouth, trying to contain the grief that fought to wail out of it. I cleared my throat. "I told you that he murdered my family. My father was—a man of importance. He had connections in the White Army. If people learn that the Bolsheviks killed not only my father but also my mother, and my sisters, and my little brother, even our servants, they will be horrified. And justifiably so."

She did not respond at once, and it was too dark to make out her expression. We continued stepping carefully along the path. I focused on putting one foot in front of the other, steady steps, moving forward. My family was gone, and I had to move forward for them.

"Important how?" Evgenia finally asked.

There was the question I could not, under any circumstances, answer truthfully. I had hoped she would not ask. I knew enough about her already to understand that she would not keep my secret. Evgenia would turn on me if she learned that my papa was Nikolai Alexandrovich Romanov, tsar of all Russia. That I was the only survivor of the royal family, and that Commander Yurovsky would chase me to the ends of the earth to exterminate our line.

I had not forgotten that they cheered my father's death in the village where we met. Evgenia had been there with them, and though she had not sung along, neither had she objected.

I still needed her help. But no Bolshevik would ever help a Romanov.

I needed a less threatening story.

"My father was merely a merchant," I said, my mind working to invent a story she would accept. "But his cousin in Petrograd was an Imperial general who now fights for the White Army." I silently congratulated myself on thinking up the lie so quickly. "He is the one in Chelyabinsk."

"Why did the Reds kill your family?"

"They never said. Commander Yurovsky and his troop of murderers came upon us in the night, and . . ." Even though the bulk of what I was telling her was nonsense, I could not go on and describe the slaughters of that night for her.

It was enough, anyway. Evgenia asked me no more questions, nor did she offer her opinion on what crimes my imaginary family may have committed. She seemed to believe me, which was all I needed her to do for the moment.

We continued walking until it grew so dark we could not see the ground in front of us. I let her tie up the horse while I crawled under a tree, and I almost immediately fell asleep. It was the second night that I spent in the forest. The first, lonely night had been a waking nightmare; I had hardly been in my right mind, and every rustling leaf or scurrying creature made me certain that Commander Yurovsky was upon me. I'd felt as though I were still in the back of that wagon, buried by my family's bodies, surrounded by Red soldiers. I feared I would never leave it. I had not shut my eyes for even a second.

Now, with Evgenia nearby, unconsciousness swallowed me into merciful nothingness.

"Did you sleep at all, Mashka?" I asked drowsily, enjoying the cushion of her legs. My sister suffered from insomnia, and I had stayed up on our last full night there to keep her company. We curled close together on the divan as she read Tolstoy in a soft voice. But I had fallen asleep before she did and woke with my head in her lap.

"Not really." She smiled. Though she had dark circles under her eyes, her round cheeks dimpled cheerily. "I was too surprised to fall asleep. I noticed that you had this around your neck, when you told us you lost your icon weeks ago."

She plucked at the pendant I wore, pulling the gold and silver cross out of my nightgown. Brother Grigori Rasputin had given each of us children a unique icon with a protective blessing; I had indeed lost mine months earlier.

"This is mine, I think?" she said.

"You were so distracted yesterday, moping over that officer of yours. Can't believe it took you this long to realize it was gone."

"Well, give it back now."

The truth was, I liked wearing Masha's things.

"No. Finders keepers."

"Nastya—"

"Look, if you let me keep it a little longer, I will wear the heavy corset today. I know it's your turn." The four of us traded off wearing the jewel-lined corset, as it was so stiff and hot. But one day of discomfort would be worth it. I calculated that Masha would likely forget about the necklace by the following day.

She sighed.

"Very well. Always the shvibzik, aren't you?" she added with a poke. Shvibzik meant "mischievous imp," and my family dredged it up often to tease me.

"Better that than a coquette." I made a face at her, and she tickled me in revenge until my laughter woke up Olga and Tatiana and they hurled their pillows at us in punishment.

"Here, I picked some berries," Evgenia said.

I blinked, startled awake, and then surprised again by the closeness of her face and the sight of the open forest around us.

I wanted to return to my dream. I trembled, shaken by this new loss. I'd had Masha back.

Evgenia had rested well. Her eyes were brighter and her expression less strained than before. She grinned, her braid mussed and half-undone, the loose curls forming a halo around her head. My heart twisted viciously.

"You smile just like my sister," I said.

Her face immediately filled with sympathy, the smile vanishing, and I wished I had kept the thought to myself.

"Here," she said awkwardly, extending a fistful of berries.

"No, thank you." I was still trying to shake the melancholy clinging to my insides. "I feel far too unkempt to think of eating." My shirt was sticking to my sweat-damp skin, and I tugged at it exaggeratedly. Overnight I had acquired a layer of grime that covered both blouse and sarafan. "If I lay down on this ground you would not be able to distinguish me from the dirt."

She snickered.

"Sleeping outside won't kill you, Anya."

I ceased picking at my shirt. She did not seem to notice that she had altered my name, as a friend would. Despite her harsh manners she must have been feeling warmly toward me. *Anya* was much better than *Anna*. Though neither was my real name, my spirits lifted a bit at her slip of the tongue.

"I know," I said, thinking of the many nights I had spent with my siblings camping in our gardens in Petrograd. "I do not mean to complain. Especially not to you, after the way you saved my life."

She shook her head. "Forget it. I was just teasing. Let's get to Mednyy and put this all behind us."

We mounted Buyan once more, Evgenia in front this time. I hoped that she was right and that we would be safe once we reached her village. I found myself gazing at the back of her neck again and again, resting my eyes on her. She could have easily left me behind once Commander Yurovsky lost our trail. There was no reason for her to bring me along to Mednyy. She was a Bolshevik, and I had told her that my survival might endanger her revolution, yet she did not turn on me. She did not even seem to care about payment anymore. Fleeing the commander together had bonded us, somehow.

Even communists could show mercy, then. For the moment, I was safest with her.

Hours later, we followed a footpath out of the woods and onto a wide field of rye, still green but with a golden wash hinting at ready harvest. Beyond, more green and brown farmland sprawled up and across the hilly landscape.

"We're here," Evgenia said.

Copses of trees dotted the fields, and down in the heart of the valley sat Mednyy. The homes here were more spread out than in Iset, scattered unevenly on either side of the dusty main road. Each of the little houses had its own barn, wild grassy yard, and chicken coop.

Low wooden fences wove in and out of the plots around each house. At the farthest edge of town, the dome of a modest wooden church peeked out of a cluster of trees. Several wagons sat on the road nearby. My heart lifted at the sight. They almost certainly belonged to the White Army.

"Mednyy is beautiful," I said, my gaze fixated on those wagons. "And very tranquil."

"It's too quiet. People should be out working the fields." Her voice was low with worry.

"I am certain no one has been harmed," I said. "The tsarist forces would not waste their energies harassing peasants."

She craned her head around to give me an astonished look.

"Sure, and cows lay eggs," she said.

My temper flared.

"The White Army is here to liberate Ekaterinburg; they are not—"

"Anna," she snapped, interrupting me. "You and I *met* in a village that was torn up by the Whites. You're not blind. You just ignore whatever you don't like."

I caught myself on the verge of a heated reply. Could she be right? I had noticed the injuries among the people of Pavlovo—and the dilapidated cabins. I had not stopped to think about how they got that way.

I took a deep breath.

"We shall find out one way or the other soon enough," I said.

She harrumphed, then led us back to the main road into town. A White Army roadblock interrupted our way almost immediately. Three soldiers lounged under the trees, rifles in their laps. Farther up the road were three more soldiers in Czechoslovak Legion uniforms, guarding their horses in the shade. The Russian men, nearer to us, stood as we rode up. They held their rifles pointed low.

The Czechoslovak Legion had fought alongside Russia in the Great War against Germany. They were fighting for their own independence, and they fought valiantly. But once the Bolsheviks took over Russia and surrendered, they had found themselves trapped on Russian land, without allies, on the wrong side of German territory. They could not return to their homeland and so had no choice but to cross all of Russia, from west to east, with the intention of then sailing to western Europe.

Except the Bolsheviks had turned on them. The Red Army attempted to steal their weapons and equipment, while the White Army offered the promise of rejoining the great global war if the Reds could be defeated. Now the Czechoslovaks and Whites fought together, and it did not surprise me to see them here side by side.

Gladness filled me. I forgot the soreness in my legs and the damp sweat on my neck and forehead. *We were safe*. Commander Yurovsky would not be able to pass such a roadblock.

Evgenia pulled Buyan's reins abruptly. While I relaxed, her back had stiffened. She tied her headscarf over her hair again.

"It's women," one of the soldiers said stupidly.

"Maybe they were sent for us!"

The men laughed. My lip curled before I could help myself. This was not what I had hoped for from White soldiers. The Imperial officers I had known in the palace were charming, well-bred men. These were crude foot soldiers. The very idea of asking these men for assistance made me uneasy. I would need to find a commissioned officer, someone from a better background with a sense of duty.

To do that, we needed to move past these men. Evgenia glanced at me doubtfully.

"We must go on," I murmured.

She inched Buyan forward, but one of the men raised his rifle. He was no longer laughing.

"Dismount," he ordered. "Now."

We quickly obeyed. Beyond them, the Czechoslovak soldiers began speaking loudly, pointing and laughing in our direction. They would be no help, either.

"Good morning," Evgenia said. "I live in Mednyy. We're just coming home now from visiting friends. Can we go through?"

"Who's she?" the stupid one asked, pointing at me.

"That's—my cousin," Evgenia answered. Her voice lacked conviction, but the soldiers did not seem to notice.

"Fine," said the one in charge. "Head to the church. The whole town's gathered there, and you need to check in."

"Excuse me," I spoke up, mimicking Evgenia's way of speaking. She turned toward me, surprised. "Who is in command of the troops here? Is there a lieutenant or commander placed in charge of the regiments?"

"Why do you want to know?" asked a leering soldier. I

had not directed my question at him, but he evidently craved attention.

"I have another cousin stationed in the south. I only wanted to learn if there are any messages being passed or any news."

"Lieutenant Sidorov is in charge," the leader said with a shrug. "He's in the churchyard. Go there. But leave the horse with us."

Evgenia's head jolted up. I tightened my hold on Buyan's reins.

"What?" she said.

"All horseflesh is being requisitioned on behalf of the loyalist army, for the defense of the Russian Empire," he droned, as though he had recited the words many times before. "Don't make a fuss, girl. Every horse in town has already been turned over. You're no different."

"No—" she started.

The soldier was already walking over, and Evgenia reddened as she watched helplessly.

"Wait!" she cried. She threw her arms around Buyan's neck. Her mouth trembled, and my insides stirred with pity. Buyan was her beloved pet, not *horseflesh*. But there was nothing we could do.

"He's an old horse, he's no good to the White Army," she pleaded.

"Then we'll cook him," said the rude soldier.

Evgenia bared her teeth. "No! You can't take him."

"Let go, girl, or we'll make you." The soldier's face grew hard, and the other men touched their rifles threateningly. Behind them, the Czechoslovaks quieted.

She stepped back from Buyan. I held out the reins for the soldier.

"Would you accept payment instead?" I asked, thinking of my jewels. I could spare another one, if it meant that Evgenia would be able to keep Buyan. "We may have some valuables at home to trade."

"Take it up with the lieutenant," he answered.

I hurried over to Evgenia as the soldier led Buyan away. She watched with heartbreak in her eyes. Buyan turned his heavy head toward her, confused, and she clapped a hand over her mouth.

She shrugged my hand off roughly when I tried to comfort her.

"There is no point in speaking with these soldiers," I whispered. "It is the officers who can help."

She balled her hands into fists as we walked away from the Russian soldiers and past the Czechoslovaks. We continued down the long road to the church in silence.

And when we stepped inside the large, fenced yard surrounding the church and adjacent schoolhouse, I gasped.

Dozens of peasants had gathered here, crowding together fearfully while White soldiers walked the perimeter. The peasants were very humble, many of them barefoot, all dressed in traditional, dull-colored, worn and dirty clothing. They were also quiet. The air was taut with anxiety. A few peasants spoke in soft voices, but mostly they watched the soldiers toss large bags onto wagons near the church.

A tall girl with bright red hair gestured for Evgenia to approach the edge of the crowd, but White soldiers stood between her and us. Evgenia shook her head. I inched closer to Evgenia to stand at her shoulder. I could make no sense of the sight before us.

Several White and Czechoslovak soldiers laughed and joked raucously with one another near the church. In front of them, an old woman was kneeling on the ground and frantically pushing spilled grain into a sack. She was doing a poor job of it, primarily because the soldiers kept shouting insults and leveling kicks at her. One soldier nearby was gripping the arms of an elderly, bearded man who watched in anguish.

I drew back, horrified. How could they behave in such a way? Where were their commanding officers? The oft-praised nobility of the Imperial army was nowhere to be seen. Had so much changed in just a year?

One man overlooking the scene wore a uniform decorated with gleaming stars on the collar and sleeves. He was an *officer*. Though he did not participate in the beatings or the taunts, he ought to have stopped them. It was his responsibility to control his men. I uttered a silent prayer that this apathetic officer was not Lieutenant Sidorov.

Evgenia watched them mistreat the old woman, too, her cheeks reddening. She narrowed her eyes.

"Do you know her?" I asked in a low voice.

She nodded. Unease gnawed at me as I considered what to do. If Evgenia acted impulsively by trying to defend the elderly woman, the way she had first stood up for me, these soldiers would be cross with us at the very least. I did not wish to get on their bad side because of Evgenia's impulsiveness.

I gently wrapped my fingers around her wrist.

"We should find your family," I whispered.

She nodded again, briefly, and started toward the crowd of peasants.

"Ey! Come deal with these *devushki*!" The officer with the gleaming stars had noticed us. He pointed one of his men in our direction.

"Yes, Lieutenant Sidorov!" Two soldiers answered readily and blocked our path.

Another weight added to my shoulders. He *was* the officer in charge. And he stood by while his men beat a helpless old woman. Would someone like that take pity on me, help me contact General Leonov?

"Who are you?" a soldier demanded. "Identify yourselves."

"I'm Evgenia Koltsova," she answered. "I've been visiting my cousin in—in Iset. I brought her back with me."

One of them flipped through his pages and then nodded, checking her name off. Then he frowned at our empty hands.

"You didn't bring anything?"

"We just got into town," Evgenia said, her voice heating, "and your soldiers took my horse on the way into the village."

"Yes, all horseflesh is being requisitioned on behalf of the loyalist army," he recited. "You still have to come back with sacks of food, tools, or weapons. Both of you. What's your name, cousin?" he asked me.

"I—I am Anna Vyrubova." I roughened my accent and used the false name I had given Evgenia. For the moment, I did not want anything about me to stand out more than my shirt, short hair, and dirty appearance already did.

"You both owe one large bag of goods. Come back with it in the next hour, or you'll be put on the list."

Behind us, White soldiers were still kicking the old woman.

Lieutenant Sidorov had turned his attention back to the unruly group, and I crossed my fingers, hoping he would finally settle them down.

"Can I see my mother first?" Evgenia asked the soldiers in front of us. "She'll tell us what to bring."

"Yes. Your family's still here somewhere. But hurry."

They moved to let us by. As we passed, the old woman being kicked dropped her bag again and spilled the grains all over Lieutenant Sidorov's boots.

"What's the matter with you, you stupid woman?" he shouted.

After all they had put her through, that insult seemed to be one too many. The old woman picked up a handful of seeds and hurled them at the lieutenant, making him flinch backward as they showered him. It was a futile, foolish gesture for the woman to make. Worse, she had done it in view of the entire town. The lieutenant would surely castigate her. No officer could allow himself to be so disrespected in public.

Evgenia and I both froze, as did most others in the yard, all of us waiting to see what her punishment would be. I gripped Evgenia's elbow, hard, just in case she was thinking of getting involved.

"You're what's the matter with me, ty *blyad*, you tsar-loving German!" the woman shouted.

My breath caught. The lieutenant would surely have to arrest her now.

Instead, Lieutenant Sidorov stepped closer to her, withdrew a revolver from the holster on his hip, and shot her in the face.

PART TWO

MEDNYY

10

EVGENIA

EVERYONE IN THE CHURCHYARD JUMPED back.
Nurka Petrova's body fell into the dirt. Her husband, Foma
Gavrilovich, fainted. He dropped to the dirt and out of the
arms of the soldiers who'd been holding him.

The whispering stopped. The birdsong stopped. Even the
soldiers stopped laughing.

And then Anna screamed.

The White officer, Sidorov, snapped his head in our direction. His angry eyes met mine. My heart squeezed. I clapped
my hand over Anna's mouth to shut her up, then half dragged,
half shoved her into the crowd of my neighbors.

Lieutenant Sidorov started hollering orders at his men. My
neighbors whispered to one another. A few of them patted me
on the back as I pushed our way through the maze of people. I
found gaps and kept moving, in any direction, as long as it got
us away from Sidorov. We needed to be far from him, and from
Nurka with the hole in her face.

"Your mother's that way," someone whispered to me, and
pointed.

There she was. I nearly ran to her, pulling Anna along as fast as I could, my hand getting wet from her spit.

"Zhenya!" Mama cried when she saw me. I let go of Anna, who'd stopped screaming, and ran to hug Mama. She held me close. She smelled like rye and fresh flax. Like home.

"Where's Kostya?" I asked.

"He's home. He's fine. Are you all right?" She held my cheek and studied me from top to bottom with her sharp blue eyes. Mama was wide and curved like me. She wore a gray kerchief over her blond hair. "We heard a shot."

Kostya was safe. The Whites couldn't know he was a Red soldier, then, because they would've killed or arrested him if they did. I let out a small laugh, relieved.

"And who's this, Zhenya?" Mama asked. She tilted her head at Anna. A few of our neighbors leaned in, nosy and staring. Anna looked at her feet. She was still pale and shaking.

"A friend. I'll explain later. Mamochka, they killed Nurka Petrova," I said.

Mama's shoulders dropped, and she put her hand on her heart. She shut her eyes, too. The Petrovs were old friends of our family. Nurka Petrova made the clay pots I sold on the road, and we split the profits. Her husband was a nice old man. They'd had their share of troubles in life. I couldn't think of anyone who deserved this less.

I wondered if Mama was praying. Mama hadn't entirely given up on her God, though she learned to keep it private after we ran the priest out of town.

"And, Mama, they took Buyan," I said. The words got thick in my throat. It'd happened so quickly. One moment he was mine, and the next, that damned White soldier was leading him away.

Mama just shook her head.

"Why did they shoot Nurka?" she asked. She hadn't been close enough to see. So I had to whisper the story to her. While I spoke, Anna sat on the ground and buried her face in her knees. The folks nearest her edged away like she had a catching disease.

Mama bent over her.

"Can you stand up, girl?"

Anna acted like she hadn't heard.

The crowd shifted around us. Then I realized it wasn't just a mess of people. We were waiting in line. Every household had to hand over their goods before they could return home. Mama had brought a small potato sack full of what had to be half our cabbage patch, cheese, old gardening tools, and three books.

"Why are you giving them Batya's books?" I demanded.

"I heard the officers like to read," she said, still focused on Anna, sitting beside the line. "Maybe we can get on their good side."

I scowled and dug through the bag.

Here was *War and Peace*. Batya made us read the whole thing aloud the winter I was eleven. We each had to read a chapter at a time. Lev was still alive then. He'd never have read it on his own, but he loved the story. Kostya had groaned through all of it. He whined most when it was my turn to read. He'd roll around the floor like he was dying of pain, while I stumbled red-faced over almost every word.

And here was *Dead Souls*. The Gogol novel was so tattered that a lot of pages were just tucked inside. Batya used to lend that book to his students. They weren't always careful with it, but they always brought it back. Everyone had respected Batya, and loved him, since—unlike Mama—he grew up in Mednyy. Even the priest had loved him, and made him teacher, even though Batya was never that religious.

"Well, they're not taking this one." I took out the Gogol. I'd spent days talking about it with Batya. I tucked it inside my sarafan, where it made an obvious bump over my stomach. Before Mama could say anything, I added, "They don't deserve it, Mama! Not after what they did to Nurka."

"Get your friend" was all Mama said. She frowned. "Who *is* she?"

I didn't know how to answer. Mama wasn't a Bolshevik, but she wouldn't be happy to hear that I'd brought an escaped prisoner home. I wasn't thrilled about it myself.

"I'll explain at home. But, um, I told the Whites she was my cousin. They said we had to bring a bag of goods for her, too."

"What?" Mama whirled to face me. I shrunk back. "No, Zhenya. We have nothing left to give. We can't shear a naked sheep."

I thought about the wagon full of goods I'd left in Iset. I should've gone back for it. I could've circled back after Yurovsky left the devil's wall. Instead, I'd run. Like a coward.

"They said they'll put us on some list if we don't bring more," I mumbled. I wasn't used to screwing things up. My role in the family was to fix things. But thanks to Anna, and my dumb decision to help her, we were now caught between two fires. Either we tried to convince the Whites we didn't know Anna after all, and leave her on her own, or we handed over more food.

Mama cursed.

"That damn list. They say if anyone doesn't bring what we're supposed to, they'll go to their homes and take even more."

"I'm sorry, Mama."

She sighed and patted my hair.

"I'll see if I can talk them out of it."

"All right. I'll catch up, Mama."

She nodded, and the line shuffled forward.

I crouched next to Anna, who was still sitting in the grass. Mama had tried kindness. I'd try something else.

I grabbed Anna's chin and forced her face up. It was even whiter than usual. Her eyes were damp, too.

"Get up," I said. "The line is moving. Do you want to be left alone? I'll go home without you."

She stilled at that and shook her head.

"Then stand up."

"That lieutenant," she said quietly. "I cannot understand how—I cannot bear to see him again. Do not make me. Please."

"You won't have to say anything to him. We'll do all the talking. But you can't stay here. Come on."

She walked so close behind me she practically stepped on my heels as we caught up with Mama. But at least she came.

Anna had brought me nothing but trouble. And she was a damn tsarist. She belonged with the White soldiers. But the idea of turning her over when she was so scared made me feel like the kind of person who'd drown a puppy. Pointlessly cruel.

When we got to the front of the line, the Whites ordered us to bring two more bags. Of course.

"I'll pick more food from the garden," Mama said as we

walked home. "These soldiers have no heart. The more they have, the more they want," she muttered.

It'd been a good year for our crops, but we needed that food to make it through the winter. I glanced at Anna, who'd cost us another sack of food. She didn't seem to care. I scowled as we followed Mama into the house.

Then my spirits rose.

Kostya sat at the kitchen table, whittling a short stick. On the table next to him sat a pile of wooden knives that he must've carved, their handles wrapped with twine for grip. Seeing him made my heart as light as a cloud.

Kostya had a broad face and narrow nose, and dark eyes like mine. His black hair stuck to his sweaty forehead. He'd clamped his mouth shut while he concentrated on his work. But his face spread into a grin when we entered.

"Kostya!" I hugged him. He was overly warm and smelled of sweat and wood. I glanced at his leg before I could stop myself. I still wasn't used to seeing it end at the knee. His pant leg dangled down, flat and empty, ending where his left shoe should've been.

He caught me looking, and his smile shrunk.

"You're back, Zhenya. And who's this?" He raised his eyebrows at Anna.

She stood near the door, clutching her elbows. Her eyes darted all over the house like she expected to find Yurovsky in a corner. But the house wasn't that big, and there weren't many places to hide.

Our house was an oak log cabin with tall ceilings six cubits high. Our white brick stove took up a lot of space. It had a deep firepit that could roast a whole goose on the bottom, and a smaller pit on top for everyday cooking. The stove was as tall as me and had a fat chimney that went straight up through the roof. On the back of the stove was a sleeping platform where Mama slept. Near that was the back door we'd just walked through, a window, and shelves where Mama kept her pans and dishes.

At the other end of the house was our sitting area. We had one sturdy wooden armchair and a few benches against the walls, where Kostya slept. A door in the floor hid more storage, and a ladder led to the loft where I slept.

"That's a very good question," Mama said. "Sit, Zhenya. You too, girl. And tell us what's going on."

I told them the whole story. I started with finding Anna, went on to being chased by Yurovsky and his men, and finished with losing Buyan and seeing Nurka die.

"If this girl's family are enemies of the Bolsheviks," Kostya said as soon as I finished, "then why did you bring her here? All we know about her is that she's a criminal."

"I am not a criminal," Anna said. She'd been dazed since Nurka was shot. Now she blinked and looked back and forth between us.

"Then why is Commander Yurovsky so determined to capture you? Why did he execute your parents?"

Anna's whole face sank, like we'd hooked anvils to her cheeks.

"She's just a girl," Mama said crossly. "Don't get all political."

"She's seventeen, you said?" he asked.

I nodded.

"That's old enough to fight. Zhenya joined the party when she was fifteen. She's been a messenger for months. Maybe this girl's father sabotaged the Reds in Ekaterinburg. Tell us, Anna Vyrubova. Did you help your father? Is that why Commander Yurovsky followed you?"

"Yurovsky's crazy," I cut in. "We can't take his word for it."

"You don't know what you're talking about." Konstantin waved his hand. "You're acting like a child."

My neck and face burned. I wasn't a child anymore. Kostya wasn't being fair. He hadn't heard the gunshots outside Stravsky's house or seen Yurovsky stalk us like prey.

Anna's lips pressed together so tight they almost disappeared. She did that when she wasn't happy about something. But she didn't answer Kostya. Instead, she turned to Mama.

"Alena Vasilyevna," she said. "I am so sorry to burden you with my presence. Your daughter, Evgenia, has been endlessly kind to me. She has tremendous heart—and I can only imagine that she learned that from you," Anna said.

I breathed in slowly to keep from blushing. It was just flattery. I peered at Mama to see if she noticed Anna's smooth talking, but Mama's face had softened. She bought it.

"I owe my life to her, several times over," Anna went on. "I beg you, please, allow me to stay here for a short while. And I can repay you for your trouble. I promise not to cause you any harm. The commander cannot get past the roadblock to follow me into town. All I need is shelter until I can find a way to Chelyabinsk."

Mama hesitated. Kostya glared at Anna, and I held my

breath. I tried not to pay attention to what she'd said about me. Me, "endlessly kind"? A good Bolshevik would kick her out, like Kostya wanted. Anna had said that her story could help rally the Whites. If she was right, then helping her put the revolution at risk.

But she'd lost her family. She froze up whenever she heard Yurovsky's voice. She'd be helpless alone. After everything we'd been through I couldn't just let her walk out the door. She was smart and sweet, in her own way. She didn't seem like a bad person. I shouldn't have wanted to, but I couldn't help hoping that Mama would keep her.

11

ANNA

"YOU CAN STAY," ALENA VASILYEVNA said.

Warmth filled my body, tinged with a thread of victory. She had taken my side—*our* side, as Evgenia had advocated for me, as well.

Her mother was a round woman with a hardened face, wrinkles at her eyes and mouth, and dark blond hair. Her blue eyes were difficult to read—she was a more guarded person than her daughter, though equally kind.

"Mama—" Evgenia's wretched brother began to object.

"That's it, Kostya. I've made up my mind. I won't kick a girl with no home and no family out of my house."

Though the brother, Konstantin, was of age, Alena clearly ruled the household. I would have to stay on her good side if I was to remain. I had been utterly wrong about White officers; I had expected them all to be noble and courteous, like the officers we knew at court. Instead, I had found riotous bullies, and then Lieutenant Sidorov. A monster who killed without hesitation. Seeing him shoot that elderly woman, an echo of things past, had broken something in me. I felt the tremors of that shock right in the center of my chest. Until I could figure out where to turn next, the Koltsovs were all I had.

Evgenia's home was extremely rustic. It was small and cramped, all one room, with low, sloped ceilings and a great stove stained with years of soot. I had been in peasant houses on official visits with Mama and Papa before, but never had I seen anything like this. Those homes had been larger, cleaner, even festive. The Koltsov cabin smelled thickly of body odor and kvass. The air was oppressive despite the open windows and doors. I could have sworn I spotted a few old chicken feathers tamped into the dirt floor, as well as several scurrying insects. The corners were thick with dust that made my nose itch. Aside from one armchair against the far wall, they used only crude benches for seating. I could not tell where they had room to sleep; there were no beds.

In the Ipatiev house, my brother and I had lamented our reduced circumstances almost daily. We were proud of ourselves for putting up with sharing a single bathroom, converting our living rooms into bedrooms at night, and sleeping on simple camp beds with satin sheets. Mama had told us that God would reward our hardships. Yet what hardships were they, compared to this?

For a moment, I thought of backing out of the Koltsov house and running. There was no way that I could stay here, not even for a day. Did they all sleep together in the same room, even Konstantin? Where did they bathe? There was clearly no electricity, no running water, not even glass in the windows. Mosquitoes and horseflies glided leisurely in the air.

But I had nowhere else to go. This was Evgenia's home.

The house had almost no decor of any kind—no wood-working, no tapestries, only a couple of icon prints and one amateur landscape painting tacked to the wall. It was signed *Koltsov*, indicating that a male member of the family had painted it; most likely Evgenia's deceased father, as I assumed Konstantin was not artistic.

"But, Anna," Alena went on gravely, ending my momentary relief, "the White troops are leaving in three days. Once they're gone, that commander will be free to enter the town. If he finds you with us, we'll all be in trouble. You must leave before then."

My heart sank. *Three days.* I quickly calculated what that meant—General Leonov's men could arrive in time if they traveled here by motorcar. They would have to depart almost right away. It would take them a day to reach us, perhaps more this far north of Ekaterinburg. Then they would have to locate an obscure, tiny village. The state of the roads in this area would not help, either.

"Then I must send a message immediately," I said. "My friends in Chelyabinsk can send someone for me if I telegraph them by tomorrow. Is there a telegraph office nearby?"

Alena shook her head. Evgenia curled her lip as though the question were idiotic, and I glanced down, feeling foolish, before I realized I had another option. "The White troops in town likely will have a portable one," I said. "However, I must find an officer here who might help me. I cannot rely on that— that brute they have put in charge."

"Sidorov is *your* ally," Konstantin said viciously. "Those are the people you and your family chose to side with, just so you could keep your land and your money. Which, by the way, should all go to the soviet."

Back in Petrograd, in summer, we used to watch the servants carry massive sheets of ice into the lower level of the palace. Those walls of ice were rock-hard, cold, and unbending. I thought of them often when I had to calm myself. If someone at the palace said something snide about me, or Papa, or Olga, I knew that lashing out in return would only embarrass us further. So I hardened myself. I did that now, concentrating on the memory of ice instead of Konstantin's hateful face. What he thought was unimportant. Their mother was the decision-maker here, and the one I needed to win over.

"I said that's enough," Alena said. "Besides, we don't have a soviet here yet, just the damned obshchina council, and we're not giving them a kopeck. This conversation is over. Zhenya, go pick out some more vegetables from the garden. I'll carry them to the church. Kostya—"

Her son was already leaving. He stood, grabbed angrily for his crutch, and ended up accidentally knocking it to the floor. Evgenia leaned over for it.

"I've *got* it," he said. He gripped his chair and bent awkwardly, bracing his shoulder on the sturdy table. He reached for the crutch, missed, and tried again. By the time he stood, his face had turned bright red. He stuck the wooden cradle under his armpit, then left the house in stony silence.

Evgenia followed him out without a word to me.

"You need a change of clothes," Alena said, drawing my attention from the empty doorway. "You can wear Evgenia's spare shirt." She opened a trunk underneath the loft and laid a white blouse over one of the benches. It would fit me awkwardly, yet still was an improvement. Then she went to the cupboards and poured out a mug of kvass that I gratefully accepted.

"You are incredibly kind," I said. "Just like your daughter. Thank you."

"Well"—she shrugged—"Evgenia's a good girl."

She was modest, like Evgenia. And it seemed to please her when I complimented her daughter.

"I mean it," I insisted. "You are both good people."

"Konstantin is a good man, too," she said, though I had not intentionally excluded him. "He's still a soldier at heart. That's how he thinks."

"I understand. Evgenia told me—forgive me—that your husband passed away not long ago. Konstantin Ivanovich must feel a responsibility to protect the family."

"He does." She nodded. "Though I've done what I could since Ivan died. A lot's happened since then."

"I am sorry for your loss. Did your husband paint that?" I pointed to the landscape, which, though simple, was skillfully done. "It is quite beautiful."

"Ah," she said. A heavier pain filled her eyes. A misstep. I had touched on a sore point. "No. My eldest son painted it. Lev. He died a few months after Ivan, in 1916—in the tsar's war with Germany."

I pressed my mouth shut. It had not been *Papa's* war. They all blamed him, when it was the Germans and their allies who had been the aggressors. Of course, I could not say that to Alena.

"I am so sorry," I said again. I had not realized that Evgenia knew how it felt to lose a sibling as well. She had not mentioned

Lev to me. It explained why she was willing to risk so much in exchange for a diamond, when she clearly was not greedy by nature. She wanted to protect what remained of her family: her mother, this strong woman who kept them together, and Konstantin, whose amputated leg and flushed skin hinted at further disease. As cold as he seemed, he was her brother. I would have given anything to save mine.

"It was a hard year, especially for the children. After that was when they got into communism, with the Bolsheviks. Kostya was working in Ekaterinburg for a few months and brought all that talk back from the factory. It radicalized them. And Evgenia followed in his wake like she always does. Meanwhile it was all I could do to keep us fed and housed."

This caught my attention.

"Are you not a Bolshevik supporter, then?"

She shrugged.

"I understand them. My children are more educated than I ever was. Ivan taught them, gave them books. They saw that things could be fairer. I admire them for it. But I wish the Bolsheviks would be more peaceable. Like the Kadets."

The Kadets were a political party popular among peasants, and slightly more reasonable than most leftist parties. They were not communist, though they did favor land redistribution. Initially they had shared power after Papa abdicated. However, they were inept leaders, and the Bolsheviks—equally inept, but more ruthless—violently seized control from the Kadets and their allies last October.

The Bolsheviks had unfortunately held on to power ever since. Not only did they surrender to Germany, they also instituted reforms that caused factories to produce far less than they used to, and price controls that discouraged peasants from selling enough food as was needed. Over the past few months, the few newspapers that reached us in the Ipatiev house spoke of growing famine in the cities.

"What about you?" Alena asked. "Are you a tsarist?"

I could hardly admit the truth to her. And in any case, my present desires had little to do with politics.

"All I want is to reach my grandmother in the Crimea," I said. I had not even told Evgenia so much. "She and my aunt are both there. Our friends in Chelyabinsk will help me reach them. They are the only close family I have left."

Her face softened.

"I'm sorry for your losses, too. I hope you get to your family. You're too young to be on your own, with the way things are today. You know," she said, "there's a Czech officer staying with us while the Whites are here. He's decent. Maybe you can talk to him about sending your message."

My heart rose, and I smiled at her for the new hope she had given me.

"I will."

"Did Mama give this to you to wear?" Evgenia asked me, fingering the linen shirt and belt her mother had laid on the bench. Alena had gone to hand over more food to the soldiers, waving off her children's pleas to join her.

"Yes. I apologize for taking your clothing—"

"Forget it," she said. "You need it."

I glanced at my stained blouse, one of the last connections

to my old life. I did not even have photographs of my family to remind me of them. And this shirt that Mama had chosen for me had outlived her.

"I would like to burn this," I said, my throat tight.

"I'll take care of it," she said softly.

"Thank you. Is there someplace private that I might change?" I asked.

Evgenia stared. "Does it look like we have private rooms here?" she asked. "Are you asking just to point that out?"

"I did not mean—"

"You want me to go through the trouble of stringing up some blankets so you can have your own space? Just change. No one's going to look."

I turned to face the corner and undressed. When I leaned over to take off the sarafan, the torn front of my corset flapped open. The lining was crumbling to pieces.

"What's that?" Evgenia asked.

She pointed. Sunlight poured in through the nearby window and reflected off my chest, creating a kaleidoscope of colored lights on the wall. Evgenia came around to see for herself, and I lowered my hand, letting the lining fall open to reveal the rows of priceless gems sewn into my undergarment.

Evgenia laughed, disbelieving.

"Well. I guess you did say you had more jewels."

"Yes."

She stared at them, and after several seconds, that familiar blush reappeared.

"What is it?" I asked.

She twisted her mouth. "I guess just one of those is probably worth more than this whole house."

"That is not my fault," I said automatically.

Evgenia's face darkened. "I didn't say it was."

Of course she had not said it outright, but it was the way she had spoken. As though I ought to be ashamed of the family I was born into. I could not stand it, I wanted to tell her off, but I kept my mouth shut.

"But now that you mention it," she went on, "I bet your parents didn't exactly fight for peasant rights, did they? They didn't get all those diamonds by sharing their profits, or telling their rich friends to pay workers more."

"My parents loved the peasants!" I snapped. "They were good—" I stopped myself just in time, before I told her they were *good rulers* and ruined everything. I was as angry with myself as with Evgenia for the near slipup. I could not allow her to goad me into admitting who I truly was.

"Good pomeshchiki?" she finished for me. "Good bosses? There's no such thing. Just because someone *has* money, or land or jewels, doesn't mean they *deserve* it. The people who do the work should own the profits."

"Oh, well done, Evgenia, you have clearly memorized the communist talking points. Do you even know what any of them mean? Do you understand that Russia will collapse if you throw out all of our educated, skilled leaders? You stole all the land but don't know how to farm it at scale. You seized factories that you don't know how to run. I shudder to imagine the state of our empire a year from now. If the communists win, we will all burn."

Evgenia looked at me as though I were a slug, as though she regretted saving me, after all. It was written all over her face.

"The days of the empire are over, Anna. It's time for people to rule themselves. We can learn the rest of it. People like you control who gets educated, then use it as an excuse to keep all the power. Maybe I only had a few years of schooling. But I know what's right. And it isn't right for one person to have all that"—she gestured at my corset—"while the rest of us starve."

My cheeks were burning, which only happened when I was on the verge of losing my temper. When Alexei would not stop pestering me, or Tatiana teased me for some mistake, or a Bolshevik guard said something crude to Masha.

"Back under the tsar, how many landowner votes did it take to elect one national representative, Anna? Do you know?"

"Two hundred and thirty."

"And do you know how many peasant votes it took to elect one?"

"There was a good reason—"

"How many?"

"Sixty thousand. But that's because the peasants far out-number landowners in Russia. Those rules existed to prevent disenfranchising the smaller classes! If you had your way, you would have stolen everything, like you're doing now. Communists want everything for free, without having to work for it."

"And how hard did *you* work for all those jewels?"

Careful, Tatiana's voice urged.

Evgenia was ignorant. She had no idea how complicated it was to run a country. My parents had exhausted themselves, daily, for their entire lives, trying to do right by our people. She did not understand what it took to balance competing interests, or how impossibly difficult it was to keep peace and build prosperity.

Then again, her family had seen none of that prosperity. They lived here.

The people in Mednyy had no hopes of educating themselves, making it to a university, and improving their lots. Konstantin, who despite his coldness appeared charismatic and intelligent, had managed only a factory job at best. Yet if his Bolsheviks won, he might earn a powerful seat on the soviet.

The appeal was obvious. Perhaps if Mama and Papa had listened to Olga, who urged them to invest more in universal education, the peasants would not have been so helpless. But that was not their *fault*. They had made the best judgments possible with the information available. They'd worked themselves to the bone for the Russian people. And if Evgenia and her ilk thought that the violent, inhumane Bolshevik leaders could do any better, then they were fools.

"Fine," I bit out. "Here. Take more of them. If I am so undeserving . . ." I scratched at the threads of my corset so I could free another jewel and give it to Evgenia, to shut her up.

"I don't want any more! Those shouldn't belong to you *or* me."

"But I thought you and your family did all the work, while—" My finger slipped through a hole in the corset lining. The diamond underneath was jagged and rough. It felt like it had been broken in half somehow, which was an insane idea, because diamonds did not break.

Unless, perhaps, they were struck by a bullet.

This was how I survived the execution. I had thought that

the power of Brother Grigori's necklace, or simply the grace of God, had protected me from the bullets. Now I remembered the tight pain in my chest after the gunshots. A bullet had struck me and ricocheted off the diamond, knocking me unconscious. The corset had saved me.

The corset that Masha should have been wearing.

My knees trembled. I sank onto the bench directly behind me and arched forward to rest my forehead on my knees.

"What are you doing?" Evgenia asked. "What's wrong?"

I opened my mouth to respond, but a wail emerged in place of words. I clamped my lips together, swallowing it, squeezing my eyes shut as tears spilled out.

Masha should have been wearing the corset. She should have lived. Not me.

"Please leave me alone," I said.

I was the reason Masha was dead. I had stolen this protection from her just as surely as I had stolen her necklace, as I had stolen her best friend at court when I was nine and she eleven, as I had stolen from her again and again because Masha was always giving and I always taking.

"Are you all right?" Evgenia asked. "Anna, you have to finish getting dressed."

The damned corset burned my skin. It branded me like a scarlet letter boasting of my shame. *Thief,* it said. *Murderer.*

"I will," I said. "I promise. Just leave me be for a little while, please." I could not look at her, could not show her my face, when she hated my family and would revel in my pain.

Briefly, I felt her hand touch my shoulder. Then she pulled away and let me hate myself in peace.

12

EVGENIA

KOSTYA WAS IN THE REAR yard. He'd dragged our old, broken wagon out and was hammering a rail into place.

I needed some peace and knew I'd find it with him. Not that I could talk to him about Anna. I hadn't meant to make her cry. But he'd be angry if he knew I was feeling sorry for her. Kostya was tougher than me. He was what a communist was supposed to be: totally committed to the cause. We couldn't let emotions get in the way of revolution.

Maybe I was too softhearted, but I didn't think she deserved to die. She hadn't done anything wrong herself. She wasn't capable of it. No one would be hurt if she joined her friends in Chelyabinsk.

I carried an herb drink to Kostya, a foul mixture Mama gave us whenever we got sick. He grimaced with each sip. I couldn't help but snicker.

"You find this funny?" he asked.

"I find your face funny. Funnier than usual, I mean," I teased.

He rolled his eyes. Kostya had come back from war so serious. The first week he'd been sick with fever and lay in bed all day, getting thinner and thinner. I'd thought he would die like Batya. When he finally came out of it, I thought things would be normal again. But the fever kept returning. And worse, he didn't laugh much anymore. As children the three of us were always laughing over something. Now I wished we could have just one day like that.

"Be a good sister and drink some for me." He held the cup near my mouth. I wrinkled my nose as the musky smell reached me.

"Because I am a good sister, I'll make sure you drink every drop." I nudged his hand back. "Go on."

"Cruel as ever." He shook his head and grimaced again as he downed the rest of it. "At least be useful if you're going to bother me." He pointed to the next wagon rail. I picked it up and held it while he hammered it into place. We worked quietly for a good while. He'd point to what he needed, and I always knew what he meant. He'd made good progress on the wagon bed, though it still had one broken wheel and no horse to pull it.

Repairs on the farm often went that way. You fixed what you could and waited for the money or supplies to fix what you couldn't. Sometimes you got them. Mostly you didn't. But you had to try.

"Sorry I lost the old one," I finally worked up the courage to say. Our wagon, all the trinkets and wares it'd taken me months to trade for, still sat in the barn back in Iset. It'd be gone by the time I ever made my way there again. "And Buyan."

Kostya sighed.

"I'm sure you wouldn't have let them take Buyan," I went on, my voice thick. Buyan had been Kostya's horse before he went to fight and I took over wagoning. "And I didn't even get you a doctor."

"I don't blame you," he said. "Not for the doctor, or Buyan. They'll take everything they can as long as they're here. I know there's nothing you could've done. You did your best."

Warmth spread through my chest. I felt a little less like a failure.

"But I'm worried about that girl, Zhenya," he went on. "If the Cheka's after her, then she's involved with something serious."

"Cheka? Is Yurovsky Cheka?"

Kostya nodded. And I wanted to cry like a spanked baby.

The Cheka were the police of the Red Army. They hunted counterrevolutionaries and killed deserters. When they arrested someone, you never heard from them again.

"*Chyort*," I said. "No wonder he's so vicious."

"Commander Yurovsky's a good man." Kostya frowned. "He's a member of the Ekaterinburg Soviet. He was the only one of them who cared about us soldiers when I was in training. He wouldn't let us fight until we had enough guns to go around. Everyone else said we could just *share*. If he executed Anna's family, he'd have had a good reason."

My mouth fell open.

"Are you joking?" I spluttered. "He's crazy. He tried to shoot me, and I haven't done anything!"

Kostya raised his eyebrows.

"I haven't!"

"You're helping a counterrevolutionary prisoner escape him. You lied to him to protect her. Why shouldn't he think you're on her side?"

"He could ask me!"

Kostya laughed, but it wasn't a happy sound. "Why would he? In his eyes, you're a traitor."

I almost didn't ask. But I couldn't keep it in.

"And in your eyes?" I asked.

Kostya didn't hesitate. "I know you," he said. "I know you're no counterrevolutionary."

That was more than I'd expected, and my tense shoulders relaxed.

"But all he knows is that you're helping this girl whose family was executed. What else could he think?"

"I don't like Anna any more than you do," I said, wishing it were true. "I want her gone. But she's harmless. You see that, don't you?"

"No, Zhenya." He shook his head. "I don't. I see a girl who somehow escaped the Cheka and led you into danger. I see a girl who is so important that a Cheka commander and three of his soldiers have chased her from town to town. Whoever she is, she's dangerous."

"Oh please," I said. I didn't know what else to say. Was Anna important? If so, then what had I done? Was I helping the Whites win by protecting her?

"The real danger here is the White soldiers," I said. "Let's talk about them."

Kostya shrugged. "Nothing we can do about it. We just

have to keep out of sight and keep our mouths shut. Some of the others from our chapter tried to fight back against the Whites. It did not go well."

I bit my lip. Kostya and I were members of the Mednyy Bolshevik group. We were trying to get more people to join us so we could get rid of the obshchina council. The council was full of old men who didn't think women deserved rights. After Batya died, they tried to take our land. Luckily Lev was still alive then, so Mama kept it in his name. When Lev died, she put the council off long enough for Kostya to come of age. But with Kostya crippled, they would try to take our land again.

A Mednyy soviet would let women vote and own land. But convincing people to believe in communism was slow going. So far only fifteen other men and a few women had joined our group, including my best friend, Dasha. And since no one outside of Mednyy cared about our government, the obshchina would keep ruling until we outnumbered them.

"What happened?" I asked.

"They arrested half our group. They killed Viktor Kossof and Natalya Popova. Everyone else scattered. Mama told the Whites that I died, a few days ago, and for now they believe it. I just hope no one says anything about you. Too many people saw you come back. The Whites are looking for more Bolsheviks."

Viktor Kossof and Natalya Popova, dead? Natalya was too old to be fighting. She'd been a loudmouth and a drunk, but also a devoted Bolshevik. And Viktor hosted our meetings with his wife. He'd been warm to me, but hard as iron when it came to communism. He wanted the revolution more than anything. And he'd died for it.

"Is Dasha all right?" I asked, my chest tight. "I saw her in the churchyard, but couldn't get to her through the soldiers."

"She's hiding with her uncle. Smart girl."

I let out a breath.

"Good," I said. "No one's going to turn me in, right? They're our neighbors. And no one likes the Whites."

"Hard to say." Kostya shrugged. "But Mama will want to keep you close to home. No going out to the fields, where the neighbors can see you." Our crops were all on the edge of town.

"What about the barley? I've already been gone four days. Without you or me, Mama can't keep up with the harvest. We'll lose the crop."

Kostya shook his head.

"She'll be worse off if we're dead. Or prisoners. We'll do what we can to make up for it once the Whites leave. And your new friend had better go with them. I doubt they'll let her use their telegraph machine."

"Those soldiers are even worse than I expected. Poor Nurka."

"Poor Foma Gavrilovich," he said. "We should check in on him. After everything else he's lost . . ." Kostya sighed. "I can't wait for the Whites to leave, either. Did Mama tell you there's one staying with us?"

"One what?"

"An officer," he said.

A chill skated down my back.

"No."

"Yeah. Most of their soldiers sleep in the church or school, but the officers are too good for that. They're being quartered in our houses. They mostly come at night, and for meals. We've got a Czech officer with us."

"I don't believe it!" I cried. "We have to *live* with one of them? How can you stand it?"

Kostya shrugged.

"We fight the battles we can win, Zhenya."

When Mama came back, she, Anna, and I sat on a bench in the shade behind the house. It was cooler out there. The evening was quiet, except for a lark singing from a neighbor's tree. I was weaving a new pair of lapti shoes. I braided together the smooth, dried strands of tree bark and pulled them through the wooden hook. Batya had taught me how to make lapti when I was ten. Now it was so easy I could've done it with my eyes shut.

Anna's eyes *were* shut. She was supposed to be stripping cabbages for dinner. Instead, she slumped back against the rough wall of the house, chin on her chest. We let her be. I hoped Kostya wouldn't notice her resting while the rest of us worked, but she needed it. I needed a nap, too, but as always there was work to be done. I made the shoes, Mama sliced potatoes, and the sun steadily lowered over the mountains.

A knock came at our front door. I looked at Mama nervously. Our neighbors called out when they visited, they didn't knock. This was a stranger.

Mama shook her head with a little frown, her sign for me not to worry.

"We're out back, Jiri!" she called loudly.

Anna woke with a start. The cabbage tumbled from her lap and Mama swooped down to pick it up, then put it and her knife on the bench beside her.

"Who is there?" Anna asked. Her voice was thick with sleep.

A Czech soldier came around the house in answer to her question. He wore the same red pants, long khaki shirt, and tall boots as the other Czechs. And, of course, he carried a rifle on his back. His blond hair was partly covered by a funny-shaped cap with a golden insignia. He smiled at Mama.

My mouth grew dry. He looked too easy to trust. Like he'd smile at you one moment and shoot you the next. I jumped to my feet to stand in front of Mama. She'd made me promise to be polite when he arrived, but I had to be ready in case he tried anything.

His eyes found me and traveled from my head to toe and back up again, a beat too long, before he glanced away. Heat rose in me like I'd stuck my head too close to an oven. If he were on our side I wouldn't have minded that look. It was almost nice. But that thought just made me madder. I squeezed my hands into fists.

"Good evening, Alena," he said in a heavy accent.

"Good evening, Jiri," Mama said. She spoke more formally than usual. "This is my daughter Evgenia—or you can call her Zhenya, like we do."

This White soldier was not going to use my nickname.

He held out his hand. I looked at it. Mama would be angry if I wasn't polite. But this was a *Czech soldier*. He and his White

allies had stolen Buyan from me. They'd shot Nurka Petrova.
And they'd cost Kostya his leg.

I knew I should shake his hand. The only problem was that
if I unclenched my fist, I'd hit him instead.

Anna rose and shook his hand just as he started to pull it
back.

"Hello," she said. "I am Anna Vyrubova." She used her
fake accent, the one that made her sound like a peasant from
Mednyy. "I am Evgenia's cousin, here for a visit. It is a pleasure
to meet you."

The Czech's brow straightened out, and he smiled again.

"It's nice to meet you, too. It's a hard time for a visit, yes?"
he added.

I scoffed. Was he talking about the fact that *his* men were
occupying our town? If he cared so much, he could leave.

Mama pinched my back with her nails, making me wince. I
knew what she wanted. Smile, be polite, make friends with the
enemy. But I couldn't do it. I wouldn't. Bringing Anna home
had been bad enough. At least she'd never killed any Red soldiers. But this?

I grabbed my weaving, last, and hook and stormed off to
the barn, leaving silence behind me. Mama could smooth over
my rudeness to keep the Czech happy. That was our job, now.
Everyone in Mednyy had to bow and smile and make nice with
them, the same soldiers who fought to end our revolution. It
was sickening.

The barn was cool and thick with the smell of hens. Kostya
sat on the floor next to our empty cow's stall, cleaning an awl
with a blackened rag. His crutch lay next to him.

"You met the Czech?" he asked. He must've heard us.

"Yes. We're best friends now."

Kostya snickered, and my chest eased some.

"You—" He stopped, and his eyes widened at something behind me.

I turned to see Mama storm into the barn.

"Mama—" I started.

She slapped me across the face.

"Mama!" I cried. My cheek burned, and I held both hands to it, forcing back tears. "What the devil?"

"What were you thinking? Are you even capable of thinking?"

"He—"

"Don't talk back to me!" She raised her hand again. I shut up. "That man controls us. He can do anything to us. Do you understand that?"

"I wasn't that rude," I grumbled. "He's staying in our house and you act like—"

"He can do what he wants," she said, her eyes still blazing into me. "Do you think he doesn't know Kostya's a Red soldier? He's not an idiot, unlike you right now. He knows we lied to Lieutenant Sidorov and said that Kostya was dead. All Jiri has to do is say one word and they'll take Kostya. Is that what you want?"

I scowled at my feet. She was right. And that stung.

"It's his house as long as he's here. What he says goes. Say it, Zhenya. It's his house."

Fuck him, I wanted to say. *Fuck him and every White soldier in town. Especially the Czechs, who don't care about our revolution*

or anything but forcing us to rejoin their war against Germany.
Fuck anyone who doesn't care about peasant lives.

"Say it."

"It's his house," I said, the words worming out of me like maggots.

"Good. Now come back and apologize and tell him he's welcome as long as he wants to stay."

I shook my head.

"I mean it, Evgenia."

"No. I'll be polite, like you want. I'll answer him if he talks to me. But he has to live without an apology."

Let him apologize for taking Buyan first, I thought. *Let him apologize for Kostya's leg.*

Mama sighed.

"You are too stubborn," she said.

"I wonder where she gets that from," Kostya called out from the floor behind me.

Mama cracked a smile, and even my chest lightened.

Mama and I walked back to the house together. The Czech still stood there talking to Anna. I felt a twinge of guilt. I'd left her alone with a strange, armed officer. And that was after she helped me by shaking his hand.

The Czech glanced at me curiously when we walked up. I fixed my eyes on the ground.

"Jiri, supper will be ready in a little while." Mama spoke slowly to make sure he got it. "Zhenya will start making the salad if you want to help her."

Curses sprang to my mouth. But as my cheek was still sore from Mama's slap, I managed to swallow them.

"He might not understand what I tell him," I said instead.

Mama's face clouded. I was pushing her limits. But the Czech laughed.

"My Russian is very bad," he said with a fake humble smile. "I wish I am in Germany. My German is better than my Russian."

I wished he were in Germany, too.

"*Sprechen Sie Deutsch?*" Anna said suddenly. I knew enough to understand she'd asked if he spoke German. Batya used to teach German at the school, until 1914, when we went to war. After that, everything German was banned. They even changed the name of the capital from Saint Petersburg to Petrograd, just because it sounded German.

Anna spoke the words easily. I narrowed my eyes at her. Her real accent in Russian was so odd. Could she actually be foreign? Even German? Her face was unusual, with her slim nose and sharp jaw. She *looked* like she could be from another country. But that was crazy. Right?

"*Ja,*" the Czech said. He spewed out more words I couldn't follow, and Anna answered back. Her face lightened, like she was relieved to be talking in another language. In *German.*

Now they had a way to talk in secret. I didn't trust the Czech, and I didn't like him cozying up to Anna.

13

ANNA

MY SLEEP WAS PLAGUED BY sweet dreams of my sisters that turned into bloodbaths. I had not witnessed their deaths, but my mind invented the images and sensations. I felt their bodies fall on top of me in the cellar of the Ipatiev house; I felt the blood from their wounds dripping onto me as Alexei's had.

The sound of the Koltsovs' front door shutting finally freed me. It took me several moments to remember where I was. The smell of tobacco, vinegar, and body odor registered first. I was lying on a lumpy, scratchy pile of hay that Evgenia had brought inside. It had taken me hours to fall asleep, unable to make myself comfortable. At one point I found a small beetle crawling through my makeshift bed. Between the sounds of Alena's and Lieutenant Valchar's heavy breathing from below, the overwhelming smells, and the roughness of my sleeping area, I had prayed for sleep, expecting it as a relief.

Instead, I was desperately grateful for the morning. On the main floor below, Alena had gone; Konstantin and Lieutenant Valchar sat at the table eating their morning meal. There was no sign of Evgenia. I felt uneasy in her home without her, her absence as discomfiting as a missing tooth.

She was supposed to have slept beside me in the loft. Instead, the evening before, she had collected her pile of hay and carried it outside. She and her brother both slept in the yard. As though they could not bear resting in the same house as me or Lieutenant Valchar.

I dreaded facing Konstantin again. Yet there was no avoiding it. Once I started down the ladder, both young men looked at me.

"Good morning," I said. They both—even Konstantin—returned the greeting. A small bit of weight lifted from my shoulders; at least he did not attack me on sight. I found it surprising that he spoke to Lieutenant Valchar when he would scarcely even look at me. Then again, it was not unheard of for soldiers to show one another respect when off the battlefield. Apparently Lieutenant Valchar rated higher in his eyes than I did.

I went outside to relieve myself and wash up with the bucket of water left for that purpose. I could not find the soap, and the Koltsovs had no glass or mirrors, so I did the best I could. I longed for a real bath; my head itched, Evgenia's clothing was musty, and my hair badly needed combing. I knew Evgenia was not in much better condition. How could she live like this?

By the time I returned inside, Konstantin had begun cleaning up the breakfast dishes, while Lieutenant Valchar was heading out to rejoin his fellows guarding the town. I hurried after him.

"Wait!" I called. He paused at the front gate and removed

his cap at my approach. I handed him the piece of bread left for me that I had no desire to eat. "You may grow hungry during the day; please take this with you."

"That's very thoughtful. Thank you."

"I am sure the food is very different where you come from. Do you miss it very much?"

He smiled wistfully.

"Yes. I do miss my home in Moravia. Especially"—he slapped at his neck, squashing an insect—"especially the mosquitoes." He laughed. "Russian mosquitoes are as fierce as their soldiers."

The mosquitoes here were indeed ubiquitous; my own legs and arms were covered in bites.

"Coming from the famously fearsome Czechoslovaks," I said, "I will accept that as a compliment on behalf of my countrymen, Lieutenant Valchar."

"You speak German so well." He smiled. "It's a relief to talk to someone easily."

"I can imagine." I mirrored his smile. "It must be challenging to stay here, surrounded by your enemies." I gestured at the Koltsov house. "Please do not think that I am as . . . hostile as they are."

He tilted his head, considering what I had said, and then shrugged.

"I don't mind them," he said. "Actually, I wish we weren't fighting. The Bolsheviks are wrong about the war, but they believe in self-determination. In people ruling themselves. That's all that we Czechs want. We don't want to be under someone else's control."

I swallowed my irritation. I had figured him for an ally, but he sounded exactly like Evgenia. No wonder he and Konstantin seemed to get along. The Czechoslovaks were fighting for their independence from the Austrian Empire, the Hapsburg allies of the Germans. It seemed that, whichever side won the war, Evgenia would be right—the age of empires was over.

"Of course," I said quickly. "Yours is such a noble cause. I truly admire the Czechoslovak Legion. My father spoke so highly of your soldiers before he died." That, at least, was true enough, as the Czechoslovaks had fought alongside our army.

"Oh, I'm so sorry about your loss."

"Thank you," I said, then found myself giving a bleak laugh. "I have lost everyone. The communists killed my entire family in Ekaterinburg. We supported the Czechoslovaks and the White Army, you know. That's why they were killed. I barely escaped. Evgenia helped me. I had nowhere else to go, and she took pity on me."

"I'm glad you found her," he said. "But I'm surprised. She seems a little . . . hard. I figured she disliked strangers, but I guess it's just me. Maybe I offended her with my terrible Russian?"

That made me smile.

"I am sure you didn't. Evgenia is suspicious by nature, but she is a good person," I said. "When I told her I need to reach my cousin, who is stationed with General Leonov in Chelyabinsk, she tried several times to help me get there. But the Bolsheviks are everywhere. I have no idea how I will ever make my way south."

His brows lifted.

"You don't need to go south. Leonov is coming. His men will help us take Ekaterinburg."

My heart rose like a balloon.

"They are coming north?"

"Yes, we're waiting for them. We will go meet them in two days. My company was separated from our regiment after a skirmish outside the city. We're trying to get back to them."

General Leonov was on his way *here*. He would not have to send someone from Chelyabinsk. Alexander, my cousin, was closer than I had dreamed. My eyes burned, and I forced down tears, glancing away so the lieutenant would not notice. He looked out at the horizon to give me privacy as I recovered myself.

"That is very welcome news," I finally said. "I would like to send a message to him right away. Do you have a telegraph set that I might use?"

"The Russians have one," he said, his eyes darkening. "Lieutenant Sidorov does not even let us use it."

The balloon in my chest popped.

"Does he guard it all the time, then?" I asked. "Are there no other Russian officers who might be more . . . generous?"

He winced.

"We want to stay allies," he said. "I'm sorry, but we can't—"

"No," I said quickly, realizing I had overstepped. "Certainly you would not want to disregard his orders. I only wondered if another officer could help change the lieutenant's mind."

"There is Captain Orlov," he mused. "He's a good man, and next in charge. He runs the telegraph and paperwork."

"Would you help me find him?"

Lieutenant Valchar smiled.

"He's hard to miss. He's a big man"—he mimed a large belly—"and runs operations in the schoolhouse."

"Thank you so much. I do hope you are reunited with your fellow soldiers soon," I said. "If there is anything I can do to assist you while I am here, please tell me."

He waved off the idea.

"No, nothing. And I say the same thing to you—if I can help you, tell me. Actually," he went on, "maybe you can convince the daughter that I'm not an enemy? I'm not here to hurt anyone."

He had a chivalrous side. Though it was silly of him to worry about making his enemies uncomfortable, it reflected well on his character.

If only he did not ask the impossible. Changing Evgenia's mind would be a tall order. She had refused to even look at him over dinner. I could only imagine what she had said—or not said—to him this morning. Yet if I could grant him his request and gain his gratitude, he would be more likely to take me with him.

"I will," I said.

I was not prepared to see Captain Orlov alone, so I sought out Evgenia. I found her working in the garden near the barn, wearing an oversize men's straw hat to shield her from the strong sun.

"You're finally up," she said as she rose. "Did you sleep all right?"

I had not. And I was annoyed that she had slept peacefully

outdoors, avoiding my presence. I wanted to confront her, to ask if she still hated me so much, but that risked provoking another quarrel, which would not incline her to help me.

"I slept fine, thank you."

She smiled, and I noticed that her hair was neater in its braid than the day before, and she looked cleaner.

"You bathed," I said, "didn't you? I could not find the soap. Where is it?"

A pink flush blossomed on her cheeks, surprising me.

"We haven't had soap for a long time," she said.

My skin prickled as humiliating heat swamped me. I knew I must be blushing but could not stop. They could not even afford soap?

Papa always said that capitalism was a flawed but efficient system. Not everyone could live as we did in our palace, but it brought the most good to the greatest number of people. He could not have known that anyone lived as miserably as the Koltsovs did. Perhaps his advisers never let him see true poverty.

Now I was living in it. I could not find words to respond to Evgenia. Her face grew tauter and redder with shame at my silence. It was no wonder that she had fallen for the Bolsheviks' utopian promises. Perhaps I would have, too, if my life had looked like hers.

"No matter," I said, trying to sound cheerful. "Please do not think I'm complaining. You and your family have been so generous, and I have more than I need here."

The crease in her brow smoothed over.

"We can stop by the stream on our way to the Petrov house," she mumbled.

"On our way where?"

"To see Foma Gavrilovich Petrov. He's the husband of the woman they shot yesterday, Nurka Olegovna. Mama wouldn't let me go work the fields with her today. She said I should go bring Foma some eggs. He's the town butcher. He doesn't have a lot of friends. I thought you'd want to come with me, instead of staying here."

"No, we must go to the schoolhouse," I said, recalling what I had learned. I quickly filled her in on what Lieutenant Valchar had told me of my cousin and General Leonov coming north.

"The Petrov house is on the way." She shrugged. "We can see him, stop by the stream, and then go send your message."

She lent me a scarf to cover my hair, and we walked to the Petrov house, climbing neighbors' fences and cutting through thick copses of evergreens to bypass the road.

His house was smaller than the Koltsov home, and in some disrepair; but its cheerful blue color made up for the few broken shutters. As we drew closer, I noticed small crescent moons and stars painted all over the blue walls. Though most of the stars were faded, some of them retained their bright yellow color. The design was pretty, and the effect would have been charming when freshly painted. I had never seen anything like it in a peasant village.

Evgenia climbed over a low, wooden fence into a garden overgrown with weeds and traipsed across rows of potatoes, beets, and cabbages competing for space. I followed her less adroitly, and stumbled on an uneven patch of ground.

"Watch it," Evgenia said sharply. She seized my elbow and pulled me forward. A sudden pinching on my ankle made me wince, and I leaned over to rub it. Evgenia began laughing. "You were right on an ants' nest."

I lifted my skirt to find a large red ant running up my leg and slapped it off. The skin around the bite burned. I scratched until Evgenia grabbed my arm again.

"It's like a mosquito bite. Scratching it'll only give you a big, fat welt," she said, still chuckling. "What would you do without me?"

Itchy and irritated, I stuck my tongue out at her. She rolled her eyes in a good-natured way.

"Come on, let's get this over with. Ey—do you hear that?"

A faint slapping noise came from the far side of the house. I could not figure out what it might be, and Evgenia looked just as baffled as she led the way around to investigate.

Foma stood over a hole in the rear yard. His wiry arms struggled with a shovel as he slowly dug out more dirt, dropping it onto a nearby pile. Next to the hole there was a small mound wrapped in a colorful blanket. My heart crawled up into my throat as I realized what it was. Nurka lay inside that blanket. He was digging her grave.

I looked to Evgenia to see what she would do; she swallowed audibly, then approached the elderly man.

"Zhenya?" he asked once he looked up. He sounded exhausted, and he appeared even older than he had yesterday in the churchyard. He drew his sleeve over his face to wipe his wrinkled cheeks and forehead. The grave only reached one cubit deep, yet his shirt was already soaked through with perspiration.

"Yes, it's me," Evgenia said. "I brought some eggs." She

placed the basket on the ground near the house. "And—I wanted to say sorry. We ran into trouble in Iset, and I lost all your clay pots. And all the money."

"Oh," said Foma. He did not seem to notice I was there, nor wonder who I was. We stood in the yard wordlessly. I wanted to back away, to pretend we never stumbled upon this painful scene. I never wished to see another corpse in my life. Nurka was just underneath that blanket, white and cold. I was even able to smell her now. I covered my mouth and averted my face. We needed to leave the man and his dead wife to carry on this quiet tragedy alone. I waited for Evgenia to turn, but instead she broke the silence.

"Do you have another shovel?" she asked. She was going to help him. That meant staying here with the body, and the smells, and the tangible thickness of Foma's grief.

"No," he answered her. "Just those." He gestured to a pair of small hand trowels on the ground. Evgenia held one out to me.

"We do not have time for this," I whispered. "We must go find Captain Orlov."

Evgenia cast me a look so vile I wanted to shrink into nothingness.

"Do you ever think about anyone besides yourself?" she demanded in a low voice. "Do what you want." She tossed the trowel at my feet.

I wanted to pull her back and say that of course I did, that I had been kind and generous to her, to her mother, to Lieutenant Valchar. Then it hit me—what had I really done for them? In truth, I endangered Evgenia and her family and offered only untradable jewels in return. My stomach churned guiltily.

I picked up the trowel and joined Evgenia.

She nodded at me before introducing me as her cousin. Foma Gavrilovich scarcely paid any attention. There was an air of emptiness to him beneath his exhaustion, and all that seemed to matter to him was completing this task. So we assisted him.

Evgenia took the shovel while Foma and I knelt beside the grave to dig with trowels. The air was thick and hot, and I had to hold my kerchief over my nose to keep out the decaying smell of Nurka's body, only a few cubits away.

We dug for hours straight, with only brief respites when I fetched water from the little stream nearby. My mind cleared as the hole grew deeper, and I forgot about the body. I stopped thinking about what it reminded me of; I stopped noticing the heat and sweat and mosquitoes altogether. I had to switch between my right and left hands as my arms tired, and I wanted to give up at several points, especially once we stood in the hole ourselves and had to lift the dirt out one scoop at a time. But Evgenia never stopped working, and so neither did I, until we had made a hole large enough to fit a body inside of it.

Evgenia and I helped Foma out of the grave, then stood beside him ourselves and stared at his wife's body. There was only one thing left to do.

"She made me laugh," he said suddenly, in a scratchy voice. "Not much left to laugh about now."

"No," Evgenia agreed.

I stared at her, appalled, and she seemed to understand that agreeing with him was hardly delicate.

"I mean, yes there is," she said, somehow finding something to say that was even worse.

"Foma Gavrilovich," I cut in, "would you like me to say a prayer for her?" It was the only appropriate thing I could think to say at what was essentially a funeral. Until communism began turning Russians away from the Church, no soul could be buried without a religious ceremony. Evgenia frowned at me. Offering to pray was risky, because if Foma were an atheistic communist, too, then he would be offended. But I wanted to try.

"Yes," he said. "Please."

I took a deep, long breath.

"Holy God, Holy Mighty, Holy Immortal, have mercy on us," I began. My voice grew thick as I spoke, but I kept on, because this was not just for Nurka. My family had received no burial. The words I recited were also for Papa, and Mama, and Masha and Olga and Tatiana and Alexei, and everyone else who had died in that cellar and then been burned instead of buried. These were their funeral rites, as well. "Lord, grant eternal rest unto your departed servant, Nurka Olegovna Petrova, and make her memory to be eternal," I recited. Foma joined in, and then, astonishingly, so did Evgenia. My eyes filled with tears as they met hers.

When we finished the prayer, he stepped nearer to his wife.

"My Nurka," he said quietly. "I was supposed to go first. You could have gone on making more art with the young ones. What good am I to anyone?" His voice broke. He got on his knees and placed his hands on her body, crying.

I was crying as well, and though I tried to stay respectfully still and quiet, the tears poured down my face. I knew exactly how Foma Gavrilovich felt; his grief seeped into me and added to the heavy darkness that swamped me. I knelt beside him and wrapped an arm around his shoulders, feeling them shake just as mine did.

"Say some words about her, Evgenia Ivanovna," Foma said when his cries slowed. "I can't."

Evgenia looked unnerved. I tried to collect myself, to stop crying so that I could speak before she said anything foolish. I rose, and Foma followed me, but as I dried my face I knew that there was nothing I could add. I had not known the woman. I glanced at Evgenia, whose throat worked as she swallowed audibly.

"Lev knew her best," she said at last. "Nurka Olegovna taught him to paint. I liked to watch them. She always made it fun. When she painted Foma Gavrilovich's clay pots, they always sold for more." She twisted her hands in her apron. "One time she painted my face on the head of a mule when she thought I was being stubborn."

A laugh escaped me, and I wiped the falling tears off my face. Foma did not react but watched Evgenia fixedly, rapt by her words.

"Nurka Olegovna was kind, and funny," Evgenia went on. "She was really brave. I'll miss her."

She stopped then and glanced at me, either for reassurance or for confirmation that she had said the right thing. I nodded at her. Foma got down on his knees once more and kissed the top of the blanket, before making the sign of the cross over it. Then he grabbed one end of the blanket and looked up expectantly.

I helped him lift from his end, while Evgenia carried the

other. The blanket was thin and scratchy, and as we raised Nurka's body, the fear and horror left me. I helped lower her into
the grave. When I released her weight, some of the dark grief
inside me went with her.

"I'll go set out some kvass," he said abruptly, before turning
and walking into the house.

I stared at Evgenia. The body still needed to be covered.

"Let's finish it," she said. I nodded, and we picked up
our tools and laid Nurka to rest, ending one of the strangest
and smallest funerals in history. I crossed myself when we
finished and said a silent prayer for someone, someday, to
do at least as much for my family. Then we looked toward
the house.

"We must be quick about this," I said.

Evgenia nodded. Neither of us felt as though we could turn
down the offer, however, so we headed inside.

"Please, drink," Foma said as we entered. He gestured at
four clay mugs on the table, filled with kvass. All three of us
noticed the unneeded cup at the same time. "I put out an extra
cup," he said in a dull voice. "I forgot."

We joined him at the table. The Petrov house was as
unusual inside as out, once more a testament to the unique
woman Nurka must have been. From waist height all the way
up to the low ceilings, the walls were covered with pictures. A
few of them were framed, while most were parchment, paper,
or canvas nailed into the wood. Nearly all the paintings were
riotously colored. Evidently blue had been Nurka's favorite
color, as it was everywhere. She had been prolific and broad
in her repertoire. She had painted still lifes of flowers, food,

machines, and landscapes, but also animals and people. The painting of Evgenia as a mule, regrettably, was nowhere to be seen.

"Thank you for the drink, Foma Gavrilovich," I said politely, after we had been seated for a while. "Is there anything you need that we can bring you?"

"No, no," he said. He didn't look up from his cup.

"May I have a look at your wife's artwork?"

He nodded, and I stood to take a closer look. The third wall, near the rear of the house, had caught my attention. It was covered not with paintings but with postcards. There were dozens of them, showing pictures of city streets, saints, flowers, churches, and more. Many of them read *Ekaterinburg* on the front. My stomach turned at the sight of those streets my family had driven over, in the city where they died.

"From his sons." Evgenia joined me and spoke softly. "They both died in the war. Germans," she added, clarifying that she referred to the Great War, not the revolution.

"The poor man," I murmured.

I curled the edge of one postcard to read the greeting, and saw *Dear Mama and Papa*. Their parents had saved every single postcard up on the wall, and now they served as a memorial.

"Foma Gavrilovich, we have to get going now," Evgenia said, returning to him. "But I'll come back tomorrow. Your garden needs weeding, and the potatoes are mature."

As I was about to join her, I spotted a postcard with a photograph of seven people on the front. My knees trembled. I put a hand on the wall to steady myself. Seeing them was like jumping into a frozen bath. It took my breath away.

The postcard showed my family. There I was, age twelve, sitting at Papa's side, with my arm around Alexei. There were Masha and Mama and Olga and Tatiana. We had taken this official photograph five years ago, to commemorate three hundred years of Romanov rule. The entire country had celebrated with us. Thousands of copies of this postcard were sold across Russia and mailed all over the world. My sisters and I had dressed in our favorite matching white gowns, Mama let us wear the pearl necklaces Grandmother had bought us for Christmas, and we giggled and squabbled for hours while the photographer attempted to take a good picture. This final photograph, the one Papa had published, showed us at ease, formally posed but serene. Only Masha and I smiled secretively, sharing some private joke that I could no longer recall.

"You should rest," Evgenia was saying behind me. She eased Foma onto a bench to lie down. "We'll be back tomorrow. Come on, Anna."

I blocked their view of the wall and carefully removed the postcard. As I walked out after Evgenia, the edges of the stiff paper pressed against my belly, comforting me. I had not thought to see their faces again, not for a long time. But my family had found me in this tiny nothing of a town. I could not wait to take the postcard out of my pocket and stare at their faces, to see them alive and happy again.

"It's not right what the Whites did to Nurka," Evgenia said. She clenched her fists as we walked. "They need to pay."

I hardly heard her. I pressed my hands on top of my pocket and held my family close.

14
EVGENIA

ANNA AND I BATHED NAKED in the stream, our backs to each other.

I splashed water on my face, trying to cool it. *Damn Sidorov. Damn all the Whites who tore up our country.* They defended the monarchy when it was the tsar who got the Petrov boys killed in a stupid war. Why did anyone want him back? I'd never seen Foma so weighed down. As the town butcher, most people avoided him because they thought his work was dirty. But I'd never seen him so alone.

We dried off quickly in the sun and with our kerchiefs. Once Anna was clean again, her short hair smoothed back, she smiled. My heart squeezed a little. I couldn't have guessed that a bath would make her so happy.

Even one without soap. She probably hated our house. Our whole town probably seemed dirty to her. Did *I*?

"Let's go," I said.

Her smile dimmed. She followed me out of the woods and down the road toward the church.

We passed three White soldiers walking in the opposite direction. I slowed down until Anna was by my side. One of the men tipped his hat with a smile, but the rifle on his shoulder wasn't so friendly. I glared. Anna greeted them as we walked by, then frowned at me like I'd done something wrong.

My body was sore from digging for so long. The last thing I wanted to do was make nice with the Whites who let Nurka die. They'd taken Buyan. Maybe they'd even *eaten* him. Now we had to go and beg them for help. The thought made me sick. But the only thing worse than talking to the Whites would be having Anna still here after they left. So we walked on.

The churchyard was full of them. Soldiers sat on the church steps laughing and probably getting drunk. More of them worked like bees, carrying papers or crates from one part of the yard to another. Just past Batya's schoolhouse I saw where they kept the livestock behind rope. Two men stood on guard. The animals bleated and grunted like they missed their homes.

My heart pinched. Maybe Buyan was back there.

"This way," Anna said. She led me to the schoolhouse. It was a squat, wide building just a few cubits away from the church. This used to be Batya's special place. Now the White soldiers had taken over.

To make it all worse, a soldier stepped right in front of us. And it was the same smirking soldier we met entering Mednyy. One of the men who took Buyan.

He blocked our way into the schoolhouse that he never should've been near. His eyes got wide when he looked us over.

"Hello, girls," he said with a nasty smile. "You two look nice. Did you come to see me?"

I snorted in disgust.

"Good afternoon," Anna cut in quickly. "In fact, we came to see Captain Orlov or Lieutenant Sidorov about an urgent matter. Are either of them inside?"

"What do you want them for?"

"I would very much like to tell you, but I think we should speak directly to them," Anna said.

This lout wasn't interested in her politeness.

"What'll you do for me if I help you?" he asked.

We were wasting our time. This idiot was just getting in our way.

"If you insist on knowing, I will tell you the reason," Anna said. She leaned into me until I had to step a bit to the side. She moved with me. "Only it is a secret, so please, come close."

His face lit up like a bratty child promised a treat. He walked over and leaned so close to Anna I smelled his oniony breath. I almost gagged.

"The truth is that we are simple country girls," Anna said. She spoke with her fake Mednyy accent as usual. It was almost scary how perfect it was. "You may remember that yesterday we told you we had been visiting friends for a few days. Do you recall us saying that?"

He nodded but also winced, like it hurt him to admit for some reason.

"Well, Evgenia here was really the one visiting, and it was my family she had come to see. We are cousins, and I am from Iset, which is a town not so far from here. It is a much bigger town, and my family is there now. So, you see, I would like to talk to the commanding officers about heading back to Iset."

The soldier winced again and started rubbing his legs. I looked down, and my mouth fell open. He was standing right on top of a red ant nest.

I shut my mouth to keep from laughing. Anna had led him there on purpose and babbled to keep him on top of it until the ants ate him alive.

"We would not want anyone to worry about where we were going," she went on. But the soldier yelped. He wasn't listening anymore. He looked down and saw at least a dozen big ants crawling over his boots.

"*Chyort!*" he yelled. He danced away from the nest. He slapped at his legs wildly, still cursing, trying to kill the ones under his pants. "Water!" he shouted. "Get me some water!"

He ran off. I burst out laughing, and Anna elbowed me, trying to shut me up. I hid my face in her shoulder so the Whites wouldn't see me. I couldn't stop laughing. I didn't even want to. My anger from the funeral was melting away.

"You scare me sometimes, Anya," I said.

Anna's eyes danced.

"We should not make a scene here, *Zhenya*," she said.

I looked at her in surprise. She winked.

"Look, here comes another soldier," she said before I could reply. "Quiet."

I coughed to hide my laughs. This new soldier had a long, honest face.

"Can I help you?" he asked. "I heard you're looking for Lieutenant Sidorov, but he's in the field just now."

I tried to catch Anna's eyes so we could share another smile. We'd agreed to come back later if Sidorov was here, so this was good news. But she kept her face serious, so I did, too.

"We would also like to speak to Captain Orlov, if he is here?"

"Hold on." The soldier stuck his head into the schoolhouse and talked to someone inside. Then he straightened and waved at us. "Go on in."

Now Anna did smile at me. We hurried past him.

They'd changed the schoolhouse. The rows of benches where we used to sit were all gone. The Whites hunched over little folding tables and wrote on stacks of bright white paper with fancy pens. One soldier rushed around like a postman, dropping off papers and collecting more from each table. Two in the rear bent over crates full of metals and made a big racket as they dug through them. It was probably all the tools and weapons they stole from us.

Up front near us, soldiers circled Batya's desk like hogs at a feeding trough. They tried to catch the attention of a big, fat officer sitting in Batya's chair. The top of his head was almost completely bald. His neck was so meaty his chin looked like ripples in water. His face was soft, but his eyes were sharp as he gave orders to each man.

The soldiers' talk died down when they saw us. The schoolhouse got quieter than on one of Batya's test days. The men stared, frowned, and smirked at us.

I looked at Anna. These were her people, after all.

"Please forgive this interruption," she said, dropping her Mednyy accent and speaking like a city girl. "Captain Orlov, is it?"

The officer's face stretched into a wide smile. Anna walked over to his desk, and all the soldiers got out of her way. Something about the way she stood and spoke had them all listening. I stayed in her shadow and pulled my scarf over my cheek to block out their stares.

"Yes, what is it?" Orlov asked. "Private, stop that." He flapped his hand at a soldier about my age. He'd been tapping away at a big, black machine near the desk.

"My name is Anna Alexandrovna Vyrubova." Anna gave a curtsy so deep I couldn't help snickering. She cast me a stern look. "This is my cousin Evgenia Ivanovna, who lives in this town."

"Hello," I said, since they were waiting for something. I wasn't about to try one of her silly curtsies. I felt a blush coming on, as if it wasn't hot enough in there. It was worse in the schoolhouse than outside, even with the shutters open. Only the Whites were stupid enough to spend all their time indoors in high summer.

"Are you not from Mednyy, Anna?" Orlov asked.

"I am not. I am from Ekaterinburg but fled here to stay with my distant relatives after the Bolsheviks seized control. They took everything from my family." Her voice shook. Some of the men leaned in. Orlov's eyes went as soft as a lamb's ear.

Anna was putting on a show. She was probably used to men falling over her like this. Mama always said that ladies lived the best lives you could imagine. Their servants did the work, their men fought the wars, and the women ruled their households. Judging by how respectful Orlov was to Anna, she was used to that kind of treatment.

"The Czech officer who is staying with us, Lieutenant Valchar, suggested that I speak with you, Captain," she went on. "He spoke highly of you. We thought perhaps you might be able to assist me."

"Come, tell me your troubles. Move." He snapped his fingers at a soldier who jumped out of his chair. Anna sat facing Orlov while I pressed close to her back and the Whites surrounded us.

"You see, I am stranded here, Captain," she said. "I am desperate to reach my family again, but I have no reliable way to contact them. The notion of being here after your battalion departs . . ." She exaggerated a shiver. "It frightens me."

"As it should, my dear," Orlov said. "I can see that you don't belong here—you seem like someone accustomed to better than these peasant houses and even that poor dress you wear."

My face burned. I pulled at my collar and wished the men behind me would back off.

"You say your surname is Vyrubov," he said. "Any relation to the Vyrubov family of Petrograd?"

"Yes, as a matter of fact," Anna said. "Though I have never met them, they are cousins of mine. And our mutual cousin, Alexander Maliukov, is the person I would like to reach. He is very close to Ekaterinburg—he serves under General Leonov's command."

She didn't say a word about Yurovsky, or her family being dead. She picked and chose bits of truth to tell. She was manipulating the White captain. I didn't care how she treated him, but it made me wonder. She'd flattered Mama when she begged to stay with us, too. Did she do the same to me?

"In that case," Orlov said, "I can bring a message to him with us when we leave town. We'll give you some paper to write a letter right now."

As soon as they left town, Yurovsky would find his way in.

"That is a most generous offer," Anna said. "It is just that, you see, I am nervous about staying here longer without anyone proper to look after me. I am afraid of the Bolsheviks coming back once you have left. And—and I miss my family so." Her voice wobbled prettily again. A tear dropped into her lap. Even though I knew it was for show, my gut twisted. She *did* miss her family. At least that wasn't a lie.

Her tears moved Orlov, too. He handed Anna a handkerchief. She dabbed at her face as gently as you'd wash an egg.

"There, there, Anna Alexandrovna. I'll send your telegraph, if it's a short one. Private, finish that communiqué. You, go get us some tea. The rest of you, quit gaping and get back to work."

The clacking noise of what had to be the telegraph machine started again. The other soldiers went back to bustling around.

Anna thanked the captain. She'd actually done it. She'd talked her way into getting her message sent, just like she'd talked her way into my wagon, and into our house. If Lenin were here she'd probably talk him into surrendering.

"Now tell me, dear," Orlov said. "How exactly did you end up here?"

Anna spun him a tale I'd never heard. In her story, her parents were still alive. Evil Bolsheviks chased them out of her house, and she lost them in a crowded square. She rode a post wagon north, and walked the rest of the way to my house.

It was a whole trail of lies. Orlov swallowed every word. He made sympathetic noises like what she told him was so terrible.

Like being far from your family and sleeping with peasants were the worst things that could happen to a *lady*.

"You have had a harrowing few days," he said. "I'm only sorry no one was there to protect you. Our country's most vulnerable and precious people, especially women and children, must be taken care of."

I snorted. Orlov's eyes narrowed at me. Anna snapped her head over so fast I swore her neck creaked.

"Just not old women, right?" I asked.

The soldier at the telegraph gasped. Orlov glared at me. Anna's lips all but disappeared.

"Evgenia," she said quietly. "Wait outside."

I stormed out. One of the men closed the door after me, so I didn't even get to slam it.

At least I could breathe outside. I wiped the sweat off my eyebrows. I should've kept my mouth shut, but I couldn't help it. They were all fakes. First Anna with her lies. Then Orlov, who only cared about Anna because she was a rich city girl. He hadn't minded stealing from poor peasants. He'd done nothing for the Petrovs.

I leaned against the shady side of the schoolhouse. Anna didn't come out, so she'd probably smoothed things over. She was good at that.

The Whites were still all over the churchyard. A few of them looked at me curiously, but luckily no one talked to me. As long as that idiot with ants in his pants didn't come back, I'd be fine.

More time passed. The itchy soldier didn't appear, but Anna didn't, either. How long did it take to send a telegraph message? I didn't know anything about telegraphs. They kind of seemed like magic. I couldn't believe that people three towns away could be reading a letter after just a few seconds.

I scuffed my feet in the dirt. There was a lot I'd never seen. Kostya had told me about the electric lights, trains, and automobiles he saw in Ekaterinburg. They even had moving pictures. Someday I wanted to go there and see for myself. There was more to the world than the road between Mednyy and Iset.

A big group of White soldiers walked into the yard. I watched them closely. The man in front barked orders at the others and sent them running off one by one.

It was Sidorov. My stomach swooped. He headed for the church, not the school, thankfully. *Look away.* Maybe he wouldn't care if he saw me, but I didn't want to take the chance.

I held my breath. He and his group reached the church stairs. He took the first step. Then he turned his head in my direction. He looked away.

Then looked again.

I snapped upright. Sidorov headed right for me.

I could have run. Behind the church the fence had a back door, and beyond that was mostly woods. It'd be easy to lose his men there. But I'd never have made it. He had six soldiers following him, and a couple of them looked fast. I'd look guilty if I ran. The Whites weren't any different from the old Imperial police. They thought all peasants were guilty of something.

Sidorov was taller than I remembered. His jaw was shadowy, like he hadn't shaved in a day or two. His men crowded around us, trapping me against the wall.

"Who are you?" he demanded. "What are you doing here?"

"Nothing," I said, but I had to cough to clear my throat and say it again. I tried to imagine what Anna would tell him and glanced at the schoolhouse door, thinking of her.

Sidorov's eyes followed mine.

"Is something happening in there?"

"No! No one's in there. I—I'm looking for my horse," I said.

But he wasn't listening anymore. He went straight to the door and pushed in.

"Wait!" I hurried after him.

Orlov jumped to his feet. His buttoned-up belly bounced, and he gave a sharp salute. Anna stood, too. All the color left her face. She looked about how I felt.

"Orlov, what's going on? Who is this?"

Orlov didn't look scared at all. His face just went blank.

"This is Anna Vyrubova, Lieutenant. She's an educated girl, from Ekaterinburg. A relative of the Petersburg Vyrubov family. She fled the Bolsheviks and wound up here. She wants to send a message to her family."

"What sort of message?"

"A telegraph."

Sidorov went silent for a long, cold moment.

"Didn't I say that all messages were to be approved by me?"

"Yes, Lieutenant."

"Then *why* did you disobey me?" Sidorov roared.

"I didn't send the message yet," Orlov said. "I was going to ask you."

Disappointment shot through me. She hadn't got the message out.

"The answer's no," Sidorov said. "Get out, girl. Both of you. I don't care who your family is. This is my machine, and it won't be used as a girl's plaything. Go!"

Anna and I rushed out together, all the way out of the churchyard. Once we were a few cubits along the road I pulled her into a shady grove where we wouldn't be seen. She still looked too pale.

"Are you all right?"

"No," she panted, out of breath. "*Chyort!* He was in the middle of telegraphing my message to Alexander. One minute more and it would have been sent. I would have been *rescued*." She'd never cursed before. She even curled her fingers into a fist, like she was about to burst. "If only I could have had a couple minutes more."

"I'm sorry. I tried to stop him. But he knew something was up as soon as he saw me," I said. "He wouldn't listen."

"Do you mean that he only came inside the schoolhouse because he saw you standing out there?"

"Yes," I admitted.

"Evgenia!" She threw her arms in the air.

"What?"

"If you had remained silent and at my side, none of this would have happened! Yet you insist on antagonizing every White soldier you meet, instead of maintaining the barest level of civility."

Something rose inside me. Sidorov had stopped us, but she blamed me.

"That's not fair," I said.

"And now you talk of *fairness*, as though that matters. You behave like a child, Evgenia. You refuse to even speak to Lieutenant Valchar, though he knows your brother's secrets. You ignore the White soldiers, who could harass or even arrest you. And now Captain Orlov—"

"Fuck them!" I felt like I did the time Batya made me recite a Pushkin poem in front of the whole school, but I forgot the words. "I won't make friends with the Whites! Not after everything they did. I'm not like you, Anna. I can't smile and lie to get what I want. I won't. I'm not a *child*. I just have principles, unlike you."

Her nostrils flared. All the color was back in her face.

"Your precious principles will get me killed. They will get *both* of us killed, and they endanger your family."

I gritted my teeth. I wouldn't let anything happen to my family. But unless I was ready to kick Anna out, then helping her send her message would keep them safe. And I wasn't ready to kick her out.

I huffed. Anna did, too.

"So what now?" I asked.

I couldn't sleep that night. We still hadn't come up with a plan, and the Whites were leaving in less than two days. I watched the stars light up one by one. Kostya snored next to me, a cloth over his eyes to block out the light. I couldn't stop worrying long enough to sleep. We'd have to get rid of Anna when the Whites left. Mama and Kostya's safety came first. But where would she go?

Something woke me up after the sky had darkened.

It was a sound like whimpering, like an animal being

beaten. I sat up and tried to place it. It was coming from the loft window of our house.

It was Anna. I stood and crept quietly inside the front door. Mama was sleeping on a hay-covered bench against the wall. The Czech had taken her bed over the oven. I climbed into the loft to find Anna squirming in her pile of hay like a dog with a burr in its side. She was caught in a nightmare.

"Mashka," she moaned.

I waited to see if she'd say anything more. But she just repeated the name again and again. I shook her shoulder roughly.

"Anya!" I hissed. "Anya, wake up."

She woke like a startled cat. For a few seconds she just stared at me, her eyes clapped on mine, her face utterly still. Then, in the faint light from the windows, I saw her eyes widen and her mouth twist a fearful grimace.

"Are you all right?"

She nodded.

"You were calling out for someone named Mashka," I whispered.

Her face crumpled. Her mouth turned down, and she buried her head in her hands. Her body shook as she started crying, quiet enough not to wake anyone.

"I'm sorry," I whispered.

She leaned into me. Even though she was taller than me, she felt skinny and small in my arms. I patted her back, like Batya used to when I cried or hurt myself.

In the silent cabin the others were still asleep. Anna cried without much noise. I wouldn't have known she was doing it, if not for the tears wetting my nightgown.

"I left them," she whispered. "What if one of them was still alive?"

"Who?"

"My family," she sniffed. "The Bolsheviks took us in a wagon to the woods. They were going to burn our bodies. They did not know that I was alive, that my—my corset repelled the bullets. I awoke in the back of the wagon, among—among my family. I freed myself and slipped out of the back of the wagon, and I fled.

"What if I was not the only one still alive? I did not stop to make sure. Mama lay next to me, and she was gone." Her voice broke. "And Alexei, too. My little brother. I saw him, and that was all it took for me to give up on my entire family and run away. I did not even check the rest of them."

"Holy hell," I muttered as she cried. "I'm sorry."

"I keep seeing my sister Masha opening her eyes, and all she sees are the bloody bodies of everyone around her. And then she screams." Anna's voice gave out, and she sank to my lap, crying harder.

I held her and let her cry. It didn't matter that I couldn't comfort her. I didn't think anything could make her feel better. How would I feel if I saw someone shoot Mama or Kostya? It'd been hard enough watching Batya die. I couldn't imagine losing my whole family.

Anna had to live with it.

"Let me get you a handkerchief," I whispered when her cries slowed.

She stilled and sat up, shaking her head. She lifted the hem of Batya's old nightgown and used it to wipe her face.

"The Reds burned them, Zhenya," she whispered. "My family will never receive a proper burial, or even a prayer like Nurka Petrova. It was not enough to murder them. The Reds had to damn them as well."

The Church taught that your soul would rejoin your body at the end of days. If your body wasn't buried, then your soul couldn't find it and go to heaven. I wanted to tell Anna it was nonsense. The Church used those lies to control people. But she still believed in it. I'd heard Kostya argue enough times with Batya to know you couldn't talk someone out of their beliefs. Batya taught those old stories at school, and no amount of arguing ever changed his mind.

"I'm sorry."

She nodded.

"As am I. I am sorry that I was wearing the corset that night, and that I lived while Masha died. She was such a good person. All of them were." Anna leaned into me again.

I held her while she cried, and thought about what kind of person I'd be if I sent her off to die alone.

15

ANNA

WHEN I WOKE IN THE morning my eyes ached from the late-night tears, but my body felt lighter. The fact that Evgenia cared enough to let me talk was a soothing balm. Nothing had changed, but at least one other person thought it mattered that my family had died.

Even better, I awoke with a new plan. I carried my hay pile outside to discard it and found Evgenia pulling dried bandages down from the line and folding them. My heart warmed to see her.

"Ey, Anya," she said. She studied my face carefully. I must have looked a tear-streaked fright, for she bit her lip. "Are you all right?"

"I feel well, thank you. In fact, I would like to thank you for—"

"Zhenya!"

A tall, slender girl with bright red hair under a clashing orange headscarf stood at the front gate, waving. Evgenia gasped—a smile lit up her round face—and she and the girl ran to each other. They embraced and chattered eagerly while the girl patted Evgenia's cheeks and arms as though to confirm she was real. Evgenia did not pull away; it was the happiest I had ever seen her.

A few minutes passed before Evgenia remembered that I stood there, staring at them like a forlorn child. She had a life beyond this house, of course. I had seen only a little part of it. After I left Mednyy, she would resume her life, unchanged, as though we had never met. My place here suddenly felt smaller, tucked in haphazardly at the edges of her existence.

"Anya, this is my friend Dasha." She led Dasha over, her face still bright. "And this is Anna Vyrubova. We met when I was wagoning. I'll tell you the whole story when we have time. We're trying to find her a way back to her friends, who are coming from Chelyabinsk."

"Anna, I'm pleased to meet you," she said.

We smiled at each other. She looked kind, and her eyes were intelligent. She studied me quickly, seemed to reserve her judgment, then turned back to Evgenia.

"Is Kostya here? I have some urgent news."

"I'll get him." Evgenia ran off to the barn. Her friend entered the house, and once more I was left on my own. I traipsed inside the house after her. If there was news to learn, I would hear it.

The four of us sat around the kitchen table. Evgenia and Dasha's lightness faded into an excited solemnity; Dasha looked ready to leap out of her seat, while Evgenia and Konstantin leaned forward, hungry for her news.

"The Red Army is coming," Dasha said. "They will be

here within hours." I gasped. Evgenia glanced at me with her brow furrowed. We were supposed to have one more day. I had thought up a new plan, but this gave me no time to carry it out. How could I ask Lieutenant Valchar to bring me with him to Ekaterinburg now, if the Reds were coming to Mednyy? I had hoped to travel with him, perhaps hidden in a wagon from Sidorov's sight, and then find Alexander once he rejoined his battalion. But if the Red Army were on its way to Mednyy, then Commander Yurovsky would be with them.

"Why are they coming here?" Konstantin asked. "Shouldn't they be defending Ekaterinburg?"

"They are," Dasha said. "But it's looking bad for us. The Whites came from the south *and* the west. We're losing the city. Pyotr just brought back the news. The Red Army is starting to retreat north. A few Red battalions are heading straight for us."

A chill coursed through my arms. The Reds would outnumber our White forces here.

"And the Romanov heir, Alexei?" Konstantin asked. "Will they leave him?"

My head snapped up. I had almost forgotten that everyone still thought Alexei, my sisters, and my mother were alive. The Bolsheviks had announced only Papa's execution.

I smoothed my features in an attempt to hide my reaction.

"They say the family is secure," Dasha said. "They're going to be moved so the Whites can't rescue them."

"If only the boy were a few years older," Konstantin said. "It'd be easier if we could just kill him and get it over with. The Whites might get it in their heads to set up a government in his name."

Ice, cold. I held my lips shut against a protest, and clasped my hands together under the table. If only Konstantin were beside me and not across the table, I might have scratched his eyes out.

"What would happen then?" Evgenia asked. "We'd have two Russian governments?"

"Yes," Konstantin answered. "And since the Whites want back in the war against Germany, they'd get support from the English and Americans. We wouldn't stand a chance." He slammed his fist on the table, making me jump in my seat. "Damn it. If they save him, we're done for."

"We can worry about that later," Dasha said impatiently. "At least three Red battalions are on their way here right now. There'll be fighting. We have to warn our comrades and neighbors to stay inside. Those who can fight will meet at Pyotr's house, but we must tell everyone else to stay out of the way."

"I'll help," Evgenia said immediately. "Who've you told already?"

"I came here first, of course," Dasha said, almost offended. "Pyotr and I can cover our friends on the eastern side of town, but that still leaves the Smirnovs, the Popovs, and the Sokolovs at the very least. Plus anyone else you wish to warn."

"We have to get Mama home," Konstantin said grimly.

Evgenia nodded. "She went to visit the basket maker near the church. All those houses are on the way. I can visit them on my way to Mama."

"Good idea," Konstantin said. "You'll move faster than me. I'll stay here in case Mama comes home before you, and make sure she doesn't leave again."

Their plan arranged, Evgenia hugged Dasha goodbye and walked her out. I rushed after them. Once her friend left, I stopped Evgenia with a hand on her arm.

"We must find Lieutenant Valchar," I said quietly.

"Why?"

"We need his protection before this battle begins—once the Reds arrive, Commander Yurovsky will have a clear path to come after us. We need protection, and we need Lieutenant Valchar to bring us to Ekaterinburg once the fighting is over."

"We can't *tell* him the army's coming!" she said, her eyes narrowing in anger. "I want the Reds to win, not be ambushed." She started down the road.

"You and I will be safer if they do *not* win."

She only shook her head.

"Look," she said. "Come with me to get Mama. I'll bring you to the churchyard and help you find a place to hide among the White wagons."

"And what of you?"

"What about me?"

"You and I are in the same position," I said. "You heard what Commander Yurovsky said, back in Iset. He wants to kill you, too."

"He thought I was protecting you. I'll tell him you went to Ekaterinburg. By then you'll be safe with your cousin, anyway. And Kostya knows Yurovsky. He can tell him that I didn't mean—well, that I'm not with you."

As long as Commander Yurovsky suspected that Evgenia knew I was a Romanov, he could not allow her to survive. Yet I could not explain this to her without revealing my identity.

Evgenia would not be happy to learn the truth. She might even tell Konstantin. The thought made me shudder. He would likely hold me until Commander Yurovsky arrived.

"Commander Yurovsky wants you dead, as well, Evgenia," I said. "You heard him say as much. Are you willing to gamble your life on the hope that *he* shows mercy?"

She scowled. "I don't have a choice. I need to stay with my family. He'll have no reason to hurt us when I tell him where you went. Now come on, let's make these visits quick."

We dropped in at two nearby houses in rapid succession, where I waited outside while Evgenia warned the families about the approaching army. My dread grew with every minute that passed. This was happening too fast. Without Lieutenant Valchar's cooperation, I had no hope of hiding successfully among the Whites. And what if they lost the battle?

As we crossed the road en route to the third house, hope appeared. Lieutenant Valchar strolled out of the patch of woods on the opposite side of the road. He was barefoot, his hair damp, his pant legs rolled up, and his shirt unbuttoned to reveal freshly washed skin. His rifle hung carelessly off his shoulder, and he walked with a merry step.

"Lieutenant, hello!" I called in German.

A smile spread across his face, and he waved before approaching us. When he noticed Evgenia behind me, he quickly buttoned up his shirt. Evgenia scowled, though a hint of pink colored her cheeks.

"Don't say a word about the army," she whispered.

I stared daggers at her.

"I must ask him for help."

"Fine. But don't tell him why. And do it in Russian."

"Anna. Evgenia Ivanovna. Good morning," he said as he reached us. "Sorry for my—I don't have shoes. Or my hat. Or jacket. Sorry." He laughed. "How are you?"

"Please do not worry yourself over your appearance," I said, forcing a smile. I gave Evgenia a second to say something polite, but naturally that was wasted time. "The truth is, Lieutenant Valchar, I am very concerned. You know that my attempt to send a telegraph message to my cousin failed."

"Yes. You say that at dinner yesterday."

"And now—you see," I stumbled over my words as I searched for a way to express what I needed from him that would not provoke Evgenia. "There is something else, Lieutenant. The Bolshevik officers who murdered my family are chasing me. I came to Mednyy with Evgenia because I knew that your forces quartering here would shield me. Only now that you are leaving so soon, they will come after me again once you are gone."

His brows furrowed.

"Why do they chase you?"

"They do not want me to tell anyone about what they did. My family was influential in Ekaterinburg. And besides that, I—I took my family's jewels with me." I pressed my hands to my waist almost unthinkingly and felt the hard corset through the cloth. "If you would help me, I will happily pay you some of the—"

He waved his hands.

"No, no. You do not pay me, Anna. You are alone, and I want to help."

Tears pricked hotly behind my eyes, and I brushed my nose, attempting to keep from crying.

"Thank you," I said.

"What do you need?"

"Will you bring me with you to Ekaterinburg? If I travel within the safety of your battalion, they will not be able to find me. And perhaps Evgenia as well, if she will come. She may be in trouble with the Bolsheviks for rescuing me."

"I'm *not* going."

"I think I can help," Lieutenant Valchar said, chewing his lip like a child struggling with sums. "Lieutenant Sidorov does not like it, I'm sure, but he doesn't command me. Not really. And this is important. Yes, Anna, I can take you."

An undignified squeak escaped me, and I grabbed his hands.

"Thank you so much!"

"It is my pleasure. I talk to my men about it tonight. We can take you both, if you want."

I released his hands as my glee faded. He did not know how urgent this was. There would be no time for him to confer with his men. I glanced at Evgenia, who was busy pouting at the very idea of coming with us.

She could be so frustratingly bullheaded. With the Red Army on its way already, I needed Lieutenant Valchar to act *now*. To find me a horse or a wagon and figure out how to keep me safe.

There was no way to avoid it.

I spoke the words quickly, in German, direct and to the point: "The Red Army is in retreat from Ekaterinburg. Three battalions will reach Mednyy in a few hours. Evgenia is warning her—"

"Anna!" Evgenia shoved me so hard I choked on the rest of my words. I staggered several steps until Lieutenant Valchar caught me. "What did you say to him?" she demanded.

"Are you sure?" Lieutenant Valchar murmured in German behind me.

I nodded.

"I need your assistance now, not tonight or tomorrow," I said.

"I must get my clothes and tell Sidorov," he replied. "Come with me. I will look for a place for you."

He navigated me around Evgenia and along the road to return to the Koltsov house.

Evgenia ran after us with an angry, red face.

"Where is he going? What did you tell him?"

"He is returning home to collect his clothing," I said coldly, rubbing the place on my chest where she hit me.

"Why? What did you say?"

I sighed.

"I had to tell him the truth, Zhenya. We have no hope of getting to safety without his protection. I had no choice."

"You shouldn't have interfered. We had a plan."

"We had a weak, inadequate plan," I said crossly, for she still glared at me as though I had betrayed her. "I am only thinking about our survival."

"That's all you ever think about!" she snapped.

I drew in a sharp breath.

"For good reason!" I said, my voice shrill.

By then Lieutenant Valchar had reached the gate to the Koltsov house; he interrupted us by pointing into the yard.

"You have visitors?" he asked Evgenia.

The gate was wide open, and an unfamiliar wagon sat underneath the large tree in their yard; two tall dark horses had been hitched in front of it. A sign hanging from the side of the wagon read *Whiskey* in clumsily painted letters. The White soldiers at the roadblock had apparently allowed a liquor seller into town. I hoped the soldiers would not indulge now, with the Reds about to arrive.

The horses were well-trained and of a fine quality. I glanced at Evgenia.

"Do you know the owner? Is that your friend Pyotr's wagon?" I asked.

"No. Something's not right," she said. Her voice was tinged with nervousness, and a chill swept down my arms. We headed for her front door. She threw it open, and I peeked over her shoulder to see inside.

Two men in peasant clothing sat at the kitchen table with Konstantin. They fell silent as Evgenia stepped in, and then one of them jumped to his feet.

It was him.

16

EVGENIA

"IT'S HER!"

Yurovsky leapt over the legs of the man next to him. I reared back and slammed the door shut.

"Commander, not my sister!" Kostya yelled from inside.

In my hurry I bumped into Anna and nearly knocked us both over.

"Run!" I gasped out, shoving her. "It's Yurovsky!"

The color drained from her face. I pulled her with me as I ran for the fake whiskey wagon. Yurovsky would be out after us right away. If we freed one of his horses, we could ride it to the churchyard. The White troops there would be our guard.

I didn't even think of leaving Anna behind. We were both prey. We both had to live.

Behind us the door opened with a bang.

"Stop! What are you doing?" the Czech shouted at the men behind us. He was walking toward the house from the fence, going in the wrong direction. We ran right past him.

"Stop!" he ordered. I glanced back to see him step in front of Yurovsky and block his way. My racing heart skipped a beat.

Yurovsky didn't bother to answer the Czech. He smacked him in the head with a hard, dark object, and the Czech fell to his knees.

I pulled my knife out. Yurovsky raised his hand. He was holding a revolver and aimed it straight at us.

I almost swallowed my own tongue.

"Down!" I grabbed the back of Anna's neck and forced her to the ground with me, just as Yurovsky pulled the trigger. The bullet shot over our heads and landed in the side of the wagon, a few cubits ahead. Wood shards scattered into the air, some of them flying into my face. I stood and pulled Anna onward toward the wagon.

Then Yurovsky's man came out of the house.

"They're both here! Get them!" Yurovsky yelled. He and his soldier started running.

We were almost at the wagon, and I realized in a panic that we'd never make it in time. Yurovsky would catch us before I could unhook the horses. We needed distance, and shelter, and weapons. And somehow, we needed to reach the White troops.

"Halt!" The Czech was up again. He pulled his rifle off his back and fired. The bullet missed Yurovsky. It also barely missed us and plowed into Batya's tree. Birds burst out from the leaves, flapping their wings in alarm.

"Stop him," Yurovsky ordered his man. Yurovsky started for us again.

Anna and I ran past the wagon. Ahead of us was the low fence that surrounded our property. We could have hopped it and kept running. Only there wasn't any cover on the other side, not for hundreds of cubits.

I forced myself to think, past the white panic that filled my head. If we could get to our barn, we could hide in the loft. An ax hung inside right by the door. It wasn't a gun, but it'd be better than nothing. The only problem was that we were running the wrong way. The barn was behind us, on the other side of the house.

My heart sped up just thinking about it. But we had to take the risk. I started veering sideways, running in a wide curve that would bring us around. Back past the house. Past Yurovsky and his man.

Yurovsky lifted his revolver. His face was rigid, and his eyes bored into us with a cold determination.

Another rifle blast pierced my ears. I flinched, but it was Yurovsky who let out a cry. He'd been shot. He dropped his revolver and clutched his arm, not running anymore, trying to stop the blood spilling out.

Kostya had shot him. He stood beside the house with his rifle in hand. He must've had it hidden in our cellar, and now he was protecting us. Or at least me.

"Valchar, the horses!" Kostya shouted.

And there was the Czech, too. Blood trickled from his head down onto his cheek and shoulder. He'd been fighting with Yurovsky's man. But he was standing, while Yurovsky's man lay on the ground, still.

Now it was two guns against one. The four of us against Yurovsky. Kostya held his position, his rifle still aimed at Yurovsky.

Anna and I stopped running. She panted beside me, clinging to my arm like rope.

Faster than a biting snake, Yurovsky swooped down and

grabbed his revolver. My heart leapt into my throat. But Kostya fired again, and Yurovsky had to duck and flee for cover. He ran for the main road, through the wagon gate, but stopped there and crouched behind the fence. His hand rose above it and took another shot. It missed wildly, but he was still aiming for me and Anna.

"Evgenia, get to the horses!" Kostya ordered.

I moved. The Czech was already loosing the horses from their harness. He freed one horse and mounted it, then shouted at Anna in German. She scrambled onto the wagon and then climbed behind him.

Yurovsky was still hiding on the other side of the fence, between us and our way out. The Czech raised his rifle and fired at him. The bullet tore through a slat in the fence, sending splinters flying, but it missed. The commander covered his head against the debris.

The Czech fired again, then nudged the horse forward and fired once more. Yurovsky started backing away, further along the fence, away from the gate.

I got to work on the second horse. I untied the reins from the pommel and unhooked the trace from the wagon posts. My hands shook, but this was familiar work, something I'd done a thousand times with Buyan. I soon drew the horse free of the wagon.

Kostya hurried over on his crutch. He couldn't walk and shoot at the same time. As soon as I was seated on the horse's back, he tossed me his rifle.

I nestled the smooth wooden butt against my shoulder and peered through the sight with one eye. I'd fired a rifle enough times before. But I'd never aimed at a *person*. And my blood was racing. My hands shook so bad I couldn't center Yurovsky in my sight.

It didn't matter. I fired. The Czech fired.

Yurovsky stayed back.

Behind me, Kostya heaved himself onto the wagon, moving slower than I liked.

"Hurry!" I cried.

He moved as fast as he could. The Czech was riding nearer to the gate, and every shot he took kept Yurovsky at bay. We needed to stay close to the Czech in order to cover each other.

Kostya swung his wounded leg over the horse's back and jumped the rest of the way on behind me. He took the reins.

"Shoot again," he said into my ear. He was winded, but his voice was calm and steadying. He kicked the horse into motion, and we caught up with Anna and the Czech.

I fired in Yurovsky's direction. Another piece of fence flew off, half a cubit from the commander's head. He cursed and stumbled back.

Both of our horses picked up speed.

"You're not safe anywhere, Anastasia!" Yurovsky screamed. "The entire Red Army is looking for you and your friend!"

The Czech galloped his horse through our gate and turned down the road. He wasn't shooting anymore. It was just my gun against Yurovsky's, and I could barely keep hold of it and stay on the lurching horse at the same time.

I fired as we cleared the gate. The shot didn't land anywhere near Yurovsky. He staggered out from behind the fence and ran toward us, blood trailing from his bad arm, his mouth open in a furious grimace.

"Koltsov, stop!" Yurovsky yelled.

He lifted a shaking hand and shot again, but Kostya had already turned us onto the main road. The wind filled my ears as we raced faster than I'd ever moved. Kostya leaned against me heavily and I had to throw away the rifle so I could grip the horse's mane. Anything to stay on.

I peered over my shoulder, past Kostya. Yurovsky wasn't following.

"Kostya, slow it down!" I cried once we were farther along. My legs clenched against the horse's muscles as I tried to stop sliding. Each step brought me closer to falling off. I wasn't used to riding, and this horse was broad and fast.

Kostya didn't answer. His hands rested slack on my thighs, and the reins were loose in his hands. That white panic started to take over my head again.

I grabbed the reins and pulled them back, slowing the horse to a trot. We were only a few hundred cubits from the churchyard now.

"Ey," I called over the noise of the horse's hoofbeats. "Kostya, is your leg all right?"

He grunted. The sound bubbled like he was gurgling water. A moment later I felt his drool on my neck. I glanced down, but I didn't see spit. Blood dripped onto the shoulder of my dress. Kostya had coughed up blood.

My heart stopped.

"Ey," I croaked. "Are you all right?"

He didn't answer.

"Just hold on."

I slowed the horse. Hopefully Kostya would stop bleeding if the horse didn't bounce him around so much.

"Kostya, we'll get down as soon as we reach the church. We're almost there."

No reply. I swallowed past my dry mouth and wrapped Kostya's arms closer around me.

We reached the center of town. The Whites were running around the churchyard like busy ants, packing up wagons and saddling horses. The Czech was already there and helping Anna dismount. I stopped next to them.

"Help me get Kostya down," I cried.

Anna covered her mouth with her hand. I looked away. I didn't want to see that wide-eyed expression on her face. I slid off the warhorse and then helped the Czech catch Kostya on his way down. We lowered him to the ground.

Kostya's face was white, except for the smear of blood streaking from his mouth to his collar. He must have bitten his tongue as well. I glanced at his leg next, where his pants fell flat at his knee. A spot of blood had soaked through there. Just like I'd feared, the ride had jostled his wound too roughly.

His eyes were closed. I crouched over him and patted his face gently.

"Kostya, look at me."

His eyes opened slowly. Everything about him looked too weak.

"You'll be all right, Kostya. We'll rewrap your bandage, and you'll feel better." He didn't even look at me. He stared straight up like it was the sky talking to him.

"He has been shot, Evgenia," Anna said.

"What?" I snapped my head over to look at her. "What are you talking about? It's just his leg."

"I saw his back when you helped him down—he is bleeding badly, from a bullet wound."

She had to be wrong.

"No," I said. I slid my hands under Kostya's shoulders and hoisted him to his side to prove her wrong.

His back was a bloody mess. A dark wave washed over me. "No."

I laid him flat again and shook him roughly.

"Ey, Kostya. Look at me. Are you listening?"

He didn't react. He just lay there like he was dying.

"Go get your medic!" I shouted at the Czech. "Go!"

The Whites in the yard were obviously preparing for battle. I didn't care anymore. They could go to the devil, as long as their medic looked at Kostya first. A ringing started in my head and drowned out the soldiers. It was like the noise of the bullets had knocked something loose inside me. My head rattled like a teakettle. Gunfire sounded from the south of town and made my head ring worse. The Red Army had arrived.

The Czech disappeared into the madness. I turned back to my brother.

"Anna, what should we do?" I asked.

She picked up a cloth one of the soldiers had dropped and handed it to me.

"Press that into the wound on his back, to try to keep the blood from seeping out."

I balled the cloth and shoved it under Kostya, up against the wettest spot on his back. Blood soaked through immediately, and soon my hand and wrist and sleeve were wet with his blood.

"Zhenya?" Kostya said softly. He finally met my eyes.

I was so relieved I almost fell over.

"Yes! I'm here, Kostya," I said eagerly, almost laughing with joy. I put my face right over his. "A medic is coming. You're fine, Kostya. We'll take care of you."

He coughed wetly. When he turned his head to the side, more blood dribbled out from his mouth. Each time he breathed in I heard liquid rattle in his throat. It reminded me of Batya on his last day. I shook that thought away. This was different.

Kostya blinked up at me. His eyes caught mine again.

"Zhenya," he said. "Keep fighting."

"*You* keep fighting," I nearly shouted. "Kostya, we'll fix you. Just hold on, all right?"

His head fell to the side. His body suddenly felt heavier on top of my arm.

"Kostya! What are you doing?" I tugged his chin so I could look in his eyes, but his eyes were empty.

He didn't blink. The rattling sound had stopped, too.

"No!" I shook him harder with my free hand and pressed the fabric closer against his wound. "Don't do this, please, Kostya. The medic is coming. Just hold on a little longer. Please."

But Kostya was gone.

It was like someone was pushing my head underwater. I couldn't fight it. I fell on Kostya's chest, and an angry scream tore out of me, climbing my insides until it exploded from my mouth. My eyes burned, and I cried out stupid, useless tears that wouldn't bring him back. *Nothing* I did would bring him back.

Swift footsteps pounded toward us from the yard. The medic was too fucking late.

"Konstantin!"

It wasn't the medic at all. It was Mama. She'd somehow found us after visiting the basket maker. I didn't want her to see him lying dead in the dirt like this. She wasn't prepared for it. I pulled my arms from under him and held them over his head, trying to block him from her view with my bloody hands.

"No, Mamochka, don't look!"

She fell to her knees and crawled over. Her face was long and taut, and seeing her pain made my insides squeeze again. She pushed my hands away and lifted Kostya's head, pulled at his eyelids to try to make him see. She put her ear to his mouth, listening for the breath that wasn't there.

17

ANNA

EVGENIA'S SOFT, DAMP FACE AND miserable gaze
tore at my heart. Between tears, she explained to her mother
what had happened. Alena Vasilyevna did not cry. She simply
laid her forehead on top of her son's and moaned, an agonized
sound that echoed inside me.

Yet we were not safe to grieve. Commander Yurovsky was
close by, waiting for his chance to come after me—after us.
And the Red Army had arrived. Evgenia and I needed to leave
before the Whites marched into battle and Yurovsky snuck his
way back into town.

While Evgenia mourned and Alena began yelling at the
army doctor who arrived, I made my way farther into the
schoolyard. Lieutenant Valchar was speaking with another soldier. When he noticed me, he broke off and approached.

"Are you all right?" he asked.

I saw no reason to feign courage.

"No," I said, my voice shaking with the fear that still
coursed through me. "That man is out there, and he is going
to keep coming after me and Evgenia."

"Who is he?"

"He is the Bolshevik commander who is after me, as I told you—I can explain everything to you, but we do not have time here. Evgenia and I must go to Ekaterinburg, where my cousin can protect us. Perhaps Alena Vasilyevna, as well. Will you take us with you?"

He jerked his head, startled.

"Anna. I ride into battle now. The Reds are here. It's not safe for you to come."

As though to reinforce his point, a fusillade of gunshots rang out in the distance. The noise came from the south—between us and Ekaterinburg. Gunsmoke rose over the distant trees. My throat tightened. We would be trapped.

Evgenia and Alena paid no notice to the sounds of battle, nor to the accelerating activity of the White soldiers within the schoolyard who were mounting horses and gathering arms. They would sit there and grieve until Commander Yurovsky caught up with us—unless I did something about it.

I seized Lieutenant Valchar's hand.

"Please," I said. "We will die if you leave us here. Can you not spare two or three men to escort us to Ekaterinburg and rejoin you there?"

His forehead creased, and he gritted his teeth, full of indecision or regret—yet whatever it was, he was not ready to agree.

"You say *three* battalions are coming. We need our men now."

Alena overheard us.

"What are you talking about?" She strode over angrily. "What's this about?"

"Alena Vasilyevna," he said in Russian, "I'm sorry for your loss. I leave now. Thank you for—everything."

"He is leaving us to face that Red commander again on our own," I said. "Commander Yurovsky is likely on his way here at this very moment. How are we to defend ourselves when he goes?"

"I'm sorry," he said. "I can meet you after. Yes? I must fight with my men, but I can find you after, and bring you to Ekaterinburg. Tomorrow."

Dozens of White cavalrymen galloped out of the schoolyard and passed us, traveling south to meet the Bolsheviks. The ground trembled from their horses. I gestured after them, desperate to make Lieutenant Valchar see.

"As soon as they are all gone, Lieutenant, we die!"

"You have to leave," Alena suddenly said. "Both of you. Now."

That finally drew Evgenia out of her daze.

"What?" she said. "Both of who?"

"You"—her mother pointed at me—"and you," at Evgenia. "Anya's right. That commander is after you both. Jiri, you said you'll meet them after the battle?"

He nodded. I clamped my mouth shut, furious. They were arriving at a decision that would do nothing for me or Evgenia.

"Tell me where, and I meet you, Anna," he said. "I help you go to Ekaterinburg then."

"Zhenya, too," Alena said. "She's not safe here anymore."

"I'm not going anywhere," Evgenia protested.

"Shut up. Jiri, the girls can meet you in Iset when the fight is over. Can you be there tomorrow?"

"I will try," he said. "Iset is the same direction as Ekaterin-burg. I can pass through Iset to pick them up."

"We will be dead by tonight," I said, my voice emerging low and unsteady. "We will never make it to Iset."

"Lieutenant!" A White officer stopped his horse near us. "We're off! Hurry!"

Lieutenant Valchar's back straightened. He looked at us with an open, decisive expression.

"I go now. Anna, I meet you near Iset tomorrow. At mid-day. You too, if you come, Evgenia. Is there somewhere safe where we can meet, Alena Vasilyevna?"

"The devil's wall," Evgenia spoke up, deciding that she wished to contribute to this infuriating conversation after all. "Anna knows where it is. It's the rock wall where we hid before," she said to me. With rising dread, I realized that she had no intention of coming. "You can ask someone the way," she said to Lieutenant Valchar. "Everyone knows it. It's in the woods outside of town."

And I was to make my way there alone, while Evge-nia stayed here to die, or even be forced to tell Commander Yurovsky exactly where he could find me. This was madness.

"It's decided," Alena said. "Meet them there tomorrow at noon, Jiri."

He nodded. He looked at me briefly, then slung the rifle off his back and held it out.

"Take this," he said. "We have extras."

I stepped away quickly; I did not want to touch that rifle. I could not use it well enough to defend myself, and I would not allow him to ease his own guilt by leaving it.

"I can do nothing with that," I said. "It is *your* protection I need."

Alena took the gun.

"Zhenya can shoot. Thank you, Lieutenant Valchar. Go on, and stay safe."

He shook her hand, nodded at me and Evgenia, then left to join the flurry of men still in the schoolyard.

I buried my face in my hands.

"You have to leave town with us, Mama," Evgenia said, surprising me. "Yurovsky knows where we live. He'll come back."

"He's never seen me," her mother said. "I'm staying. But you're not." She looked down at the body of her second dead son.

"Why do I have to go while you stay?" Evgenia demanded.

Another troop of White soldiers marched out of the schoolyard while the battle raged on to the south. We needed to leave soon. Commander Yurovsky could sneak in here at any moment.

"Evgenia," I tried.

"I'm not leaving you, Mama!"

"I won't leave Kostya. Or the farm," Alena said, her mouth firm. "The moment I do, the council will take our land. I'll stay and bury Kostya. And when this is over, you'll have a home to come back to."

Evgenia's mouth opened and shut a few times.

"When's it going to be over?" she finally asked. Her voice sounded tiny.

Alena took her daughter's hands and squeezed them.

"That Yurovsky's trying to hide what he did to Anya's

family," she said. "He's after you both to keep it quiet. So you need to make it public. He's leaving a trail of bodies behind him. If the secret gets out, he'll have to stop."

My heart lifted—she understood. Alena saw exactly what we had to do. I nodded eagerly.

"Yes," I said, "and if we tell the world what he did to my family—especially to my sisters and my little brother—they will be outraged. People will rally against the Bolsheviks. Zhenya, you will be safe once it is known that my family is dead and I am alive."

She jutted her chin out and shook her head; she did not believe me. If she knew that I was a Romanov, the daughter of the tsar, and that my entire family had been massacred—she would understand, then, why the world would care about their deaths. Perhaps soon I could tell her the truth.

"Then we should go," Evgenia said tiredly. Her capitulation took us both by surprise. "Before the Whites are all gone."

At that very moment, Lieutenant Valchar returned, riding a tall horse and leading a second one behind him—a short, squat, older horse that looked distinctly unprepared for war.

"I find an extra horse for you," he said. "We don't use this one to fight." He held out the reins to me.

It was Buyan, Evgenia's horse. My heart lifted. I watched Evgenia closely, eager to see her joy. Yet instead of smiling, her face fell. She let out a sob and threw her arms around Buyan's neck. For several long seconds she cried into his side.

"That is her horse," I explained quietly. Lieutenant Valchar's eyebrows rose, and he nodded before riding down the road, off to battle.

Evgenia turned to her mother and they hugged tightly, while I led Buyan over to a tree stump so we could easily mount his bare back. She knelt by Kostya's side and bid goodbye to him for the last time.

"Be careful, Zhenya," her mother said before Evgenia mounted. "You are all I have left. I won't lose two of my children today. You be careful, and smart. Do you hear me?"

"Yes, Mamochka."

"You'll see me again soon enough. Go find someone who can stop Yurovsky. Then you can come back. Your home will still be here, waiting for you. I promise. Understand?"

Evgenia nodded.

"Good. Now go."

18

EVGENIA

MY BROTHER WAS DEAD.

Anna guided Buyan along the forest path, following my directions. She didn't try to talk. I wouldn't have minded if she did. Dark waves rushed through my head, beating me over and over with the same thought: *It was my fault. It was my fault.* I wanted Anna to talk and distract me. But we rode in silence, and I fought to push the thought away.

Every time Buyan took a rough step and jolted us, I felt Kostya falling against my back. He'd been dying behind me the whole way to the schoolyard, and I hadn't noticed. I'd just let him die. Now I was leaving Mama behind to face the man who killed him.

"*Keep fighting*," he'd said. He wanted me to do what I couldn't.

Would Yurovsky go after Mama?

That question dogged me, too. What could Mama do if he went after her? She wasn't safe with Yurovsky in town. He'd killed Kostya, who, even with one leg, was the strongest of any of us.

Anna and I had entered the woods behind the church and headed for the mountains bordering Mednyy. This path would take us a long, roundabout way to Iset. We'd have to sleep in the woods at night and then go on at sunup to reach the devil's wall by noon.

"Zhenya, look!" Anna squeezed my elbow. We'd reached a bare patch of woods where so many trees were chopped down you could see clear to the town below. Big clouds of smoke rose up where the fighting was thickest. The armies clashed at the north end of town, and again at the churchyard. Mama better have gotten out in time. She'd better have moved *Kostya* in time.

"*Zhenya.*" Anna pointed up the road. As far as you could see, all the way into the southern mountains, the road was moving. It was a river of khaki budenovki. Red Army soldiers on horseback and on foot were going to flood Mednyy.

"Let's go," I said. I nudged Buyan along.

"If Lieutenant Valchar does not survive the battle—"

My heart pinched, like a ghost had reached in and squeezed it. The Czech—Valchar—had turned out all right. He'd stood by us. One moment he was an enemy with an annoyingly nice smile, and the next, he turned into a fierce soldier fighting beside us. Like a comrade.

"He'd better."

We broke off the path at a small stream. Buyan drank and nibbled at the grass along the bank. I stroked his neck. He seemed happy. He'd been Kostya's horse before he was mine, and now he had no idea his former owner was dead. He kept butting his head into my side in a friendly way, like he was glad to be with me.

"Do you—? Is there anything that I can do for you?" Anna asked.

I looked up in surprise. I'd almost forgotten she was there. "I'm fine," I said.

"You ought to have something to drink, at least," she said. "If only we had something to use as a cup." She patted her apron pocket.

I snorted. That was Anna for you. I got on my knees by the stream, cupped my hands, and drank.

Anna followed my lead to drink but lost her balance and stuck her arms straight down to catch herself. She soaked her shirt to the shoulders. On a different day, I'd have laughed or teased her.

Something in my own pocket thumped my knees. I dried my hands and pulled out *Dead Souls*. Batya's book. I'd picked it up during my morning chores. Seeing it now was a gut punch. I'd read this with Batya and Lev and Kostya. I was the last of us left. Just like Anna.

But I still had Mama. *She'd better have got out in time.*

"Clearly I am not as agile as I might have hoped," Anna said lightly. She twisted her shirt sleeves to wring water out of them.

"What book do you have there?" she asked.

I lifted the spine to show her. Her face went suddenly blank.

"Where did you find that?" she asked sharply, like I'd stolen it.

"It's mine. It was my father's."

"Forgive me," she said. She shook her head. "It is only—it

is quite the coincidence that you should have that novel. It used to be one of my favorites. Last year, my sisters and brother and I all fell sick with measles, one after another. We grew as thin as pencils. My mother read this one aloud to us." She gave a little laugh. "I still remember listening to it and trying not to cry while the doctor shaved my head to keep the disease from spreading." She got quiet for a moment. "Have you read it?"

"Why else would I have it?"

Anna knelt in front of me.

"May I?" she asked when she'd dried her hands. I handed the book to her. She turned the pages gently, her long fingers careful not to bend the paper. "There was a passage in particular I never forgot—here it is. 'There are occasions when a woman . . . will become not only harder than a man, but harder than anything and everything in the world.'"

That line always stuck out to me, too. Most books I'd read had silly, useless women in them. But Gogol saw more.

"I remember that," I said. "It made me think of Mama."

"I think that must be us, now," she said.

Mama always knew what to do. She'd kept our land after Batya died, even though the council didn't let women own property. She held on to it after Lev died, though it was in his name by then. Now that Kostya was gone, they'd really come after our home. That was why Mama stayed. She'd fight them off. She'd hold on long enough, until the Reds changed the laws to make women equal, like they'd promised.

I couldn't be strong like her. I wasn't harder than anything. If Kostya didn't survive the war, what chance did I have?

"Anyway," Anna said, "it is a very funny novel. My—my

eldest sister, Olga, and I used to laugh over it together. No one captures the absurd quite like Gogol."

"Yeah. He showed what those tsarists were really like."

"Hmm," Anna said, shutting the book. "Gogol was a tsarist, actually. He sought to satirize the weakness of human nature."

Right.

Anna was still a tsarist. Even seeing what the Whites did in Mednyy didn't change her mind.

Yurovsky killing Kostya didn't change mine. But Yurovsky didn't speak for the whole party.

Anna probably saw Sidorov the same way.

"He was a true traditionalist, despite his imaginative writings," Anna went on. She gave *Dead Souls* back to me. "Perhaps, given time, he might have seen the flaws in the tsarist regime—well. It hardly matters. He was very devout, in any case. I always liked that about him. His faith brought him a great deal of comfort late in his life. As mine has brought me."

My eyes burned. I couldn't even think about what she'd said about tsarists. I looked down so she wouldn't see, and acted like I was fumbling with the book. But the tears spilled out, and Anna went quiet. I wiped my face, but couldn't stop.

"I wish I still believed in all that," I said. My voice came out shakier than I wanted.

"Oh, Zhenya," she said. She slipped next to me and put her arm around my shoulders. I leaned into her. "God will accept you, even if you have turned from Him."

I laughed, only it came out like a sob, and I started crying for real.

Anna might know a lot about Gogol, but she was dumb about the world. She thought peasants couldn't read. She thought her God could keep her safe. She thought the White Army cared about poor Russians. And she'd probably never read Marx. I had. Pyotr and Kostya brought his pamphlets when they came back from the city. We learned about how the Church took money from the poor while bishops lived in luxury. They allied with the tsar to hoard land and power. And they told pretty lies to keep us quiet.

Now I missed those lies. I wished I could believe that Kostya and Batya and Lev waited for me in heaven. But I knew better. They'd lived, and now they were gone. They'd winked out like a doused fire.

I dried my face with my apron and tucked the book away.

Sorry, I was about to say, but a noise cut me off.

Shouting. A man's voice in the distance, somewhere in the woods.

"D'you hear that?" I whispered. She tilted her head, and her eyes widened when she heard it. She nodded. "Hang on."

I had to pry her arm off me. I needed a clear view. A spruce tree nearby looked promising. I stayed close to the trunk and climbed a good ten cubits up, pausing now and then to look out. In high summer the woods were thick, and the spruce itself blocked my line of sight. But a third of the way up, I spotted them.

More horses than I could count. Soldiers in green shirts and caps. And one man shouting orders at them all. He was too far to see his face. But I knew that straight back and dark hair. I knew that voice. Yurovsky was coming. He knew we were here.

My head spun with rage. We had Valchar's rifle. I could do it so easily. I'd sneak up on them, find some cover, take aim, and kill him. Let him bleed out just like Kostya had.

"Well?" Anna hissed from the ground.

Right. It was just the two of us. For now, we were the ones being hunted.

I scurried down like a squirrel.

"It's him. They're after us. He's got a few men with him on horseback."

Anna's face went white.

"How close is he?"

"Close. We should get off the trail. Come on."

Part of me wanted to meet him. But Anna's face was making my heart pound, reminding me we didn't stand a chance against him. I untied Buyan and led him and Anna into the brush. We pushed forward quietly. I used the rifle to hold back the few branches and bushes blocking our way. We moved off-path for a little while, before we heard them again.

"*Shh.*" I crouched and tugged Anna down next to me. Buyan was behind a bush taller than him, which was the best hiding spot I could hope for. And at least he was brown, not dressed in bright blue or red.

We could just make out Yurovsky and his men through the trees. They moved quietly down the path. If Yurovsky hadn't raised his voice earlier, they would've stumbled right over us. They were so close now that I could see his face. His dark eyes looked out into the woods, his head turning steadily back and forth.

He stopped his horse at the stream. His three new men

stopped, too. Yurovsky turned his horse and nudged it into the tree line, coming in our direction.

My throat closed up. Anna sucked in a breath next to me.

Yurovsky swung off his horse. He was still staring straight at us. I couldn't see any bandage from here, but someone must have treated his arm, because he moved like he wasn't in pain. He was favoring his right arm, though. He bent down and picked something up off the ground.

Anna's hand flew to her head. She'd taken off her scarf. *Chyort.*

"They were here." His low voice carried clearly. "Spread out."

His men dismounted. They fanned out on either side of the path. Yurovsky held his course. Every step brought him closer to us.

This was it. Kostya wasn't here to save us. It was me against him. I slid the rifle off my back.

Anna yanked my arm. Her eyes were wide and horror-struck. She looked like she had pissing herself in the woods, when we first ran into Yurovsky. Any moment now she was going to panic.

I held my finger to my lips. Behind us was another thick copse of bushes. It was too risky to move Buyan, big as he was, but we could hide ourselves better. I pointed so Anna could see what I was thinking. She nodded, sense coming back into her eyes.

I crept as low to the ground as I could. I crawled with my elbows bent, so slow my knees shook. Every fallen branch, pine cone, or dried leaf was a risk. Yurovsky might hear us before he saw us. I gritted my teeth and clenched my gut, holding every muscle so nothing went out of place.

Sweat beaded on my eyebrows and dripped onto my lashes. I shook them away.

"Commander!"

My breath caught. One of Yurovsky's men, somewhere west of us, was shouting. Anna and I froze.

"What is it?" Yurovsky called. His voice flew over our heads. He hadn't turned away.

"I think they lit a fire here!"

My arms wobbled. Some hunting party must have spent the night near the stream. *Go look at it*, I urged. *Stop coming this way.*

Yurovsky started moving again. My heart skipped a beat, and then I realized he was walking away from us. Toward the stream. He hadn't seen Buyan, or us.

They talked over the fire and decided it was old. Not ours.

"They can't be far," Yurovsky said. "They stopped here for a drink. We're on their trail. We keep going—and *quietly*." The word sliced into the air like a threat. His men smartly didn't answer.

Then they got back on their horses and rode on.

I fell onto the dirt. A cool leaf pressed into my cheek. A black beetle skittered right in front of my eyes. I breathed in deep, my chest opening.

"Dear Lord," Anna whispered.

When we finally sat up, she looked at me helplessly.

"What do we do now?"

"We stay put," I said. "Let them get as far as possible."

She nodded. I dropped my head onto my knees. That'd been way too close. And now Yurovsky was between us and the devil's wall.

There were wolves in these woods. And lynxes. But when the sky grew dark we couldn't risk a fire. Anna and I huddled close together under a big tree and watched the dark take over.

Frogs sang out from a far-off pond. Owls hooted, and water trickled over the rocks in the stream. Cool air skated over my face. It was like sleeping in our yard, except Kostya wasn't at my back anymore. Anna didn't snore comfortingly like he did. When she wasn't trapped in a nightmare, she slept in quiet.

"I am so sorry about Konstantin," Anna whispered. She hadn't been asleep at all.

She should be. She'd brought Yurovsky down on our heads. Kostya died protecting her.

No. He died protecting me.

I'd brought Anna home. I'd argued for her to stay when Kostya didn't want her. And he'd paid the price.

"I know what you must be feeling now," she went on. "You looked up to him. It was like that with my sister Tatiana. She was so skilled at everything she did. Sometimes it frightened me, to be honest, how perfect she always was. Now I tell myself that even if she is gone, she can still be a model for me. She would want me to work hard and improve myself. I can still do that for her."

The grief in her voice called to the pain in my chest like an echo. It was the same I'd felt two years ago when I woke up to find Batya dead on that black winter morning. Or when we got the yellow letter in the mail: *To the family of Lev Ivanovich*

Koltsov. We regretfully inform you that the soldier in question has been declared missing in action as of May 14, 1916, and is therefore considered by this, the Imperial Russian Army Command, as lost to enemy hands.

Our family was being picked off one by one.

Did we deserve it?

"Kostya wasn't perfect," I said. The words stopped up my throat and tried to stay inside, but I forced them out. I wanted to tell her. "He made mistakes just like I did."

"Of course, everyone does," Anna said softly. She put her hand on my elbow.

I shook my head.

"Not as bad as we did." I swallowed. I'd never told this story before. Everyone in Mednyy knew it, and it wasn't something I bragged about while wagoning. But now it burned to come out. "We did something last year. Kostya and I'd been going to all the Bolshevik meetings in town for months. We were ready to do something about it. We were tired of talking. So after one meeting in Iset, Kostya got some of the members together. He told them it was time to stop the bourgeois from hoarding all the land.

"I spoke up, too. I was *angry*. We all were. We had nothing, and there were these two rich families near Iset living in big mansions. They paid us mere kopecks to work their land, while they sat around and drank tea all day. They banned us from hunting in their forests since no one could afford the fees."

I swallowed, trying to moisten my dry mouth. Anna didn't say anything. She looked at me with wide eyes. I couldn't tell what she was thinking. She waited for me to continue.

"I have a big mouth," I went on. "I said their names.

Gersky and Ilyov. I said we should go to their houses and take back our land. So we did. We all got weapons. Those who had rifles brought them, and the rest brought shovels and pitchforks and torches.

"We marched to the Ilyov house first. We sang the Marseillaise on the way, and then we went in and tore apart their house. We broke their windows and their dishes, anything we could. They were having supper when we got there, and they just stood and yelled at us while we did it.

"Kostya gave them one day to get out of town. Their land, animals, and anything left behind would go to our peasant collective. Someone started a fire outside and burned their paintings and books. I tried to stop that, because we could've used the books. But no one wanted to hear it. By the time we left, the Ilyovs were gone. They took their carriage and the one horse we left them, and rode out of town.

"It was like a festival. We hugged and we toasted one another with the Ilyovs' wine. We drank and sang and talked about how it would change everything to have more land. Then we went to the Gersky house."

I stopped again. I couldn't tell the next part. But Anna stayed quiet. She hadn't gasped or made a horrified face. She just listened. I swallowed dryly again and spoke past the cold guilt in my chest.

"The Gerskys were waiting for us. They stood outside in the yard holding guns, and they shouted for us to stay back. But we were like a swarm of locusts. There were dozens of us. Kostya and I tried to stop the others from shooting, but no one listened. The Gersky couple ran back into their house to protect their children inside.

"It was dark out. By the time they set the house on fire and dragged the Gerskys outside, it was bright as summer noon. Someone tied the Gerskys together with rope, and they were bloody and beaten. Kostya tried to free them, but the others shoved him away."

I closed my eyes. I'd never forgotten the sound of their screams.

"They put the Gersky couple in a pit and set them on fire," I finished.

"What happened to the children?" Anna whispered.

"Someone helped them escape."

"Thank God for that."

"We just stood there. While they burned."

Anna let go of my arm. Cool air rushed in where she'd touched me, and I felt exposed. Dirty. Guilty. But then she stroked my hair. Her thin fingers were gentle. Calming, like the feeling you get from watching waves lap at the shore. She didn't hate me for what I'd done.

"Is that why you rescued me?" she asked. "So it would not happen again?"

Warm relief washed through me. It felt so unfairly good that I jerked my head away from her hand. I *had* tried to make up for it by saving her from the fire. But nothing could change what we'd done. The Gerskys were gone. And now Kostya was, too.

"I guess," I mumbled. "Kostya and I stopped going to meetings in Iset after that. We stuck with the Mednyy chapter. He never meant for any of that to happen. Me neither."

"It was not your fault that the mob lost control. They went too far. You didn't want that. Your communism is about fairness, and equality. I see that, Zhenya. That is who you are. Do not blame yourself—I don't."

I tried to argue, but the words choked inside me. I hung my head and let myself cry. Anna's fingers started smoothing my hair again, and I closed my eyes.

19

ANNA

NOT LONG AFTER HER WHISPERED confession, Evgenia drifted into sleep, her head resting on my shoulder. Knowing she was awake had been a security of some sort; once her breathing grew heavier, the sounds of the forest became louder. Each rustle seemed more alarming. A wolf howled long, low, and far too close, and I considered waking Evgenia to ask if we should not light a fire after all. But there was a worse creature out here than wolves, and a fire would surely bring him to us.

I let her sleep even as she drooled on my shoulder like an infant. Waking her would only return her to her troubles. The fact that she had contributed, in some way, to the murders of innocent people did not change what I thought of her. Nor even that she had left orphans behind. Perhaps it ought to have mattered, but I knew she was not the kind of person to wish that violence on anyone, even her enemies. She had shown me kindness again and again, despite her beliefs. Even Konstantin had tried to protect me in the end.

There were many kinds of Bolsheviks. There were those who would burn innocents or shoot an entire family. But there were others, like Evgenia, who wanted only the betterment of her people. They saw inequality and refused to wait for those in power to come around. Evgenia had not scorned me just for being rich. She had been provoked by my unwillingness to change. The entire White Army had risen up to restore the monarchy—to put a tsar or some aristocrats in power once more, and make everything like it used to be.

But those days were gone. People like Evgenia, Konstantin, and Lieutenant Valchar were ready to govern themselves. And it was folly to think that they would go back to their former helplessness. The Bolsheviks had a strain of poison within, but at least they were trying to improve peasant lives. They needed people like Evgenia to keep them on the right track, and to fix things when they went wrong.

Papa must not have known what their lives were really like. If he had been able to spend time with a family like the Koltsovs, he would have seen just how much they were capable of. And perhaps if he had given them more freedoms, more support, more power, they never would have chased us out of the palace. Never would have fallen prey to evil creatures like Commander Yurovsky, and the leaders who ordered our executions.

Perhaps we could offer suggestions when we reached Alexander and General Leonov. If the White Army wanted to win over the peasants, they would have to listen to them. They would have to be willing to ally with other parties, like the Kadets and Socialist-Revolutionaries, who had wanted to make peaceful change. And I could think of no better duo to convince them of this than me, a Romanov, and Evgenia, an activist peasant.

We only had to make it to Ekaterinburg first.

Find Alexander, Tatiana's voice, which I had not heard for days, spoke clearly inside me. *Stand for all of us, and help Russia.*

I will, I vowed.

The sun rose eventually, heralded by nightingales. As light seeped through the leaves, I shifted from underneath Evgenia. My left leg had turned numb overnight. I smiled, thinking of Masha, who had once done the same for me.

As I relieved myself, I eyed a patch of deep blue berries and thought to ask Evgenia if she knew whether they were edible. When I returned, however, I realized that we had spent the night underneath a towering wild apple tree. My mouth watered at the sight of the dangling fruits.

The day before, Evgenia had climbed a tree to serve as lookout for us. I had been too frozen with fear to even think of joining her. But now it was my chance to both gather our breakfast and search our surroundings for the commander.

I found a low, sturdy branch and gripped it tight, walking my way sideways up the trunk until I was able to loop my legs over the branch and swing up onto it. I scaled several levels of the tree until I found the most appetizing apples, and I took a crisp, juicy bite.

"Nastya ate my apple!"

Three years ago, on vacation in the Crimea, our family had picnicked on the beach—even Papa, escaping from his never-ending duties for an afternoon of fun. We had eaten apples that tasted just like this one—a little sour, full of juice, with the perfect amount of sweetness. Masha, Olga, and Tatiana had run off to play in the waves without me, and I wanted their attention. Alexei, ten years old then, had been lying with his head in Mama's lap. His hand in the air, gesturing wildly with the apple as he told some pointless story about the Cossack guard, presented me with an easy target. I had snatched the apple and danced away, taking enormous bites as he whined.

My sisters rushed to his rescue, as I had known they would. Olga and Tatiana each caught me by one arm, while Masha tickled me until I collapsed and dropped the apple. All I cared about was being back in their midst, surrounded by my sisters. When they returned to the water they pulled me with them.

Tears dripped onto my apple, turning the next bite salty. I threw it, no longer hungry, and it tumbled to the ground directly in front of Evgenia.

She startled awake. Her head swiveled as she sought to track down the source of the noise. A giggle rose in my chest. I brushed away my tears and picked another apple, then tossed it on the other side of her.

She flinched and finally tilted her head to peer up into the tree. Her perturbed face lightened, pleased to see me, and the heavy ache inside me eased.

"Anya. There you are."

"Good morning," I said. It was quiet enough that we had no need to raise our voices. "Would you like some breakfast?" I dropped another apple directly above her head. She caught it with a flash of her arm.

"Stop throwing those at me."

"I am only looking after your appetite," I said, loosing another apple. This one she batted away from her, sending it rolling over the dirt.

"Very funny. Get down before you fall on your ass."

"Make me," I said, and threw another fruit.

She stared for so long that the mischief bubbling inside me settled, and I felt wicked for teasing her so soon after her brother's death. Then she leapt to her feet. She began to climb, and another laugh squeaked out of me. I reached for the next branch and climbed higher, tossing another apple at her head as I ascended.

She caught up soon enough, and perched on a fat branch adjacent to mine. She extended her hand.

"Give it over," she said. I pretended to huff and gave her my last weapon. Evgenia snickered, a sound that lifted my heart, and bit into her apple.

"You're a surprise," she said. "I wouldn't have guessed you knew how to climb trees."

"I am not as delicate as you seem to think. I have climbed scores of trees in my day."

She looked out beyond the leafy brush, scanning the forest for Commander Yurovsky.

"See anything from up here?" she asked.

"No. He is nowhere in sight, thank heavens."

She grunted in agreement and continued with her snack. Her eyes grew distant, lost in thought, and I maintained what I hoped was a courteous silence until she surprised *me* with the turn of her thoughts.

"You must've been a handful as a kid."

I smiled.

"Certain people have said as much. I remember one time, when my family was sailing on the *Standart*—a cruise ship— that I was so bored I convinced Masha to sneak belowdecks to the sailors' quarters, where we were forbidden to go. We snuck into one of their bunks and dressed up in their spare hats and clothing, leaving a dreadful mess behind us. The next day we heard through our parents that the sailors thought there was a ghost onboard.

"After that, playing 'ghost' became our new favorite game. We would move the sailors' belongings around, move their pillows from one end of the bed to the other, that sort of thing. Soon we started to overhear the sailors telling one another ghost stories, and when we were alone we nearly collapsed from laughing so hard. Naturally someone caught us after a couple of days of this. Goodness, my parents were angry. Masha and I had no desserts or playtime for a week. It was well worth the punishment, however."

Evgenia laughed with her whole body, her shoulders hunched and her lovely brown eyes crinkling. My heart pinched tight. It felt suddenly, overwhelmingly cruel that she would never have the chance to meet my family. She would have adored Masha for her friendliness and warmth. She could have appreciated Alexei's adventurous side, so much like hers. And my family would have loved her in return. Once they saw past her tough exterior they would have seen the good-humored, compassionate girl I had come to know.

"So you were a little troublemaker," Evgenia said.

The ache in my heart deepened.

"My family thought so. They always called me 'shvibzik,'" I said.

"Well, shvibzik," Evgenia said as I dried my eyes. "Why don't we go find Valchar and get you to your cousin? Then you can drag him into all the trouble you want."

We rode Buyan through the forest a couple of carriage lengths away from the path, to avoid catching up unexpectedly with the commander and his men. Every hour or so one of us would scale a tree to scan our surroundings, and each check reassured us that he must have put significant distance between us.

We reached the devil's wall as the sun neared its highest point in the sky. Our luck had held so well all night and day that I was almost certain Lieutenant Valchar would be there, waiting for us, victorious and ready to parade south after defeating the Reds in Mednyy.

He was not there. We dismounted Buyan in the center of the clearing, which was open and bare and quiet around us. The wall cast the entire area into shadow, leaving it chilly and damp. There were no birds singing here, no gentle summer's wind. It was desolate.

"He may still be coming," I said, breaking our tense silence.

Evgenia's eyes were heavy with worry that only made me feel worse.

"It may not yet be noon, and anyway, he said we might have to wait until tomorrow."

"We should take cover," was all she said.

I dreaded approaching the gray wall, where I had last

huddled and trembled as Commander Yurovsky stalked above us. Yet Evgenia was in the right. I followed her to the little cavern on the other side of the wall, where we had hidden Buyan before. It smelled of mildew, and the walls were slimy. Evgenia slid down the wall to sit down, not seeming to mind, but I wrinkled my nose.

She took out *Dead Souls* to read while we waited, but put it aside only a moment later. I found a dry-looking spot near her and sat, shifting my apron under me to avoid sullying my sarafan. Then I picked up the novel.

"Are you going to read this?" I asked.

She shook her head. I flipped the book open and attempted to distract myself.

I had been reading for only a few minutes when Evgenia perked up.

"Did you hear that?" she asked.

"Hear what?"

She stood, and I followed her out of the cave. Try as we might, there was nothing to be heard. No one was approaching. She had simply imagined it. We headed back into our covered space.

"What's that?" Evgenia asked. She pointed to a little slip of paper on the floor where we had been sitting, then swept it up before I could respond.

It was the postcard of my family. My heart gave an erratic beat. It must have fallen out of my apron pocket when I sat down. Evgenia peered at it, but in the dim light she could not see the image well.

Perhaps this was the moment for me to tell her the truth. I took a steadying breath and opened my mouth.

"Is this the tsar and his family?" she asked, and then spat at the dirt in disgust.

Perhaps not.

"Hand that to me, please," I said between my teeth.

Evgenia smirked.

"Make me," she said. She darted to the edge of the cave. I whirled to chase after her, and my heart pounded again but now for an entirely different reason. This was *not* the right time to tell her. She could learn who I was once we reached Alexander and we were safe together. Not now. Not yet.

"Zhenya," I snapped. "That is personal. Give it to me at once." I reached for the postcard, but she danced back again, holding it playfully out of my reach. I was taller than her, but she was much stronger, and enjoying herself far too much. "This is no joke, Evgenia!"

"So says the shvibzik," she said. Then she turned the postcard over, and her laughter faded. She put out an arm to restrain me.

"This is from the Petrov boys. Why the devil did you take this?"

"I only took it by accident," I said irritably. It was a poor lie, given my protestations, and Evgenia cast me a suspicious look.

"It's just a harmless letter home," she said.

Then she turned it over once more, looking again at the picture. I tried to snatch it, but her arm cut across my chest and shoulders, keeping me back while she studied the image.

She brought the postcard closer and stared directly into the face of twelve-year-old me. She glanced at me, in the flesh, her eyes traveling over my features, then again at the postcard.

"No," she said, looking back and forth between the card and me. "What is this?"

"It is nothing important," I said, and this time when I attempted to snatch it from her, she let me. I hid it in my pocket, but she did not have to look at it anymore.

Her face lengthened, and her mouth fell open.

"I only liked the picture."

"Your brother's name was *Alexei*," she said softly. "And you called your sisters Olga and Tatiana. And *Masha*. Like Maria Nikolaevna?"

"What on earth are you talking about?" I said crossly. A terrible shadow rose within me as her face grew more shocked—and more horrified.

"I've heard of the *Standart*. Everyone has. I'm so stupid. The royal family was locked up in Ekaterinburg. Everyone knew that, too, even though it was supposed to be a secret." She gave a dark laugh that made me cringe.

"What are you saying? I cannot begin to follow—"

"Are you Anastasia Romanova?"

I forced out a laugh of my own.

"What an incredible idea. Of course not, Zhenya." I thought I sounded believable, but her face became even more distraught, and her eyes darker.

"I feel sick," she mumbled, turning away.

"You are being absurd! Perhaps I resemble her—I do not see it, but perhaps you are right." I hurried after her, making her listen. "I only took that postcard because I thought it was pretty. It reminded me of how the world used to be. You are seeing things that aren't there."

"Stop lying!" She spun to face me again, and she was red with anger. "You lie all the damn time. I'm sick of it."

I breathed in sharply. It was no use. She had figured out the truth—but maybe if I denied it fervently enough, we could pretend it had all been an amusing mistake.

"Don't look like that," she snapped. "You know who you are. Now I do, too. Fuck!" She balled her hands into fists and covered her eyes. "Are you saying Yurovsky killed the whole royal family? That's why he wants you so bad?"

"I am saying nothing of the kind. I am not her."

"Shut up!" She jabbed her finger in my face. "Shut up until you can say something true. All this time, I've been helping you . . . They'd kill me for this. Not just Yurovsky. Any Bolshevik would kill me for hiding a Romanov."

"You would think it a crime to help me if I were born with a royal name? That is hypocrisy and cruelty, Evgenia. I have done nothing wrong and neither, I am certain, has she." I gestured at my pocket. "Do we deserve to die for nothing?"

"It's not nothing. While you lived your easy, coddled life, your father ruined this country. He starved us, he sent us to die in a pointless war, he shot us when we protested. *Nikolai the Bloody* earned his name."

"You be quiet about him! He was a great man, and a loving father!" The words tore out of me.

Then I froze in place. Both of us did.

I had just admitted the truth.

I felt light-headed. I shook myself, trying to clear my mind. But I had lost my temper, and there was no way out of this anymore. She knew.

And the look she gave me held no compassion, no good humor, no affection at all.

The sound of approaching horses came from the far side of the wall, moving swiftly. I caught myself against a nearby tree as terror swept through my body. I was trapped between a furious, still-Red Evgenia and possible death at the devil's wall.

I forced myself to move. If Commander Yurovsky had come for me, I needed to get away before Evgenia decided to help him instead of me.

I found a wide crack in the wall and peered through. Evgenia pushed in next to me, not giving me any space to maneuver. We competed for a good view of the other side of the wall until I spotted the men in the clearing.

It was Lieutenant Valchar and another Czech soldier. They sat on horseback, their clothing roughened and their faces filthy, but both uninjured from the recent battle. They spoke in low voices as they surveyed the clearing, looking for us.

I fell to my knees, resting my head against the stone, almost trembling with relief.

"He came after all," I said to Evgenia. Instead of responding she straightened and headed for the cavern. I rushed after her. "Zhenya, we made it. Thanks to *you*. We made it."

She ignored me. She loosened Buyan's reins and led him out of the cave, then mounted him, for all the world as though she planned to ride off without me. I picked up *Dead Souls* from where I had left it on the ground, hoping to entice her off Buyan. But she was already riding him around the wall, back in the direction of the path. I chased after her.

"Hello!" Lieutenant Valchar called merrily when he saw us.

He trotted over, he and his man blocking Evgenia's way without realizing they had done so. Evgenia tugged on Buyan's reins, clearly annoyed.

Lieutenant Valchar removed his cap politely. Despite the bloodstains on his shirt and hat, the wretched state of his uniform, and several red scratches on his face, he smiled broadly, thrilled at finding us.

"Good to see you alive," Evgenia said. "Take care of yourself."

The lieutenant's smile fell. He finally noticed my alarmed face.

"Is something wrong?" he asked.

"I'm not going with you," Evgenia said.

"You *must* come with us," I insisted. "He knows what you look like, and your name, and where you live, and he said the army was after both of us, Zhenya. You are a criminal in the eyes of the Red Army. You have no one else to turn to. This is— this is nothing but temper!" I said, growing more heated. She could not leave now, when we had so nearly reached our goal. Not now, when she knew my secret and might tell anyone. I held out the novel. "Look, you are so insensible that you forgot your father's book. You are not thinking clearly. Come down from there and stay with us."

She glanced at the book briefly.

"Keep it," she said. "You and your family already took everything else from me."

It was like all the breath was drawn out of me. I dropped the book. *How dare she?*

"Move your horses, Valchar," she said.

He obeyed, guiding his horse away so she could continue on.

"You can come, too, Evgenia," he said. "I tell your mother I help you both."

"No."

"All right. Please be safe. If you need us, we are in a big house north of town. We wait for the Reds to leave Iset so we can pass. The house is white, with many gardens, and it is burned on—on the top," he finished, forgetting the word for *roof*.

Evgenia let out that ugly laugh again. I wanted to shake her.

"The Gersky house. Of course that's where you'd go," she said. "You won't see me again."

She rode away without once looking at me, without saying a word. I watched her disappear, leaving me alone and turned to ice.

PART THREE
ISET

20

EVGENIA

I'D SET OUT TO HELP Kostya and ended up trading his life for the tsar's daughter. I'd screwed up worse than I ever imagined.

It wasn't just *who* Anna was. It was how she lied even after I saw the postcard. Like I was so stupid I wouldn't believe my own eyes. Like she thought all peasants were that dumb.

I'd thought we were friends. She was rich, and I was poor, but we liked the same books. We laughed at the same things. I'd thought we were the same.

And the whole time she was a Romanov. She wasn't just rich. She was richer than the Church. Richer than God. And instead of helping anyone with all that money, her father sent Lev to die. He sent his bureaucrats and police to steal from us. He taxed us until we had no bread left, then let the landlords take our crumbs.

All while his otrodye daughters danced, drank tea, and wore fancy clothes. That was Anna's life. She never cared about people like me. She'd probably never even thought about the peasants who paid for her palaces.

She's got no choice now.

I couldn't forget how she'd screamed about her father, either. She loved him just like I loved Batya. She loved her sisters, like I loved Lev and Kostya. She'd lost them all just like I had. That made my stomach turn, too.

All she'd wanted was to stay alive. The real problem was *me*. I was the one who took in a Romanov because some twinkling jewels called out to me. My greed got Kostya killed. My softness let her tears change me. If I'd been a better communist, like Kostya, none of this would've happened. Kostya would be alive. I'd be home with him and Mama, working the land, working for freedom together.

Instead, I had no one but a Romanov and a Czech soldier, and the Gersky house where they went to hide.

I couldn't be around them. I needed my own people.

I led Buyan to Iset. It was only a few versts from the devil's wall. I tied Buyan to a tree in a little hollow, where he could nibble on wildflowers and drink from the stream. It was a risk leaving him, but safer than bringing him to town.

The heart of Iset was the church, perched on a big hill. A few small houses and shops nearby made something of a town square. Today wasn't a market day, but it was as lively as one. Red soldiers poured in and out of the church like ants from moldy bread. Dozens of townspeople had come to offer vegetables, seeds, and cloths. There was a whole line of people waiting to hand baskets of goods over to the soldiers.

It wasn't like Mednyy, where the Whites bled us dry. Here

the people laughed and were friendly with the soldiers. They wanted to help the army. They gave what they could afford, and the Reds didn't demand more. They understood we were poor. They were fighting for *us*.

Peace, land, and bread. That was the Bolshevik motto. The Bolsheviks ended the war with Germany. They let us take our land back from the pomeshchiki. And they left peasants alone to grow enough grain to feed ourselves and sell. That was all the Reds wanted.

It was all I wanted. And I could go back to helping them, as long as no one recognized me.

"*Keep fighting*," Kostya'd said. Not *go make friends with our enemies.*

"Good afternoon, comrade," I said to a soldier. He was managing the line of villagers waiting to donate food. He looked around Valchar's age, nineteen or so, with a round, chubby face and bright eyes.

He smiled after a fast glance at my chest.

"Are you chatting me up, lovely?" he asked.

I snorted. And my neck grew hot. "No."

His grin slid off his face, so I hurried to make my point.

"I just wanted to ask if I can help. I'm a party member."

He laughed at that. I gritted my teeth.

"You? Aren't you a little young?" he asked. I'd heard it plenty of times before, but it always stung.

"I'm not an elected officer. I'm a messenger. And Med—I mean, I come from a small town. I helped start our chapter even before October."

"Well, aren't you special," he said, still pointing the way for people in line. "Hang on a moment. Yes, we can use you. Ey!" He called over another soldier. "Take over. I'm going to bring her inside."

"Oh yeah?" his friend said suggestively.

The chubby soldier winked, then waved for me to follow.

I slowed down. Anyone could be inside the church. He wasn't about to let me check before going in.

"What's inside?" I asked nervously as we headed for the steps. The Iset church was huge, made of red brick with a tall, white onion dome on top. We dodged the soldiers hurrying up and down the stairs on our way.

"We need to organize all the gifts people are bringing. I think a woman's touch is called for."

We neared the doors. I stopped and grabbed the soldier's arm. I couldn't walk in blind.

"Have you heard anything about Commander Yurovsky?" I asked shakily.

He lifted his eyebrows. "You're an admirer of his, eh? Lucky man."

I held my breath, waiting.

"I've heard the name. He's a Cheka commander, isn't he?"

I nodded.

"He might be at the jail. The Cheka officers traveling with our company set up there, to guard their prisoners."

The jail was on the other side of town. I smiled at the news.

"Oh, you're going to go off and look for your hero, aren't you?" He put his hands over his heart. "My loss."

"Very funny," I said. "I still want to help here. Show me."

I ducked my head as we entered. The church was dark,

and so tall that the large windows mainly lit the ceilings. Just enough light to see trickled down to our level. The soldiers had set up rows of benches to sleep on. The men walking up and down the center aisle kicked up so much dust I coughed before getting used to it. I peered carefully at the faces of everyone inside the building but saw no one I knew.

Then I saw the altar. The soldiers were dumping all the food and goods into heaps many cubits high.

"What a mess," I said. We walked down the aisle alongside another soldier who emptied a basket of old rags onto the top of a pile.

"This is what I mean. We can use your help straightening this out. What's your name?"

"Um, Anna Vyrubova," I said, taking on Anna's fake name before I could think about it. "What's yours?"

"Assistant platoon leader Agapov." He stuck his chest out, proud as a peacock. "But you can call me Vlad, Annushka."

"Wow," I muttered. He was getting awful familiar awfully fast. "All right, Agapov," I said sternly. "How should we do this? And why aren't you putting this stuff directly into wagons? Aren't you heading north?"

He shook his head.

"Our orders are to retreat. But some of our company are still fighting in Ekaterinburg. We're giving them time to catch up. They should be here soon. Or we might get ordered back into the fight. I *hope* we do," he added, but he looked at me so intently I knew he was showing off.

"It's just your company in town now?" I asked. One company could be as many as 150 men.

Agapov's face dropped.

"What's left of us. We have two platoons back in the city, and we lost a good number of men during the fighting. Those Czech *svolochi* are worse than the Whites."

"They're all rotten," I agreed.

"Yeah. Now let's get this organized so our cooks can actually find what they need to feed us tonight."

It was soothing work, like gardening. I made piles of cabbages, rows of grain bags, and covered the altar table with neat lines of carrots. Agapov had a big mouth. He talked more than geese in flight. He told me about his friends, about army life, and about his family stuck in Omsk, an Eastern city under White control. I let him talk. He was decent company.

My thoughts wandered to Anna as he chattered. She was alone in that empty, dead house with the Czechs. But she'd be fine without me. They'd all go to Ekaterinburg. She'd be safe from Yurovsky, and I'd never see her again.

She'd spend the rest of her life thinking I hated her. She was the tsar's daughter, and a liar . . . but she was still *Anna*. I couldn't hate her.

What would she think of me, for leaving her like that? The only way to find out was to go to the Gersky house and apologize. But what if she was still angry? What if *she* didn't apologize for lying? I couldn't decide if I wanted to risk it.

The donations stopped coming in after a while. That made it easier to fix everything up, and we finished before I could make a decision. Agapov and I stood back to look at our work.

"Not bad," I said.

"Pleasure working with you, Anya," Agapov said. "Are you hungry? I can go find something for us to share."

I was hungry. But he was too eager, and I wanted to check on Buyan.

"My family will be looking for me. I'd better go. But I'm glad I could help."

"You sure? You seem sad. I can cheer you up. How about a song? *Ey, little apple, where are you going to? My wife bores me, I want a young thing like you!*" He sang a dirty version of an old folk song, doing a silly little dance. I wanted to laugh. But inside I felt like an egg sucked dry.

"Sorry," I said. He was nice, and almost as cute as Valchar.

I shook myself for the stupid thought. Anyway, Agapov deserved better than my lies.

"Look, Agapov—"

A strong, bony hand landed on my shoulder. It pulled me off-balance, and I spun around, alert but annoyed.

I glared up to see who was bothering me.

It was Stravsky.

The instinct hit me like a falling tree trunk: *Run.*

"You," he said in an oily voice. He pressed his fingers around my shoulder, hard as a blacksmith's tongs.

I knocked his hand off, elbowed him away, and ran. I jumped down from the raised altar and dashed into the aisle, past a Red soldier carrying hay.

"Stop that girl!" Stravsky shouted. "She's a spy!" My heart flew into my throat as the few soldiers in the church turned their attention to me. A hand darted out to block me and I twisted out of its way. But I stumbled into a bench and smashed my leg against its sharp corner. I pushed myself off of it, swallowed the pain, and ducked between the long rows so I could race to the side of the church.

Stravsky kept yelling. Two soldiers came down the row after me, their boots pounding on the old wood floors, their guns slapping against their backs. I pumped my legs and ran even faster. At the end of the row I looked left. Two more soldiers had come in the front doors and joined the chase.

I veered right. There was a door in the back of the altar. If it led outside or even to a basement, I'd have a chance to escape. I was only a few rows away. Stravsky screamed again, and he started running at me, too. I pushed myself harder.

Agapov stepped into my path in front of the altar, five cubits in front of me. Would he let me by? Behind me, the four Red soldiers were still coming. The wall trapped me on the left. My heart sped up faster than the soldiers' footsteps, and my sight narrowed on Agapov. He didn't move. He wasn't going to help me.

My shoulder barreled into his torso, then I shoved him with both hands. I was almost clear of him when he yanked me backward. I fell against him, hard. I elbowed his gut, stomped on his toes with my heel, and he finally coughed and loosened his arm from around my waist.

I broke free. Without thinking, I sprinted for the door again, getting nearer. As soon as I got through it, I would get the hell away if it led outside, or barricade the door if I found the basement.

Agapov crashed into me from behind and knocked me to the floor, landing on top of me. My left shoulder and hip slammed into the floor first, then his weight flattened me. All the air flew out of my chest.

He shifted, and I gasped in a breath. Agapov's wide, confused eyes met mine. In a moment the rest of the soldiers would reach us.

"Let me go," I said, sounding weaker than I'd hoped. "I'm innocent."

He studied my face. A look of sympathy washed over him but vanished quickly. He locked his jaw, pushed me flat beneath him, and held my head to the floor. The rough wood scraped my cheek. Agapov tugged my right arm behind my back so harshly I grunted with pain. I couldn't move.

The footsteps stopped and leather boots surrounded us.

"Good job, Agapov," Stravsky panted. "You three, take her to the Cheka and make sure they secure her. She's a counter-revolutionary. Then cable Commander Yurovsky. He'll want to come see her himself."

21

ANNA

IT DID NOT TAKE US long to reach the dilapidated mansion where Lieutenant Valchar and his men had taken shelter. The path we followed in the forest ended at the base of a wide, green hill, and we rode up through an elaborate garden where unkempt rows of hedges and rosebushes were being strangled to death by weeds.

The house was three stories tall, or had been, before the fire. The uppermost level was half gone, as the roof had caved in. The mansion's white exterior was streaked with black. The colonnaded entrance must have once been grand but now looked as outlandish as makeup on a smallpox victim. The second-floor windows were broken and capped with soot stains. More than anything else it resembled a haunted house from a ghost story.

We left the horses tied up in a shady grove behind the house and entered through a back door, stepping onto a split staircase. On the right, the stairs descended past cobwebs into a dark basement. We took the stairs up to the ground floor instead, into a marbled entry hall that stretched from the rear to the large double front doors. It smelled moldy and damp inside, and though they had left the front doors open, there was little hint of fresh air.

The ground floor, at least, was largely intact. Elaborate molding rimmed the hallway ceiling, and the wallpaper remained, though it was torn and scarred in many places. The meager sunlight penetrating the transom caught streams of dust in the air and revealed cracks and chips in the marble floors. A chandelier was in tatters, and there was no furniture at all.

I followed Lieutenant Valchar into a door on the right. My eyes widened in surprise.

Several more Czech soldiers were inside the drawing room. They were all bare-chested in the heat, and they lounged casually, leaning against a broken sofa on one side of the room, or crowding around a game of cards near the far windows. The men stood as we entered. At least a couple of them looked embarrassed to have been caught so off guard. Two injured soldiers slept on the floor and did not stir; one's leg was bandaged while the other sweated profusely, clearly racked by fever.

"This is Anna Vyrubova," Lieutenant Valchar introduced me in German. "I told you about her this morning. She'll come with us to Ekaterinburg."

A tall, pale soldier leaning against the window with his arms folded said something quickly in Czech, and an uneasy ripple traveled across the room. Lieutenant Valchar's face sharpened. He answered back crossly, and the men stilled.

I cleared my throat.

"Thank you for allowing me to take shelter here with you," I said. "I promise that I will be as helpful as possible, and as little a bother to you, as we await passage to Ekaterinburg. You have no idea just how great a service you are rendering. God bless you all. Lieutenant Valchar, would you kindly introduce me to the men? I would like to know their names."

He presented me to each of the men in turn, and I shook hands with them, just as Papa would have done for any soldiers on guard. Most smiled and greeted me politely. Only a few avoided my eyes, while the tall soldier near the window glared outright. For some reason, my presence discomfited him.

"You can sleep here." Lieutenant Valchar led me into a small sitting room on the other side of the hall. The walls here were covered in peeling, filthy, pink-flowered paper. An old armoire had been torn to pieces, its drawers and doors gone and the shelves broken. The floors were littered with half-burned books and old, soiled clothing. We kicked the debris aside to make a path. "At least it's a little more private."

"Thank you. I am not worried about the state of our accommodations. I am more concerned with how soon we can leave. Is the Red Army merely passing through Iset, or are they digging in to stay?"

"We don't know." He shook his head. "We're watching the road to see if they start heading north. Nothing yet."

"How many are still there?"

"Too many for us to get past," he said. "We couldn't get close enough to count them exactly. They'd recognize our uniforms."

"Am I safe with you here, Lieutenant? I noticed that some of your men appeared less than pleased when I joined you."

He winced.

"I'm sorry. It isn't you. They're worried about three of our men who were captured yesterday. They aren't ready to leave without them. And, Anna, please, call me Jiri."

"Certainly, Jiri," I said in a rush. "But do you even know where they are being held? Or that they are still alive?"

Jiri frowned.

"We think the Bolsheviks took them to Iset, but we're not sure where. Some of the men want to rescue them. Some don't."

"What do *you* want?"

"I haven't decided," he said. As the commanding officer, the choice ultimately rested with him. I sighed as frustration washed through me. Evgenia had left me alone and at the mercy of these men, who had their own agendas.

"Is it wise to risk the lives of ten able-bodied men in exchange for three? You may end up handing the Reds more prisoners of war."

Jiri moved to look out the window; a beam of sunlight caught the back of his golden hair. His head was still bowed, and he seemed to be considering my words carefully. I knew him to be chivalrous. He had repeatedly risked his own life to rescue others. He was rather like Evgenia in that way.

Evgenia, who had turned her back on me the second she knew my true identity. As though I were *evil* because I was a Romanov. As though my family were evil. How could she still think so poorly of me after all we had been through together? She knew me. Why had that not been enough to convince her that my family and I were not bad people?

I struggled to hold back tears. If Evgenia was so blinded by fanaticism, then she might truly betray me. She might have gone in search of Commander Yurovsky herself, to tell him where I was, just as she had threatened the last time we were in Iset.

A chill passed through me.

"I will be entirely alone if I lose you and your men, Jiri," I said. "With no hope of reaching Ekaterinburg alive. If you deliver me safely, I promise my cousin and the general will reward you richly. *Richly*."

When he faced me, his eyes were wounded and his mouth tilted downward. My heart fell. I had miscalculated.

"I'm not interested in any reward, Anna," he said. "As a friend, I'll do my best to help you. But as a leader, I'm responsible for all of my men."

"Of course you are," I said. "I understand how important your soldiers are to you. And I know that leadership is no easy burden. Forgive me."

After he left, I paced in the empty room, tossing aside insect-infested tomes to clear a space where I might sleep. The house was quiet, and smothering, and I was restless for something to do.

At home in the palace I had often been irritated by Mama's puttering. She never sat still and continually pressed us children to always be busy with chores or needlework or study. "*Life is for work, not pleasure*," she liked to say.

But in the eerie quiet of the Gersky house, even I could not sit still. I wandered upstairs, cautiously climbing the creaking staircase to the second level, and wandered in and out of the bedrooms there. The second floor was in far worse condition than below. The walls were crumbling, the ceilings blackened, and many of the floorboards broken. In one room I heard scurrying creatures behind the walls. I tried to imagine which rooms had been for the Gersky children, and which for the parents. This was the house Evgenia had told me about, where the Iset townspeople burned the owners alive.

I could not feel the presence of the family who had once lived here. In the Ipatiev house we had periodically found reminders of the family who had been evicted so that we could be imprisoned there—they left behind toys, furniture, children's drawings on the walls. But there was nothing of the Gersky family left here. Instead, all I felt was the memory of the mob's anger. Its marks were everywhere.

I hurried back downstairs. I kept the basement stairs out of view, not even wanting to look that way as I headed to the drawing room. As soon as I rejoined the Czechs, I found work to keep me occupied.

There was not much I could do for the injured men—we had no medicines and no supplies. But I fetched cool water for them from outside, and applied cold rags to the feverish young soldier. I chatted with the two men casually, for one spoke Russian well and the other passable German. Often the best thing to do for someone in pain was to entertain them.

I had done the same thousands of times during the war, when Masha and I visited hospitals for the enlisted men. If my sisters were here, they would have known what to do even without medicine. They knew much more about nursing than I ever learned.

If Evgenia were here, she likely would have bitten the heads off all the men for supporting the White Army. Her brand of knowledge did not extend to healing.

Just as her friendship was limited to people like her.

She liked me before she knew how badly I lied. She had never truly minded me when she believed I was a wealthy merchant's daughter. It was the enormous scope of my lie—the lie that I was *forced* to tell for my own survival—that appalled her. She had confessed her worst secrets to me, while I kept even my name from her.

Though I was furious with her for what she had said, I still wanted her here with me. I wanted her safe from Commander Yurovsky. I hoped she was not thinking of going home to Mednyy. The only place for her now was by my side—but she had shunned it.

Perhaps she would return.

"Russian bitch."

My back snapped straight at the words hissed to me in Russian. I pulled my hands from Ambroz, the badly ill soldier who had been falling asleep under my ministrations.

The words had come from behind me. The tall, pale soldier strode past me, casting a glare so ferocious that I shivered. I thought back over my words and deeds, wondering what I might have done to offend him so.

"Ignore him." Ambroz's wan green eyes opened. He nudged the damp rag on his forehead farther up his hairline, so he could see me better. "Josef is grieving. He lost his brother last month, and his best friend yesterday. He blames all Russians for the acts of a few."

I could not ignore him, for Josef stood in his corner post and pinned his angry eyes on me, watching my every move. If he decided to attack me, would anyone stop him? Jiri had left, and the other men did not notice—or pretended not to notice—Josef's behavior. My hands began to tremble until I finally gave up. I excused myself from Ambroz and left the parlor to try to find my only remaining ally.

Before I took even a few steps, someone shoved me from behind into the corridor wall. I cried out as my head collided with it painfully, and then a filthy, merciless hand closed over my mouth and nose, smothering the sound and my breath.

"You bitch," he growled in my ear, now speaking German. He leaned his weight against my shoulders, pressing me against the wall with his arm.

I tried to escape, but he was so strong I could hardly move, and I could not draw in enough air to scream. My eyes watered.

"We won't abandon our own men just to save Russian garbage."

Spots danced in my vision and, desperate for air, I fought against him harder, only to hear him laugh in a low voice.

"I could kill you right now and Valchar couldn't do anything about it. He's so soft I bet he'd apologize to *me*," he said. "If you say anything about this to him, I'll kill you and find out if I'm right."

He released me so abruptly that I lost my balance and fell to the floor, gasping. The pain in my lungs eased, but I held my hands to my throbbing forehead. By the time I looked up again, Josef had vanished into the parlor. I hastened to my feet and out the front door, putting as much distance between us as I dared.

22

EVGENIA

THE JAIL WAS BIGGER THAN I remembered. The courthouse was made of red brick same as the church, but behind it the jailhouse jutted out like a knocked-down tombstone made of pale, sturdy lime. Agapov and his comrades dragged me past three officers working in the courthouse, down a dark, wet staircase, and into a darker, wetter basement. A cloud of stink greeted us. It reeked of sweat, piss, and blood, like the Petrov barn on a butchering day. Thin windows near the ceilings let in just enough light to see the thick layer of filth on the floor and the cobwebs covering the empty candleholders on the walls.

It was as quiet as church. There were six cells here, two on the left and four to the right. Each was the size of a cow's stall. Three were occupied. In one, a man slept in a heap against the back wall. I hoped he was sleeping, anyway. In another cell, the prisoner was leaning against the metal bars. He watched us silently. He wore a loose collared shirt, so he probably wasn't a Czech officer. His bare toes poked out between the bars, like he didn't mind the sludge that was already seeping through my lapti.

The soldiers shoved me into the second cell. I landed on my hands and knees, the blow shooting straight to my aching shoulder. Agapov slammed the door shut and closed a padlock over it, then left.

I scrambled to my feet. The ghosts of Agapov's and his comrades' grip on my arms were still there, and I rubbed at them, trying to make the feeling go away. My whole body was on edge. Somewhere upstairs, a man screamed. The horrified sound died abruptly, then came again. Ice tiptoed down my back.

The Reds had thrown me into the hell of a Cheka jail. Either they'd kill me, or Yurovsky would when he arrived.

I had to get out. I tried the door, but of course it held tight. Next I ran my hands over the walls. The sides of the cell were wooden, coated in chipped paint and dust, and broken in a few places with small, jagged holes. I felt along the gaps and found an old, rusty nail that might be useful. I shoved it into my apron pocket. Otherwise all I managed to get were splinters in my fingers.

The rear wall was made of limestone, with a small window tall as my hand and three times as long. The sunlight melted away in the dust and dark of my cell. I checked the aging window frame to see if it could be loosened, then stuck my fingers through the bars. There was warm, springy grass right outside.

Tears prickled at my eyes.

"Fuck!" I rattled the door again, pulled it as hard as I could, trying to tear it down. Then I tried slamming my shoulder into it. Once didn't work, so I kept going, hitting it over and over. I wasn't just going to sit here and wait to die. That fucking door would give in before I would.

It didn't. My arm and side couldn't take any more hits. I sat down, my muscles throbbing angrily. I wasn't any closer to getting out than when I'd started. And the poor guy upstairs was screaming again. I dropped my head.

"The mountain won't give way to Muhammad," a smooth voice broke into my thoughts. The man in the third cell sounded close, like he had approached our shared wall. Was he talking to me?

"What?"

"You tried to break down the mountain. I'm sorry to say, my unfortunate lady, that it will not work." He spoke oddly, like Anna, and not like a peasant.

"What the devil are you talking about? What mountain?"

"Never mind. You sound young. Very young. What did you do to land yourself a prisoner of the secret police?"

"What did *you* do?" I snapped. My head spun, my chest felt like it was caught between a wolf's teeth, and this enemy of the Reds was confusing me.

"I'm a journalist," he answered. "The Cheka didn't like what I wrote, sadly, so they arrested me. Apparently they enjoyed my company so well that they brought me with them when they fled Ekaterinburg. Now it's your turn. What brought you here?"

My stomach turned. I didn't want to think about it.

"Nothing. I don't know why I'm here. It's a mistake."

"Ah," he said. "That strikes me as unlikely. But then again, the Cheka are not known for showing due diligence before arresting someone. What is your name, my dear? And how old are you?"

"Anna Vyrubova," I said shakily. I could hardly follow what he was saying. But sticking to my fake identity seemed smart. Maybe if I stuck to my story, I could convince the guards here that they had the wrong girl. "I'm sixteen."

He made a disappointed *tsk*.

"This is no place for a child. My name is Anton Ulyevich Utkin, by the way." He sounded educated and rich, like Anna.

"Where are you from?"

"Originally? From Moscow. I was sent to Ekaterinburg for a story, to cover the imprisonment of the royal family. And believe me, I regret taking the assignment."

My mouth fell open. I'd never met anyone from Moscow before. But then he mentioned the royal family, and my heart skipped a beat.

"You—" The words caught in my throat. "Did you see them? The Romanovs?"

"No, I never expected to. They were kept under house arrest and behind a tall fence, under heavy guard. But I spoke to servants who went in and out, to the guard, the neighbors. The Cheka decided they didn't like me poking around so much, and so here I am."

I couldn't believe it. He was here for almost the same reason I was.

"Do—do you know what happened to them?"

"Well, I heard they executed the tsar. I suppose the rest of the family must have been freed when the White Army arrived.

After all the work I did, some other newspaper will get the scoop on that story." He sighed dramatically.

I laughed shortly.

"Tough luck," I said. Too bad we couldn't have met him the last time we were in Iset. He could've published Anna's story, and the Bolsheviks would've stopped Yurovsky then. I never would've had to bring Anna to Mednyy. Kostya would still be alive.

I squeezed my eyes shut against the wave of anger and grief that hit me. I wanted to cry. Instead, I held my breath and hoped it would pass.

"Who else is here?" I asked next.

"A couple of Czechs. They don't speak much Russian. I won't say I'm glad you're here, Anya, but it is a relief to have someone to talk to."

That didn't deserve a reply.

"Who's upstairs?" I asked.

He knew who I meant.

"I don't know," Anton said, his voice lower. "They haven't brought him down yet."

They never did. A revolver shot cut off one of the man's screams a little later, and that was the end of it. The Czechs howled with rage, so it must've been one of their friends. But their shouting couldn't help him now.

The day dragged on. The light turned golden. I figured out that the corner of the stall was my latrine, which explained the stench. I couldn't sit still. I paced back and forth, trying to ease my jittery skin, and every noise made me jump. I'd fight Yurovsky if he came. Better to die quick than to suffer like the prisoner upstairs. Yurovsky would want to know where Anna was. He'd happily hurt me to find out.

No. They'd taken my knife, but I was strong. Yurovsky had an injured arm, thanks to Kostya. I imagined digging my thumb into his wound, knocking him down, and running for the stairs. The fantasy stopped there. I didn't know how I'd get past the Cheka officers in the courtroom.

The guards came for me. Three against one. I'd never have made it past them.

"Step back," the first armed guard ordered. He smacked the bars with the rifle butt, and I let go, backing up quickly. A second guard unlocked the door, while a third stepped into the cell.

"I hear Commander Yurovsky is excited to see you, girl," he said. He was only a little taller than me, but he was built as wide as a barrel. And standing way too close.

"I wonder why that is," he went on. "What's so special about you, *Evgenia*?" His white teeth caught the fading light. He was smiling.

I backed up, tensing.

"You must be important. I guess we'd better take good care of you." He lifted the bowl of water he was carrying. Instead of handing it to me, he turned it and poured it on the floor.

I almost cursed him, but kept my mouth shut. *We fight the battles we can win.*

"You make sure to tell him how good we treated you when he gets here." He upturned the second bowl in his other hand, and thick, gloppy stew splattered to the floor and onto my skirt.

My heart thudded as the guards locked me in again. I slid down the wall to the floor, breathing in great, big gulps of air.

Yurovsky was coming. I was screwed.

"Are you all right?" Anton Ulyevich called out.

"Best I've ever been," I said, waiting for my heart to beat normally again.

"Hmph. I know Commander Yurovsky, my dear. He is very high up in the scheme of things, or at least he was in Ekaterinburg. Why would he be looking for you?"

"We're old friends," I said without thinking. I felt light. Giddy, from fear. "We used to pick mushrooms together."

"Anya—only your name isn't Anna, is it? Nemov called you Evgenia. Is that your real name?"

"Yeah," I admitted. There didn't seem to be any point in lying. Nemov and his comrades weren't going to listen to anything I said.

"Evgenia, do you know Commander Yurovsky?"

"Yes."

"Are you from Ekaterinburg?"

"No."

"Will you tell me why you're here?"

My chest tightened. The fog around my head cleared a little.

"Forget it, damn it. Leave me alone."

But Anton wasn't one to stay quiet.

"We'll both get through this," he said.

Right. And cows lay eggs.

23

ANNA

THE DAY PASSED SLOWLY. I ricocheted between tending to hopeless flowers in the gardens and injured men indoors. Always I stayed within screaming distance of the house, for I could not predict where or when an attack might spring—from Josef, inside, or from Commander Yurovsky, who might appear from the forest.

Jiri had gone to investigate the road heading north out of Iset, leaving me feeling especially exposed. He returned late in the day, and while my heart lifted to see him emerge from the trees, I immediately noticed that he led a horse behind him—a squat, stubborn brown horse that kept resisting his lead and that looked far too old to be of much use to anyone.

My blood ran cold. I could not move, and I waited in the middle of the overgrown, twilight yard as Jiri and Buyan approached. The lieutenant's eyes were dark and as heavy as my immobile feet.

"Where is she?" I asked, my voice strange and hoarse. Visions of Evgenia's body riddled with bullets—of her tossed into a ditch somewhere, of Commander Yurovsky standing over her, demanding to know where I was—all played through my head like a grotesque movie.

I knew at once with utter certainty—Evgenia was still my loyal friend. She loved me. If Commander Yurovsky had captured Evgenia, she would not tell him where to find me.

"I don't know," Jiri replied. "I found him in the woods closer to town, but she wasn't there. I figured maybe she'll come here if she finds him gone."

Evgenia would never have left Buyan alone in the woods so close to dark. And she would have died before turning me over to the man who killed Konstantin.

Which meant that she was already dead. Commander Yurovsky had found her and taken yet another person I loved.

"Anna," Jiri said urgently. "We'll find her. I have more men out watching the road. I told them all what she looks like. If they see her, they'll bring her back."

"If he has found her—"

"I know. Let's hope he hasn't. Let's hope she's just being as difficult as always."

I could not muster a smile. After securing Buyan alongside the other horses, Jiri brought me inside to eat supper with his men. We sat in small groups around the parlor, a few candles providing light as the shadows lengthened outside. I was able to keep my back turned to Josef so I would not have to look at him, and sat together with Jiri, Ambroz, and Karol, the other wounded man who had greatly improved.

After dinner Jiri went out onto the front porch for a smoke. I followed him.

"May I join you?"

"Do you smoke?" Jiri asked in surprise.

I nodded, and we stepped onto the porch together.

He pulled out a matchbook and lit a cigarette for each of us. I inhaled deeply; it was poor-quality tobacco, weak and cut with something sweet. Yet it kindled a warmth in my chest that was like a hug from an old friend.

It had been a month since my last smoke. We had been in the Ipatiev house. As Masha's, Tatiana's, Mama's, and my birthdays were all in June, the Bolsheviks allowed a gift package from Grandmother to reach us. Usually they stole any nice things sent to us, so it was a rare treat. My sisters and I had unwrapped the items with glee. During the hour we were permitted outside in the yard, the four of us sat in the shade, leaning all in a row against the side wall, smoking peacefully in silence. I had savored every drag, and when the last embers crumbled through my fingers, I leaned my head onto Masha's shoulder and closed my eyes. She had smelled of citrus perfume and tobacco.

"Thank you," I said now to Jiri. The memory weighed on my heart like a stone, but I was grateful for it.

He nodded, leaned back against a column, and looked down the hill toward the trees. The rising moon cast a soft light over the slope.

"She still has not come," I said unnecessarily.

"No."

"Are you still thinking about your men?"

"Yes, always. I worry about them."

"I wonder," I said gently, "what your superior officers would want you to do."

He harrumphed at that.

"They don't know my men like I do," he said. "They don't know their names, their family's names."

That was the point, of course. It was precisely that distance between generals and their soldiers that allowed them to make unemotional decisions. Jiri, who was attached to his men, could not bear the thought of leaving them. But should his own affection for them overcome him, we would all be doomed. It was the burden of military leaders to count lives as the cost of victory.

Just as *Nikolai the Bloody* had done.

Evgenia's use of that detested nickname still infuriated me. Papa had been the gentlest man I knew. He was praised—sometimes even mocked—by our relatives for his moderate temperament and kind heart. He dreaded sending men into war. He was not only our father but the father of everyone in Russia, and he loved the peasants as his own children. If he had to arrest and execute liberal agitators, it was only to protect the health of the empire.

"People like you control who gets educated, then use it as an excuse to keep all the power. It's time for people to rule themselves."

Papa wanted to take care of everyone. But the Russian people were not children. They wanted to take care of themselves. "I know this impacts you, too," Jiri said, pulling me from my grim musings. "I'm sorry for that."

"Oh, don't apologize." I sighed. "What kind of war would it be without impossible, life-threatening decisions?"

He smiled. "A short one, probably."

"If only we were so lucky," I said.

"What will you do when you reach Ekaterinburg?"

I was glad for the invitation to think forward and not backward.

"My cousin Alexander is there. He can help me travel safely to the Crimea, where my aunt and grandmother are. I long to see his face." I smiled. "He and my eldest sister used to get into the most ridiculous squabbles. They were so competitive in everything—cards, games, who could memorize more poems, who knew more words of French. They quarreled like beasts whenever we visited. And Alexander always cheated." I laughed. "He is so smart, yet he could never bear to lose. When Olga caught him at it, he would scrunch up his nose in the funniest way." I imitated it for Jiri's benefit.

"You'll see him soon," Jiri said.

"And what about you? What will you do?"

"I'll rejoin our army. We want to leave Russia, too, and get back into the fight. If we can help the British and the French win, they'll give us our independence from Austria. We can have a Czechoslovak government. And I'll get to see my parents again."

"You must miss them very much."

He laughed bitterly.

"I haven't seen them in ten years," he said. "The Austrians put them in jail. They're nationalists. And my father is Jewish, which some people didn't like, either."

I felt another twinge of guilt. Papa had had the most antiquated views on Jews. My sisters and I had groaned over it whenever he blamed protests on *yid conspirators*. He had once said that our nation would be better off if we exiled every

Jewish person on Russian soil. He would have been instantly suspicious of Jiri.

He had been wrong about so much more than I ever realized. Jiri was one of the best people I had ever met.

I stubbed out my cigarette, sickened by everything.

"I am sorry," I said. "You would have been young ten years ago—who raised you?"

"My uncle. Anyway," he said briskly, "Austria and Germany are losing now. I want to get back and help finish them off."

Ironically he and Papa would have been allies.

That evening I could not sleep a wink and spent the brief night out of doors, far from Josef, near the horses. Near Buyan, in the hopes that his owner would come. I felt wretched, trying to reconcile the parents who loved me with Evgenia's hatred for them. I couldn't. There was no reconciling the two. Mama and Papa had been good—even great—people. And yet for some reason, they had been blind to the suffering of their own subjects.

Whatever their faults, whatever their attributes, they were gone. And perhaps Evgenia was gone with them. By midday she still had not returned. I kept myself busy, puttering again. Between washing Ambroz's face and neck and cleaning out the traces of our morning meal, I took a few minutes to kneel and pray for her.

Running feet approached and entered the pink room. Jiri appeared in the doorway, his face long and drawn with some grim knowledge.

I rose slowly, my hands shaking.

I could not bring myself to ask.

"Our lookout overheard Red soldiers talking," he said. "Anna, they captured a girl who killed a Cheka officer in Mednyy. Now she's in the Cheka jail."

She was still alive.

I reached my hand out, and Jiri was there to catch me as my knees weakened. I dropped my forehead on his shoulder. After a moment it was as though some of his strength seeped into me, and I stood, my mind no longer spinning so wildly.

"Do they know if Commander Yurovsky is there?" I asked.

"No. This is all we know about it. But he also heard that the Red soldiers are leaving Iset today and tomorrow. The fighting in Ekaterinburg is over, so they're going. The Whites won."

Dread crawled up my spine.

"He will torture her," I said.

He furrowed his brow.

"No, Anna. She's a girl, and a pretty one. They'll go easy on her."

As though being pretty had ever protected anyone.

"You do not know the Cheka, Jiri. They are a merciless secret police force, and whatever they want, they will get. They torture their prisoners." My voice broke, and I covered my mouth, trying to steady myself. "He will torture her until she tells them where we are. Then he will kill her and come here for us."

"I'm going for my men," Jiri said. "I'll save Evgenia, too. I can't leave any of them to that. Now that the Reds are leaving, we have a chance. We'll go tonight. At dark."

Hope and dread warred in my chest. They might save

Evgenia's life, keep her from being tortured, liberate her before Commander Yurovsky arrived and found out where we were.

Or it might be a futile mission—a few Czech soldiers against dozens of Bolsheviks. Evgenia could already have given us up. She might even already be dead.

I groaned and fought to exorcise the image of her slain body from my mind.

"If you're worried about your safety," Jiri said, "don't be afraid. I'll leave some of the men back as protection. Whatever happens, I'll get you to Ekaterinburg."

"No, you must take them all!" I burst out. "Please. Lead them. Take all the men with you. You must do everything you can to save Evgenia."

24

EVGENIA

AT NIGHT MY CELL GOT dark and quiet, like a grave. Then the rats came out. Their small feet scratched along the stone floors faster than Batya plucking his balalaika strings. One rat sidled right near me. A quick bang of my lapti against the wall sent it scurrying away. Mostly the rats just wanted the spilled stew. I let them enjoy their feast, even if the sounds of their munching turned my stomach.

It was a long night.

Anton woke in the morning, a good while after the sun rose.

"Evgenia?" He knocked on the wall between us like he thought I could open it. "You still there?"

"Yeah."

"Oh. I wasn't sure if I might have dreamed you up. I think I'm sorry I didn't."

I sat on the floor, my back toward him, and I let my head fall onto my knees. I hadn't relaxed once. My body buzzed nervously, making me jumpy on top of tired and thirsty.

From outside the jail came the sound of busy activity, men calling out, wagons bouncing on gravel. A buzzing noise, like a bee in my ear, grew louder until it filled the cell around me. I'd heard that sound once before. It was an automobile.

"What's going on outside?" I asked Anton.

"They've been moving around out there all morning. Automobiles, wagons, horses. We think it's the last of the Red Army from Ekaterinburg, preparing to go north."

"We?"

"The Czechs and I. Havel's next door to me; he speaks a little Russian. Yesterday the soldiers talked about leaving a small company behind in Iset, to look after the trash. We think they were talking about the retreat. The trash presumably referring to us, of course."

I grunted. That made sense.

"How long have you been here, anyway?" I asked.

"In this town, just since the troops fled Ekaterinburg. That was two days ago. But they arrested me nearly two weeks ago."

"Did they question you?"

"Like the unfortunate man upstairs, you mean? They did at first. But after they brought in their Czech prisoners, they left me alone. Short attention span, these Cheka officers."

I wondered what Anton looked like. Did he have scars from the Cheka interrogations?

I studied the walls, the window, the metal bars. I rattled the padlock again, on the off chance it had weakened overnight. Nothing.

Hours passed. Anton talked some more. The Czechs woke and spoke to each other. Havel asked me, "You girl?" in bad Russian. He followed it up with "Be careful." Like I had any way of doing that.

Nemov came in the afternoon. He was grinning.

"You have a visitor," he said. "Someone who's eager to see you."

My mouth dried, and my back broke out into prickly sweat. I knew who my *visitor* was.

Nemov unlocked the door and grabbed my arms tighter than a bear trap.

"We're going to have some fun, girl." He pushed me up the stairs. He kept poking my back with his fist as we walked. It wasn't hard enough to be a punch, but it wasn't soft, either. I would've pointed out that I was going where he wanted me to go, but I couldn't speak. I couldn't think clearly. He was here.

The hall upstairs was longer and brighter than I remembered. Halfway down it was an open doorway. It looked to be roughly where the screaming had come from the day before. I stopped and tried to yank my arms free of Nemov, but his hold didn't give.

"Walk, *suka*," he growled.

Up here I could see him better. He had an angry face to match his voice. His eyes were wide apart, bulging, and full of hate.

I walked.

We turned into the open room. It was as small as my cell and smelled just as bad. Right in the middle there was a single chair bolted with metal planks into the floor. Against the wall to the right was a table, and another chair, and Yurovsky sitting in it.

My heart stopped. Nemov had to push me in. Yurovsky's nose was sharper than I remembered, his eyes narrower. He wore his army uniform, and the stars on his sleeve were bright red. His hand rested easily on the revolver in his lap. My skin prickled with sweat. I tried to breathe normally, but it entered my mouth like a croak. He was going to kill me.

I looked at the revolver again. It was the same gun he used to shoot Kostya. Heat rose inside me, and I lost my head, baring my teeth furiously. I tried to jerk my arms free of Nemov. If I could reach the gun fast enough I'd kill Yurovsky. It would be worth it. If nothing else I'd at least get in a few hits. But Nemov's grip was like iron.

"Tie her down," Yurovsky said.

"Fuck you!" I screamed. Nemov and another guard forced me into the chair and tied my hands behind the back, then each of my ankles to a chair leg.

Yurovsky stood. I glared at him, waiting for his next move. He stepped forward, and my knee jerked wildly, my thigh muscles flinching. Then I saw that he had the gun in his hand.

He pressed his knees against mine. His smell filled my mouth, old wool and gunpowder. The door to the room closed. I didn't know who'd left or who was still there. All I saw was Yurovsky leaning over me, his neat hair slipping over his forehead as he came closer.

He put the barrel of the gun on my temple. It was cold and unforgivingly hard. I wasn't breathing anymore.

"Tell me where Anastasia is," he said quietly.

I squeezed my eyes shut. He could kill me just like Kostya. I wouldn't help him kill anyone else. I wouldn't say anything. I was dead anyway.

But a word slipped out from my lips. It sounded as weak as a child's whimper.

"Speak up," Yurovsky said.

I whimpered again, then pushed the word out.

"No," I said.

Yurovsky pressed the gun harder into my head, like a trowel into land that won't give. He pushed until my head lowered all the way to the side, my ear digging into my shoulder.

"Where is she?"

He cocked the gun with a machinelike click. I gasped, trying to breathe or beg for my life.

Let him do it. For Kostya. I wouldn't help his murderer. I'd die first.

"No!" I cried.

The blast came. I flinched. But no—I'd imagined it. I'd *almost* heard it. It was coming, and I'd never see Mama again. Tears trickled into my hair and snot dripped onto my cheek. I gritted my teeth, readying for the shot.

Yurovsky pulled the gun away. My temple throbbed with relief, but I stayed still, waiting.

"So you are not yet afraid of dying," Yurovsky said. He moved away. I slowly lifted my head and relaxed my tense body as I looked at him. My head felt like it was going to fly off. My whole body felt light. He hadn't shot me. I was alive. But why?

Yurovsky put the revolver on the table with a solid, heavy thud. The room was so small. Nemov stood by the door with his arms crossed. He wore his rifle slung under his arm, ready to use. On his belt he'd strapped extra ammunition and a knife. He watched me with furious eyes. If Yurovsky didn't end me, Nemov would.

"Maybe you don't believe I'll really kill you," Yurovsky went on. "You think your knowledge of the grand duchess will protect you."

I held my breath. Would it?

"You don't understand your position. Let me explain it to you." He sat in his chair and crossed an ankle over his knee. His stare was as hard as icicles on the border of Lake Iset.

"You either tell me what I need to know, or Captain Nemov here will help our conversation along. So. Where is Anastasia?"

I glared at him. His face changed when he realized I wasn't going to answer. He nodded at Nemov, and I looked over just in time to see the butt of Nemov's rifle headed toward me. It smashed into the side of my face, and my cheek and jaw exploded with pain. Blood pooled in my mouth, warm and metallic, as I accidentally bit my tongue.

I'd been hit in fights before, but never like this. My head pulsed like a heart, pain beating against the sides. I spat out some of the blood. It splattered onto my apron and the floor, where it landed on older bloodstains.

"Do not play games with me, traitor." His voice was still quiet, and dark as granite. "You see, I already know everything about you. I know the details of the crimes you committed, and I know you're hiding the Romanova. Let us try again. Tell me where she is."

It took me a moment to understand him.

"I don't know," I said over my numb, thick tongue.

He nodded. I closed my eyes. Nemov punched me on the same cheek. Then he punched with his other hand. My head flew, the world went black and dizzy. All I knew was pain. I was sure the next punch would break my face in half, but it came and I was still whole. It felt like my nose was twisted sideways. He hit me in my gut, he punched my chest. My face was a mess of blood and bruise, and my torso felt like a flattened pancake when he finally stepped back.

My head fell forward. Blood burned as it streamed out of my nose and poured to the floor like milk from a spilled pitcher. There was even blood in my eyes, and on my eyelashes. For a while all I saw was red. Bolshevik red. When I could finally lift my head, I saw Nemov standing in the corner like nothing had happened.

The commander stared at me. His eyes looked the same.

"Tell me where Anastasia is," he said.

I tilted my head back. The blood slowed to a trickle. It felt warm and dirty, like someone pissing on my chin. Yurovsky repeated his question, but I didn't have an answer for him. I couldn't even think straight.

"I don't like to be ignored. Captain, wake her up."

Nemov grabbed my hair and tugged my head back, hard.

"Answer the commander," he growled. He reared his fist again.

"Hold on, Captain," Yurovsky said mildly.

Nemov let me go, and I gasped with relief. I couldn't get enough air, I couldn't steady my jumpy heart. I could barely see. Everything was spinning.

"I will not waste my time," Yurovsky said. "The men in my command have given their lives to fight against the capitalists. Yet you betray us. You help people who want to keep us in the dark ages." He turned to gesture at Nemov.

"I'm no traitor!" The words burned in my throat. "You are. This isn't communism. You can't make things better by killing people or hurting us. You'll only make more war, and more violence!"

Yurovsky's face frosted over.

"You," he said, "are the worst kind of traitor. You can see the path that will bring us peace and equality, but you're too cowardly to take it. You're willing to let your own people suffer. You don't realize that the path of compromise is lined with false hope. *I* will make sure we are not swayed. I won't let you sabotage our future. Captain, bring in the box."

Nemov's face lit up, and my heart skittered. He came back a moment later, laid something heavy and metal on the table, and took great care with whatever he'd brought. Yurovsky waited patiently. A box lid creaked open. Nemov placed several thin metal objects that I couldn't see onto the wooden table with distinct clinks. It sounded like he was setting places for dinner. Sweat broke out on my forehead. I wished I could see him better. I wished I knew what was coming.

"Your brother spoke highly of you," Yurovsky said.

"Think how sorry he'd be to see you now. Tell me. Where is Anastasia?"

I spat at him. He did not even flinch.

"This question demands an answer of yes or no. Will you tell me who turned you?"

"You don't—"

"Go ahead, Captain," he cut me off.

Nemov walked behind me and started untying my hands.

"What are you doing?" I gasped.

He tied my right hand to the metal chair, the rope cutting deep into my skin. He came around me, his steps heavy in the quiet room. My left hand was free. I could have hit him. But a weak punch while I was still tied to the chair wouldn't do me any good.

Nemov grabbed my left wrist in his huge, rough hand. He squeezed my fingers together so hard I thought they'd break. Then he pulled out my index finger and wrapped his fist around it to hold it still.

My breath started coming out in short pants. Something bad was coming. He was going to break my finger in his hands.

"Please don't," I said.

"Too late," Yurovsky answered for him.

Nemov picked up a pair of old pliers. He slipped one hot, sharp jaw under the nail on my index finger. A moan started deep in my throat and slipped past my lips, ugly and animal. He dug the modified tool in deep, stabbing into my finger wrongly, like a bone poking through skin. It hurt, but I knew what was about to happen would be worse.

"Don't," I cried.

"Spineless," Yurovsky said coldly. "You and your brother both. I wonder what your mother will say when she learns she raised two traitors."

An icy wave washed over me. I looked from my finger to Nemov's eager face to Yurovsky's glare. Only one thought came through.

"Leave my mother out of this," I said.

"Why should I?" Yurovsky said. "She bears some responsibility for what you are. I have children, too, you know. It's the worst traits that get passed on from generation to generation—greed, like the pomeshchiki and kulaks teach their children. Or weakness. My own father was soft. I had to be the one to change, to show my children that we can make this world better by acting, not with empty prayers.

"Your mother must have bred her cowardice into you. I will have her arrested and questioned, if you won't answer me now."

"No!" I cried. "She doesn't know anything! She doesn't even know who Anna is—no one does! I only just found out myself, a day or two ago. My mother doesn't know *anything*, she didn't do anything!"

"Then if you want to protect her, tell me where the Romanov girl is."

"Leave my mother alone." I hunched forward to hide my face in the arm that Nemov still held.

"Answer my question."

"Fine," I moaned.

Nemov let go.

I'd tried to hold out. I kept my mouth shut as long as I

could. But I had no choice. I wanted to kill Nemov. I wanted to be far away from the Cheka jail. I wanted Yurovsky dead, or to die myself. I kept wishing for the ground to open up beneath us. For an earthquake to rattle the building and crumble us all into dust. But nothing came.

"I'll tell you," I said.

25

ANNA

"WE HAVE A PLAN." Jiri found me at the horse enclosure again; I could not resist the foolish part of me that imagined I might see Evgenia creeping out of the woods to fetch Buyan. The scout's information could turn out to have been wrong. Perhaps Evgenia was never caught at all—she simply wanted nothing more to do with me and so was avoiding the house. The idea of Evgenia's hatred seemed preferable to the alternative.

"Tell me," I said.

"I am leaving three men behind to watch you and the wounded men."

That meant that only seven soldiers, including Jiri, would attempt the rescue. In a town fortified with dozens of Red soldiers.

"That is hardly enough—"

"The Reds are already leaving, going north. The jail is at the south end of town. They're the last ones to go. Not many men are left. We think the jail will be emptied tomorrow, so tonight is a good time to attack."

It made sense; there would be fewer Red soldiers around to rush to the aid of the Cheka officers. And since they needed the cover of dark to sneak into town undetected, we had no better choice. It could work—as long as Evgenia stayed alive. And as long as Commander Yurovsky did not find us here before then.

"Very well. Then I will wait here with the rest of your men. We ought to prepare to leave at a moment's notice, in case you return with the Red Army chasing you. Or—" I stopped my own train of thought, but Jiri understood what I nearly said.

"Or if we don't come back. Yes. We'll have one man watching the end of the road. If he sees any Red soldiers coming this way, he'll shoot once into the air. If you hear that, you have to run, Anna. Run to where we met, the devil's wall. One of us—or all of us—will meet you there by morning."

I swallowed nervously. "And if no one is there by morning, then I will be on my own."

He clenched his jaw and nodded.

"I trust you will do everything possible to ensure that does not happen," I said.

"Let's meet here tonight"—he smiled—"and smoke some cigarettes with Evgenia to celebrate."

"That is your finest plan yet."

"But listen," he went on. "It may not be safe for you to run. If you hear *two* warning shots, that means the house is surrounded. Don't run. You should hide in the basement, then. My men will split up and try to draw them away. You have to hide."

I coughed in a vain effort to clear the lump from my throat. "Where shall I hide?"

"I'll show you." He led me in by the rear stairs, and for

the first time I descended into the basement. My feet landed heavily on each step as I pushed myself forward; every corner of my body wanted me to stay away from that dark, underground space. The wooden stair rail was unnaturally cool under my hand, and the air grew thicker, more oppressive, even menacing. I remembered the last time I was forced down into a basement, and my muscles spasmed nervously. We went lower and lower.

This basement was a cavernous space lit sparsely by a little sunlight penetrating its small windows. Tall piles of old crates filled the center of the room, and there was one door on either side wall. Otherwise the basement was wide open; not what one might hope for in a hiding place. Jiri led me over to one of the doors and opened it to reveal a small, cobwebbed closet. It was as dark as death inside, and it reeked of mold and rot.

I cleared my throat again.

"It is a bit obvious as a hiding spot, is it not?"

"It's the best we have," he said unhappily. "If you hear two shots, come here. Don't come out unless you know it's safe."

I pictured myself cowering in the filth, blind, while the Czech soldiers fell to an army of Bolsheviks upstairs.

I would not be able to do it.

"It will not come to that," I said aloud. "You must rescue our friends and come back for me, Jiri. That is the only way to salvation for us. You must return."

"I will do my best," he said.

We left the house, and I returned to Buyan, took Masha's necklace in both of my hands, and prayed.

26

EVGENIA

"I'LL TELL YOU."

"Speak, then," Yurovsky said impatiently.

He was a demon. I didn't even believe in demons anymore, but he was one.

Still. I had to give him what he wanted.

"She's at the devil's wall," I said. "There's a little cave on the south side of the wall. She's hiding there with my horse. That's *if* she's where I left her. Maybe she's run since I haven't been back."

Yurovsky sprang to his feet.

"You'd better hope she hasn't," he said, his voice thick with excitement. "Put her downstairs," he said to Nemov. "Then meet me at the stalls. I'll bring two more men, and we'll saddle up. I know the place she's talking about. It'll take us almost an hour to get there, and the sun's already going down. We'll want to go in quietly. Hurry."

He raced out of the room. I was forgotten. Nemov didn't even bother to taunt me or poke at my wounds. He untied me from the chair and dragged me down to my cell.

"What is wrong with you people?" Anton yelled while Nemov locked me in. "You're torturing a child, a girl! Do you not see how inhuman that is? Have you no souls?"

The Czechs shouted, too. They yelled in Czech, but Havel managed a "She is girl!" in Russian, so I guessed they were defending me after seeing the state I was in.

"Shut up!" Nemov banged his rifle against Anton's cell door. The sound rang out like a muffled church bell. "Or I'll do the same to you."

I didn't try to get up. I didn't move at all. The bruises and wounds liked that best. I sucked on my finger with the loose nail, but that hurt, too. So I just lay there. The stone floor was a cool relief on my sweaty skin. How long had I spent in that room? I'd completely lost track of the day.

Anton was calling my name, like a faraway echo.

"*You'd better hope she hasn't.*" What was Yurovsky going to do when he reached the devil's wall and Anna wasn't there? It was nowhere near the Gersky house. They were still safe, and Yurovsky would find nothing.

What would he do to me when he found out I lied?

I fell asleep with my left hand curled protectively under my chin. Some time later the door to my cell opened and woke me up. I lifted myself on my elbows, sliding back in the filth, away from my visitor. An oil lamp flickered. The flame lapped against the glass sides, burning it black. Its light sent the rats scurrying into new shadows, and showed me that it wasn't Nemov after all.

It was Agapov.

"Mother of God," he muttered. He knelt and passed the

lamp over me from head to toe, surveying my injuries and wounds. "What did they do to you?"

Suddenly I was moving faster than I'd thought I could. I grasped Agapov's knee, squeezing him tight so he couldn't leave.

"Help me escape," I whispered. "He's going to come back and kill me. They're going to *kill* me. Just let me slip past you. No one will know."

"I—I can't," he stammered. He stared at the cuts on my face. "This isn't right."

"No, it isn't. Let me out, please!"

"There are still men on guard upstairs. Most of our company is leaving, but a few of us are here to watch the jail with the Cheka officers. They'd see us."

"There has to be a back door. Or a window I can go through. *Think.*"

But he shook his head.

"There isn't. The only way out is through the courtroom."

All the energy that shot through me fizzled like a snuffed match. I fell onto my back, my head bumping the floor, my arms falling flat.

"Fuck you," I mumbled. He'd caught me in the first place. Now he would leave me to die. So much for the smiling, nice-guy act he'd played when we met.

"I brought you water," he said stiffly. "Are you thirsty?"

That got me up again. I downed half the bowl before I could stop myself. My head felt a little clearer, more awake then, and I got another idea.

"Can you get a message to the Bolsheviks?" I asked. "To the nearest Red Army command, or the regional soviet? Can you send a wire? Tell them what he's doing to us. I'm a Red, a party member. Tell *your* commander—can't he stop Yurovsky?"

"Commander Yurovsky *is* the officer in charge here," he said. "He was left in command of our company. And, Anna." He sighed. He still didn't know my name. "The regional soviet knows what he does here. He gets cables from them every few hours. He even gets messages from Moscow. Commander Yurovsky outranks everyone here—by a lot."

It was like he'd blown out the lamp. Why had Agapov even come? He'd brought water but would take every last drop of hope away with him.

The party *knew*. They let the Cheka and Yurovsky do whatever they wanted. It didn't matter that I'd been a party member for almost two years. No one would stop Nemov from beating me into dust or stripping my nails off.

It was as bad as learning that Anna was a Romanov. Everyone had pretended to be on my side. Everyone had lied to me. I wasn't just going to be tortured. I was going to die alone, and they'd call my death justice. The Bolsheviks would say I deserved it. That I was a traitor.

Maybe I did deserve it. Here I was, protecting the tsar's daughter. If Anna lived she'd tell the world about her family's murders. She'd rally outrage against the Bolsheviks. And I was helping her do it.

No wonder Yurovsky hated me.

Agapov promised to come back. Like that would do me any good.

"Evgenia?" Anton called out.

I grunted.

"I won't ask if you're all right. I already know the answer. Can I help you somehow?"

Tears sprouted and spilled down my cheeks. For some reason his kindness hurt more than Nemov's scorn.

"Only if you have a key," I said.

He sighed heavily. "I would say that I'm shocked at a girl your age being subjected to such brutality, but by now there is little I would put past the Bolsheviks."

I pictured Kostya in his uniform. He'd come home a few days after enlisting, in new boots, with a shiny rifle and neat budenovka. He was so excited to join the revolution. I'd been jealous of him. I'd dreamed of going to Petrograd as soon as I turned twenty to join the Women's Battalion of Death. I'd wanted to be like Kostya.

I pictured our last meeting in Mednyy. Pyotr, Dasha, and Natalya talked about forming our own local soviet. We wanted to replace the unfair council of elders who controlled the village. The same council that drove Mama to stay in Mednyy even when her life was in danger. We'd wanted a better government.

"It's the Cheka," I said. "Not Bolsheviks."

"You're defending them?" Anton laughed. "The Cheka *are* Bolsheviks. Vladimir Lenin knew what he was doing when he created the secret police. He can't win this war without the Cheka. And what they do is no secret—everyone knows. The Red leadership allows them to exist."

Did our leaders really know? The answer hit me right away, like Nemov's fist. Yes, they knew. *Chyort, I'd* known that the Cheka did unspeakable things. I'd heard the rumors, and

I was nobody. The Bolshevik leaders knew. So why didn't they stop it?

"Are you against the revolution?" I asked.

"No," Anton said firmly. "I'm not. I want communism. I want *democracy*. I want a Constituent Assembly to represent the people. But the Bolsheviks are blocking all of it. They chase off every other political party that tries to work with them. The Kadets, the Socialist-Revolutionaries, the Mensheviks—everyone. The Bolsheviks care more about their own power than about communism."

I was too tired to argue with him. I'd heard it all before anyway. Communists from other parties did nothing but talk, and they complained when the Bolsheviks took action.

But I was starting to wish someone would take action against the Bolsheviks.

Hours later, a noise from the stairs woke me again. Thundering boots pounded toward us. My whole body froze. Here came the oil lamp again, but it wasn't Agapov. Nemov was back. And he was coming for me.

"You little *suka*," he snarled. His comrade unlocked the door, and then each of them caught my arms and lifted me from the floor. Their anger washed over me. Nemov was going to hurt me, bad. I kicked out and knocked the oil lamp from his hand. It broke on the floor and winked out, but they didn't stop at all. While I kicked, they carried me upstairs, shoved me into the chair, tied me up. The ropes bit into my wrists and ankles like a dog's bite.

Yurovsky was waiting. The other men backed off as he

came to stand over me. His eyes blazed. I shrunk down in my chair, but there was nowhere to hide. I couldn't get away. Yurovsky lifted his arm and backhanded me across my face. My cheek, already puffed and sensitive, exploded with pain. My lip split open and loosed a spray of blood onto Yurovsky's wrinkled shirt.

He'd never touched me before. It had always been Nemov. But now Yurovsky couldn't restrain himself. He was sweaty and hot with wild eyes. His clothes and hair were rumpled. He'd lost his mind.

He grabbed my jaw with one hand. His fingers stabbed into my skull just under my ears, squeezing, until I was sure I'd pop open like a cracked nut. I heard myself moan, but it sounded distant. Yurovsky's breath was louder. He stuck his sharp nose close to mine.

"You lied to me," he said, his voice like grinding rocks. "There was nothing in that cave. No sign of anyone camped there. No fire, no horse shit, and cobwebs in the entry. She was never there at all, was she? Answer me!"

My head pounded from the pressure. I couldn't answer him. I barely understood the question.

Yurovsky shouted in frustration. But he let go. My head spun while the world tried to straighten itself and blood pulsed in my ears.

"Why are you protecting her?" He clenched his hands into fists that I watched carefully. Only he put them against his own temples instead of pounding them into mine. "You were a Bolshevik once. Your brother was a Bolshevik. How is it you're now willing to die for a cause that only recently recruited you?"

There was something wrong with any cause that let Yurovsky fight for it. How could the Bolsheviks let the Cheka exist? And how could the revolution ever win if it kept destroying people like Kostya and me?

"Fuck you!" I screamed. I was losing my mind, too. I could feel it slipping. "You killed my brother. What good did being a Bolshevik do him? He would've died for the revolution."

Yurovsky grabbed my jaw again. Then he poured nasty words straight into my ear.

"He *did* die for the revolution. Though I was aiming for you. And now I will finish you unless you tell me where the Romanov girl has gone. I won't let you destroy our party. Do you know what I've done for our cause? I killed a *boy*, just because he was born to the wrong father. I killed young women. Innocent servants. Now I live with that memory every day. I won't let you make it all for nothing. Anastasia escaped once. She won't again."

He let go, and I flinched away from him, but my relief died quickly. Yurovsky untied my hands and grabbed my left again.

"Nemov." He snapped his fingers. A moment later Yurovsky slid the metal pliers under my loose fingernail and pulled.

I screamed. He pulled, and I screamed more as he peeled my fingernail away from my skin. He didn't stop until the nail was gone, and I didn't stop screaming at all.

Then he did it again.

My hand fell limply to my lap when he let go. I stuck my fingers into my mouth and didn't even notice the taste of blood. I sucked to soothe, but it didn't work. My fingers throbbed, and my hand shook from the memory of the pain. It was a hundred times worse than any of Nemov's punches. Tears coursed down my cheeks, making my eyes sting, too.

"I can keep going," Yurovsky said. He tapped my chin so I'd look at him, but I couldn't lift my head. I quivered, wishing the pain would stop. The two of them waited quietly.

"If this is too gentle for you," Yurovsky said, "there are other things we can try."

I sobbed. My fingers still burned. I couldn't imagine anything worse.

"Then we continue," Yurovsky said. He took my hand again and slid the metal tool under my next fingernail.

"Fine!" I burst out.

Surely Anna was gone by now. I wasn't sure how long I'd been in jail, but the Reds in town had packed up and left. Surely Anna and the Czechs took their chance to head south. She had to have gone already.

If she hadn't, then he'd kill her. I couldn't protect her any longer. I couldn't even protect myself. Yurovsky had won.

"She's at a mansion north of town. The old Gersky house."

Yurovsky stilled.

"Look at me, Evgenia."

My head flew up. Yurovsky leaned over with his hands on his knees. His face was level with mine. He looked calm again. He peered at me steadily.

"If you're lying, then you'll die a long and painful death," he said. "Captain Nemov is going to sit here with you until I return. If we don't find the Romanov girl where you say she is, then it's the fire for you. You'll burn until you answer, or die.

So tell me, and take a moment to think about it. Is that really where she is?"

"Yes."

He stood.

"Good. Now—"

The air around us exploded. A booming noise came from down the hall. The room shook as falling bricks crashed into the walls outside. For a moment I thought I'd imagined it and had truly gone crazy.

Yurovsky ran to the door.

"Czechs!" someone screamed.

27

ANNA

AFTER THE SUN SET AND the sky deepened into a dark blue, Jiri and his rescue team departed. They would enter Iset town at dark. They went off on foot, equipped with rifles and bandoliers heavy with spare ammunition. They were somber in their preparations, quiet, purposeful; Jiri merely tipped his hat at me on their way out, and then they vanished into the forest. I made the sign of the cross and sent a prayer after them.

I sought shelter indoors, for with night falling and only a few men remaining on guard, it was too dangerous outside. I sat in the parlor with our injured men. Karol crouched by the rear window, rifle resting atop his lap. He nodded at me as I entered; his too-long dark hair spilled over his forehead, and he had to toss it back.

"It will be a long night," he said in Russian. He was one of the only Czechs who spoke my language, and did so better than Jiri. "I hope Ambroz will sleep through it." He nodded at the other wounded soldier, who, for once, slept peaceably instead of his usual fretful moaning. Ambroz was dying of infection.

I had merely cooled him with damp cloths to ease his suffering. It was a matter of time for him now.

Russia had left the war only to fall into another, and it seemed like the dying would never end. I did not want Ambroz to die, I did not want Evgenia to die, I did not want one more person to die just because someone disagreed with them. It was all so *unnecessary*. They could have been arguing in parliament instead of shooting one another on the battlefield. Was anything worth this?

Night fell slowly at that time of year, and the house cooled by degrees. I sat across from Karol and joined him watching the rear yard. I could see Buyan from there, and it was like looking at a piece of Evgenia. I kept imagining her darting out of the forest to claim him, sneaking away in the night. I wished she had gone back to her village instead of leaving with me.

I wished I had never asked for a ride in her wagon.

Around us, shadows spread from the corners to fill the empty parlor in unnatural shapes. In my peripheral vision they loomed like sneaking enemies, and I couldn't stop checking to ensure no one was there. We did not light our candles. Should anyone pass by the house we wanted it to appear empty; the two men standing guard on the front porch hid behind columns to stay out of sight. Any light or activity from inside would only give us away.

While we sat in the dark, the nearly full moon cast a delicate light over the gardens and forest. The world turned silver and black. Trees writhed in the violent breeze that had picked up, and the horses, no more than dark shapes now, shifted occasionally in their sleep. The window beside me grew cool as night went on and chilled my skin whenever I brushed against it.

Karol and I soon ran out of things to say to each other. Time passed at an agonizingly slow, tense pace. And my thoughts would not settle.

When I was ten years old and Tatiana fourteen, she had saved Papa's life. She, Olga, and Papa had been attending the opera when someone began shooting. As soon as one shot had been fired, Tatiana jumped from her seat and locked Papa and Olga out of the box to keep them from the line of fire. That night, when it was all over, she would not stop crying, no matter how many times we called her a hero.

Now I understood why. I had been growing comfortable with grief, but this was the first time I had to sit in terror for the life of someone I loved.

I needed Tatiana's strength.

You've always had it, shvibzik.

Another hour passed. Ambroz began tossing in his sleep, so I did take the risk of lighting my candle; as efficiently as I could, I washed the perspiration from his face and neck and changed the bedsheet underneath him to make him slightly more comfortable.

A loud bump sounded from the front porch. I looked at Karol in alarm. He gestured frantically at the candle. I blew it out, sending the coppery smell of its smoke trickling up my nose. My hand trembled, and a bit of hot wax dripped over onto my palm.

I dropped the candle and it landed with a too-loud *thump* on the wooden floor.

"Shhh," Karol urged. He rose and carefully crept over to the parlor door, then out into the hallway, where he disappeared into the dark.

I stood perfectly still. Jiri had given me a hunting knife that I kept in my apron pocket, right next to the picture of my family. I could not imagine actually using it to stab someone, but I did what Evgenia would do if she were here and drew it out. My hands perspired as I gripped the knife with all my strength; I had to wipe them dry on my skirt a few times.

I listened keenly. Karol's injured leg made a soft shuffling noise as he dragged it down the hallway to the front door.

The front door creaked as he opened it. I shut my eyes. I was shaking harder than ever, and I clasped both hands over my knife hilt, raising it in front of me. I prayed, begging for there to be nothing and no one out there.

The front door shut again. My heart pounded harder than ever against my ribs. I silently begged Ambroz to stay quiet, not to moan, not to reveal that there was anyone in the parlor. If a stranger entered the house, perhaps they would ignore this room altogether.

A shuffling noise. It was Karol, coming back down the hall more noisily than before. I breathed out in relief.

"Anna?" He entered the room again. He did not bother to whisper. "It's all right. One of the men just nodded off and dropped his rifle. I gave him a talking-to. You—you can put that down now."

I still clutched the knife in front of me. I gasped in relief and placed it back in my pocket. My hands felt stiff from how tightly I had held it; I shook them loosely to ease the cramps.

"What sort of a soldier falls asleep while on guard?" I demanded.

"Ach, he's not so bad. He's been worrying a lot about one of our friends in the Cheka jail. Hasn't slept much lately."

"We'll all end up in jail if he lets the Bolsheviks surprise us tonight," I said crossly.

Karol did not answer. I took a breath to steady myself; my blood was still racing in my veins, and I had let my nerves unsettle me.

"Never mind," I said. "As long as he stays alert from now on, I am confident we will all be fine."

"He will," Karol said loyally. He stretched his arms and back before taking his seat again. "Guess it's still a waiting game," he said.

More hours passed—so many that the sky began to lighten again, as the sun slowly reemerged. It was not yet in sight, still hidden behind the distant hills, but the moon set and night was ending. The early morning remained quiet, undisturbed except by the rise and fall of chirping cicadas and, once or twice, a wolf crying from the forest. I had not thought about the wild animals out there. If I fled this house, I might encounter some. I had traveled safely enough through them once before, after I escaped Ekaterinburg and fled blindly to Pavlovo, the town where I met Evgenia.

I only vaguely recollected that time; I had the impression that I had spent two nights in the forest on my own. At the time, the only fear that pervaded me was the idea that Commander Yurovsky and his men would catch up to me, or that I would wander until I died. Now I remembered that there were wolves in those woods, and bears, and all manner of untamed creatures.

A gunshot pierced the silent morning.

I flinched wildly; Karol flew into the air and was on his feet before the sound receded. It was nearly dawn, and I had begun to hope that, perhaps, all our caution would be unneeded. But the shot was unmistakable. It had come from in front of the house, from the direction of the road. Our lookout, Leos, had fired the warning. One shot. I faced Karol, my throat too tight to form words.

"You must go," he said urgently. Worried lines framed his eyes.

I could not move. I crouched back against the wall behind me. He wanted me to run outside, where the Bolsheviks were. Into the forest with the wolves, where I might never see him or Jiri or Evgenia again.

"Move," he snapped. He yanked my arm roughly. I cried out in pain, but he pulled until I had to stand or dislocate my shoulder. Once standing I felt less frozen, and I nodded at him, more composed.

"I will go—" I started. A second gunshot sounded.

Two shots meant that it was not safe to go outside. They meant that we were under attack.

Karol's lips trembled. He looked as confused as I felt.

A third shot rang out. We *were* under attack. The Reds surrounded us. They were coming to kill me. I opened my mouth to explain this to Karol, but what came out instead was a long, terrified whimper. I clamped my hand over my own mouth.

Karol pulled himself together. His face firmed up, and he swung his rifle into his hands, ready to aim.

"You have to go into the basement," he said.

The basement was worse than the forest. The Bolshe-viks would find me there. I turned and walked slowly; Karol shoved me from behind, and I picked up my pace. Soon I was running—out of the parlor, down the hall, to the stairs. I paused at the back door halfway down.

The basement *was* worse than the forest. My entire family had been trapped and slaughtered like animals in a basement just like this one. I did not want to go down there. I turned the knob to the back door, planning to risk running outside, only it stuck. Someone had locked the door. I felt around wildly for the lock before seeing that I would need a key to open it. I could not get through.

It did not matter. It was an insane idea to flee for the woods when, according to Leos's warning, we were surrounded. We had a plan, and I needed to stick to it. I hurried down the stairs and into the dark underground room.

28

EVGENIA

GUNSHOTS BURST FROM OUTSIDE AND even closer. From the courtroom.

"They've come for their men," Yurovsky said. "Watch her. Stay with her, let the others fight them off. Kill her if they come in here. I'm going for the grand duchess."

Then he was gone.

Nemov's mouth hung open stupidly. When he noticed me watching, he glared and shut the door. He slung his rifle onto his shoulder, where he could grab it faster. Then he crossed his arms.

"You're done," he said almost cheerfully.

"So are you," I spat. Only my voice broke, and it didn't sound as strong as I'd hoped. The Czechs were *here*, but Nemov would never let me get to them. I'd be dead before the door opened.

"You lied again, didn't you? I may as well kill you right now."

"They'll shoot you, too. The Czechs are better fighters than you Cheka cowards."

Footsteps raced down the hall—my heart leapt, but they passed right by our door. More gunshots sounded from the courtroom. A man screamed.

Nemov walked over to me. He gripped my braid, making me cry out. I clenched the cloth of my apron inside the pocket and gritted my teeth. My fingers brushed against something hard and sharp. I held it between my fingers. Nemov leaned closer and stuck his foul face right in mine.

"You killed a good man," he said. "You and your fellow traitors murdered Captain Kuzmich. He was my friend and a good man. I'll enjoy killing you for that."

He was talking about the man who came to Mednyy with Yurovsky. Valchar had killed him. I could've told Nemov that the man he wanted was probably here, attacking the jail.

But my hands were free. Nemov was closer than he should've been, and I still had the rusty nail I'd found in my cell.

I pulled the nail out of my pocket and jammed it straight into Nemov's eye. I screamed. He howled and reared back, raising his hands to cover his eye. Blood oozed out past his fingers. He didn't stop screaming. He bent his whole torso over as if trying to make the nail fall out.

I stood. My legs were still tied to the chair, so I couldn't move anywhere. I reached down to try to quickly untie them, but I was too slow.

Nemov swung out with his fist sloppily. I ducked, and he stumbled forward, knocking into me and sending me back into my seat. He caught himself on my shoulder and swung with his other hand. The punch caught me right in my cheek. My skull rattled from the force of it, and then Nemov pulled his fist back again. He was going to pound me until I couldn't see straight. Maybe until I died.

The world spun in front of my eyes, but I didn't need to see to remember what Nemov looked like. Over the past days I'd stared at him endlessly. I knew every detail of his uniform and his body. I stuck out my hand for his belt, felt along the line of his stomach, and clasped the hilt of his knife just as he punched me again.

My head roared with pain. I still couldn't see, but he was so close I didn't have to aim. I plunged the knife into Nemov blindly.

He gasped. It sounded like a draining funnel. I'd gotten him right in his gut. He let go of my shoulder. I yanked the knife out of his clinging flesh, then stabbed again, higher.

He clawed at his own chest, trying to find the knife. He fell onto the floor. At first he backed slowly away from me like a dying buck. Then he stopped. Dead. Blood spilled out from his belly into a dark puddle on the floor. His nose, mouth, and chin were covered with blood and pus from his eye.

Bile filled my throat, making me gag. I forced it down and made myself face Nemov. I'd only done what I had to. He deserved it. After everything he did to me, he deserved this, and worse. *He deserved it.* I kept repeating it in my head. I had to believe it to get myself moving.

Then I noticed his rifle. I untied myself from the chair legs and reached for him, even though everything inside me told me to keep back from the disgusting sight. I slid the rifle strap over his heavy, unmoving arm. It was a large gun, almost as tall as me. I slung it on my own shoulder and held the gun with both hands, ready to shoot if I had to.

I was free.

I ran out of that room without even checking to see if the hallway was clear. But there was no one there. More gunshots rang out from downstairs, off to my right. To my left, down the hall, were the remains of the courtroom. Two walls had collapsed from the explosion. Rubble fell in piles, covering the pews and floors completely. I counted two dead bodies that I could see from this distance. Neither wore the Czech Legion's red pants.

Maybe one of them was Yurovsky.

The air was cloudy and smelled of gunpowder. Silvery early-morning sunlight poured into the building. I ran toward the courtroom, toward the men sprawled out on the piles of broken bricks. I didn't recognize either of them. A third man was partly buried under the bricks, half his face coated thickly in drying blood. Something about his full cheeks drew me closer. It didn't take me long to figure out why he looked so familiar.

It was Agapov. My heart thudded. His mouth hung open, and his eyes looked fearful, all his good cheer knocked out of them. I'd known him for all of two days. It was like he'd blinked in and out of life in the flap of a butterfly's wings. Now he was dead, gone the way of Lev and Kostya and millions of other brothers who died too young.

I crouched and shut his eyes. When they found him, he wouldn't look afraid.

Yurovsky had either left or gone downstairs. I needed to

get the hell away from the jail. But as I made to run out, I stopped. *Anton.* Was he even alive? No gunfire had sounded for a while. I had no way to know what was happening downstairs. There'd been at least three Cheka officers to begin with, plus Nemov and Yurovsky. Then Agapov and some of his comrades had joined them. How many were downstairs? Was the fighting still going on down there? If not, who'd won?

If Yurovsky was down there, the best thing I could do was run to the Gersky house, get Anna, and get the hell out of here.

Before I could decide what to do, the door to the stairs flew open. It slammed into the wall, sending my heart into my throat, and then seven Czech soldiers and three filthy prisoners poured down the hall toward me. The tall Russian had to be Anton. He was safe. He was even smiling. He was younger and lankier than I'd pictured, his nose longer, his dark hair shaggier. His beard went down to his collarbone. He loped behind the soldiers like an awkward fawn, and it did me good to see him.

At the head of the pack was Lieutenant Valchar. His face and uniform were coated in dust and his mouth tight with anger. But when he saw me, his expression cleared into his usual smile. Maybe he'd come to save his men, but he'd saved me, too, and looked pretty happy about it. My stomach flipped nervously.

"Evgenia!" He came over like he wanted to hug me but stopped short. His eyes flashed once he got a closer look at my bloodied, swollen face. He grabbed my shoulder and squeezed once. Like he wanted to comfort me. "I'm happy you're alive."

I could still feel the warmth from his hand after he let go. It was a nice change from Nemov's fist.

"Where's Anna?"

"She's at the house. She's fine. I leave three men to guard her."

My head spun again, like I was back in the room with Nemov. I wanted to lash out, to scream that three men wouldn't be enough against Yurovsky, but that wouldn't do Anna any good. We just had to get to her. I gripped the rifle in my hands to steady myself.

"No," I managed. "Yurovsky's headed there now. I gave her up. He's going to kill her."

Valchar turned to his men and barked orders at them in Czech.

"We meet again here," he translated for me and Anton. "If I'm not back in two hours, you all leave."

"Let's go," I said.

He shook his head.

"Evgenia, you stay," he said. "You look . . . bad. You can't help."

I must've looked a bloody, purple and red mess. But I hardly even felt the bruises. My body was shaking impatiently. Standing still only made it worse. The thought of hanging around here, waiting for it all to end, was worse than anything.

Anna had looked so scared when she'd admitted who she really was. She'd been afraid that I was going to give her up.

And I had.

I started running. Valchar followed, and that settled the question.

"I have a horse," he said.

So I let him lead and mounted his great warhorse behind him. The pain did come back then. I squeezed Valchar's strong waist as the horse galloped across open fields. Every leap sent my ribs into my lungs. I gritted my teeth to keep in the moans. If I cried out in pain Valchar might slow down. I couldn't let him do that. Yurovsky had a good lead on us. I wasn't sure how much time had passed since the explosion.

"How did you blow up the jail?" I asked to distract myself.

"We make bomb," he said over his shoulder. "The Reds mostly run. It's easy to save our men now that the army leaves town. And to save you. Anna insists we come for you, and I don't want to leave you, either."

On top of the pain, my stomach twisted with guilt. She'd sent Valchar to save me, and I'd sent Yurovsky to kill her.

I stopped asking questions.

"We're here," I said needlessly when we reached the bottom of the hill where the mansion sat. "Let me down." I could climb the hill almost as fast as the horse, and it would hurt less.

"Good idea," Valchar said, misunderstanding. "Let's be quiet." He tied his horse to a tree, and we started up, through the garden, to the house.

My heart started beating faster. How could we stop Yurovsky? He'd torn me to pieces to find Anna. He'd die before letting Anna go again.

The house was too quiet.

We found Valchar's men first. Two lay on the front steps of the house. One had a bullet in his chest. A cord of rope was twisted around the other's neck. His eyes and mouth bulged open, and his skin had taken on a sunset-purple tint. Yurovsky had snuck up behind him somehow. He'd killed him quietly.

Ice swam through my veins. Yurovsky might be waiting for

us. Watching us. I glanced at Valchar to see if he was thinking the same thing. But his face was drawn with anger. These had been his men. Friends. I touched his arm. He nodded, his face cleared, and he held his fingers to his lips. We went slowly into the house.

We found two more dead men in a parlor. One was flat on his back, a bullet in his head. The other sprawled near the door.

I looked behind us and in every corner. It felt like Yurovsky was waiting to pounce. He had moved through the house like an assassin. We were like flies caught in a spider's web. Here were the ones who'd been killed before us. We were next.

A muffled thump came from above us. Valchar and I looked up, then at each other, realizing the same thing. Yurovsky was upstairs.

"Go to the basement," Valchar whispered. He grabbed my wrist to make me listen. "I check upstairs."

I made a face that said all I thought of *that* idea. I was here to help Anna and make up for betraying her. I wasn't about to run and hide.

"I tell Anna to hide in basement," he insisted. "If something happens, I tell her to hide in a closet there. Go find her."

"Come with me," I whispered.

He shook his head.

"I go stop him," he said.

My heart still wasn't working right. It twisted as his eyes met mine. I put my hand over his and nodded. Then I let him go up to face Yurovsky all on his own.

And I went down.

29

ANNA

A VOLLEY OF GUNFIRE SOUNDED from upstairs as I crawled into my basement hiding place. My world had ended in a Ekaterinburg basement; now I wagered my life on one sheltering me.

I collided face-first with a cobweb and reared back in alarm, bumping my head. I scrabbled to pull the faint, sticky strands off my skin. Only for a few seconds did I react so uncontrollably; I soon remembered that a spider in my hair was nothing compared to the danger behind me. I moved in farther, sliding my palms over the grimy layers of dirt on the hard floors. I hadn't been able to force myself into the cramped, black closet, as Jiri suggested. Yet I wasn't sure this spot was any better.

I pulled my knees up to my chin, making myself as small as humanly possible. My heart beat frantically. In the quiet of the basement the heartbeats took over, filling my eardrums, faster and faster. The shooting upstairs had stopped. For a moment the sound of running feet—a loud crash—and then nothing.

The silence stretched on. My heart rate slowed marginally, but every hair on my body stood alertly, waiting for the next onslaught. Masha's necklace around my neck shifted when I moved my knees slightly; I clutched it and prayed. My lips mouthed the prayers while my mind spun with questions. Was Commander Yurovsky upstairs? How many had come? After Leos's warning shots I expected a louder attack, a swarm of Bolshevik soldiers from every direction, tearing the house apart as they searched for me. There ought to have been more than a few gunshots; there should have been more noise altogether: doors slamming, men shouting. Where was everyone? Had they all killed one another?

Was Commander Yurovsky upstairs?

I squeezed my eyes shut and prayed harder. *Do not let him come. Anyone but him. Do not let him come.*

It stayed maddeningly silent. I began to wonder if it was safe for me to emerge. But the quiet, too, was threatening—as though the Bolsheviks were holding their breaths, waiting for me to reveal myself. It was a tense, heavy silence, full of ghosts and anger.

The moment I considered slipping out, my chest tightened in fear. Yet I could not stay down here forever. If they were all dead upstairs, I could not remain buried under another house full of corpses.

A creak came from the stairs. My skin jumped, but not violently enough to make a sound. Another creak—two steps down onto the basement floor. Someone was alive, after all.

"Anastasia," his voice came.

I ceased breathing. A wave of terror lifted me from my body, and I shut my eyes as I floated.

"I'm tired of looking for you," Commander Yurovsky called. "If you're down here, come out now. It'll be worse for you if you make me wait."

My teeth chattered from the trembles racking my body.

I clenched my jaw to muffle the sound. If I kept perfectly still, he would go away. He had to go away.

The other door slammed into the wall. My throat tightened, suffocating me—he would search every corner until he found me. The best thing to do was to run. I needed to run out of the house and into the forest to try to lose him. To somehow, miraculously outrace him.

Yet I could not move. As it had every other time I heard his voice, my body froze completely. All I could manage was to lean forward, slightly, and peer out through a crack. I could not see him. But I heard him shut the first closet door after failing to find me there.

I did have a clear view of the staircase, however, illuminated by light from the rear door transom. And there was Evgenia, walking down the stairs.

My heart soared. Evgenia tiptoed carefully down and surveyed the basement, then darted into the shadows and melted into darkness. I waved at her frantically before realizing that she could not see me.

She had come to rescue me. I needed her to find me before he did.

30

EVGENIA

THE BASEMENT WAS A HUGE, open space. It was long and wide, with a line of pillars across the middle. Narrow windows like the ones in the jail lined the walls near the ceiling. They let in just enough light to see the wooden ceiling beams and thick clouds of dust in the air. The middle of the room was shadowy. Tall piles of wooden crates crowded between the pillars.

There were two doors on opposite sides of the basement. One of them had to be Anna's hiding spot. A man closed one of the doors—Yurovsky. I quickly moved away from the light behind me. If he spotted me, I was dead—and so was Anna.

Yurovsky was holding something in his hand, pointed up. A revolver. He was circling the room, moving away from me, heading toward the other door.

Before I could think how to stop him, he leapt in.

As the door slammed against the wall, one of the piles of crates in the middle of the room wobbled. I looked over in shock. Sticking out from the pile of crates farthest from

Yurovsky was a hand waving crazily for me to approach. My throat choked up again. It was *Anna*. She was trapped.

I sprinted for her. There was a gap between two crates that I darted into. Anna had found a little cavern within the wooden boxes. We could see the far side of the basement, where Yurovsky stood. And the gap that I'd crawled through showed the way to the stairs.

The second closet door slammed shut.

"Come out, Anastasia!" Yurovsky called. "If I have to drag you out, you'll regret it."

He was coming for us. I crowded in next to Anna. There was barely enough room for the two of us. The back of my shoulder pressed into the front of hers, our bent knees bumped together, and Anna's breath landed heavily on my ear. She was shaking worse than I was.

I pulled Nemov's rifle in after me. The only way it fit was if I stuck the barrel out of the other end, between the crates. I peeked over the gun to see Yurovsky searching the crates near him.

I faced Anna and pointed toward the back door. I mimed running and pointed again.

She shook her head. I nodded insistently and made to move. She gripped my shoulder and shook her head again. Then she brought her hands together and made like she was snapping a twig in half.

She mouthed a word that I couldn't make out, pointed at the door, and made the motion again.

I got the message. *Broken*. The back door was broken. To get out we'd have to run out the front door. It was too far. Yurovsky would catch us.

I nodded, then peeked out of our peephole again. Yurovsky had moved on to the next pile of crates. He peered and poked at them, making them wobble. He'd figured out that Anna was hiding here. Now he was only ten cubits away.

Where was Valchar? Why hadn't he realized that Yurovsky wasn't upstairs? If I could stall Yurovsky, that would give Valchar time to get down here. But the only way to stall Yurovsky was to make some noise.

Maybe a gunshot would bring Valchar running. I lifted the rifle and angled it as far as I could toward Yurovsky. He was too close to the crates for me to hit him, but maybe I could scare him a little.

I fired.

The shot tore through the quiet air and made both me and Anna jump. Yurovsky threw his arms up protectively, but recovered fast and stuck out his revolver. Now he knew we were here. But he also knew we had a gun.

He crouched near the crates and aimed his gun in our direction.

"So you're armed," he said. "I will find you, Anastasia. Your rifle isn't going to stop me."

He started toward us. I popped out the old shell and shot again. He stopped, leaning against the crates.

I opened the bolt and stuck my fingers in to check how many rounds I had left. Two bullets. I'd save those for kill shots. Hopefully the rifle blasts would bring Valchar down here and it would be two against one.

"Stay back, *svoloch*!" I shouted. "I won't miss again."

"Koltsova," he said, full of disbelief. "How the devil did Nemov let you out?"

"He's dead! Just like you if you come any closer."

"And the first thing you did was come here, to protect the Romanova? So much for all your protests. You're a traitor through and through. Your brother would be ashamed of you."

"I'm here to stop you," I spat. "He'd want that more."

"This isn't about me, Koltsova. Look past the lies that girl has been telling you. Is she here with you? Hand her over and you can do whatever you want to me. I'll give you my own revolver. But she *has* to die. She is a threat to the revolution."

Anna whimpered. She clasped her hands together. *Praying.* For all the nothing that would do.

"Your brother didn't want this for you. He told me that I could have the girl, as long as I left you alone. Don't you want to honor his sacrifice?"

"Stop talking about my brother," I said between my teeth. He was lying. And even if Kostya did want Anna dead, there wasn't anything he could do about it now. And who was to blame for that?

I checked the action on the rifle again. If only I could point it straight at Yurovsky. I'd shoot him and laugh while he died.

"You had two brothers in the army, no? That's what Konstantin said. Don't you want to honor them both? That girl you're helping stands between Russia and freedom. She wants to destroy us before communism can ever take hold. What would your brothers say to that?"

I looked at Anna. She still mouthed the words of her prayers, her hands tucked under her chin. Just like she had at Nurka's funeral. She hadn't even known the woman, or Foma Gavrilovich, but she'd helped bury her and comfort him. She'd held me and stroked my hair after Kostya died. She'd cried over her sisters. *Masha.*

"She's just a girl!" I cried. "She hasn't done anything wrong. You can't keep killing anyone who gets in your way!"

"I can, and I will," he said. "We *must* kill anyone who stands in the way of victory. Don't you see? How can you hold one life against freeing the whole world?"

He was getting closer. My body tensed. I adjusted the gun but still couldn't get him within its sights.

Anna's eyes opened, and she looked at me. She heard him coming, too.

I pointed to the stairs. *Run*, I mouthed. I pushed at her shoulder, shoving her to get her moving. She waved for me to follow her, but I just kept pushing her until she started crawling.

Yurovsky was still coming. I eased the rifle in so he wouldn't see it sticking out. And I waited. As soon as he got within range, I'd kill him.

I glanced over my shoulder again. Anna was still crouched by the gap, looking back and forth, frozen like a scared rabbit. What was she waiting for? I kicked her, trying to make her move.

"Come," she said softly, urgently.

Yurovsky started running. He'd heard her.

"Run!" I shouted.

Anna ran. I held my breath and waited for Yurovsky to pass me. He flashed into sight—I fired.

I missed. He ran past me, around the crates.

I scrambled out. Anna reached the stairs and started to

climb. I dragged the rifle out and lifted it to my shoulders, just as Yurovsky came around the pillar, revolver first. He stopped at the edge of the pillar and fired.

The bullet hit Anna in the back and she jerked forward with a cry. She fell to her knees, and then face forward onto the stairs.

"No!" I shouted.

Anna didn't move. My head swam, and then hot rage exploded inside me. He'd killed her. After everything. I'd been through hell to save her, and now he'd won.

I was going to tear him apart.

I ran toward Yurovsky. I had to get closer for a better shot. He was still partly hidden behind the pillar. He backed around it, taking cover, but I came around and faced him.

We both fired. We both missed. And now I was out of bullets.

I screamed and leapt at him. I threw myself forward and plowed into his stomach with my shoulder. My body protested, the blow shaking my aching torso, but I couldn't stop. He had to pay. He staggered back when I hit him but caught his balance. I gripped his belt and tried to pull him down.

He smacked me across the temple with the butt of his revolver. For a moment my vision blacked, but instead of letting go of him I pulled at his forearm. I bit into his hand, digging my teeth in to tear his skin apart. He yelled, and the revolver clattered to the floor.

He shoved me roughly away. My shoulder hit the floor, and I rolled onto my back, right on top of the gun. Yurovsky followed me. He tried to push me off the revolver, tried to reach under me so he could get it and end me. I twisted my arm under my back and found the gun first, then sent it skittering away from us, across the floor, until it bumped into the crates.

"I don't need a gun to kill you, traitor," Yurovsky snarled. He knelt one knee onto my chest, flattening me. I could barely breathe. I punched up with all my might and hit him right under his chin. His head snapped back, but it didn't break his hold. In a flash, his hands were around my throat.

His mouth twisted, and his eyes glared fire at me. He tightened his hands around my neck. I couldn't breathe. I clawed at his hands and punched him again. Nothing worked. My vision started fading. The last thing I'd ever see was Yurovsky's face. The hate in his eyes filled my chest instead of breath, and my life melted away.

One of the tall stacks of crates teetered above us. A moment later the pile collapsed and sent the wall of boxes crashing down onto us, knocking Yurovsky off me.

I sat up and took a huge gasp of breath, just as another crate fell and smashed into my face.

31

ANNA

I SCREAMED, THE SOUND DRAWN as much from
my terror for Evgenia as the pain in my shoulder. Had I killed
her? The crates, though empty, were extremely heavy. The
last one to fall had crashed into Evgenia and knocked her flat
beneath it.

Commander Yurovsky lay still, not far away. I hurried first
to Evgenia and pushed the box off her, crying out again from
the effort as pain coursed through my wound. Evgenia's face was
horribly swollen. Fresh blood streamed out of her nose, over her
mouth and cheeks. This was not only from the crate—the Cheka
must have beaten her badly. But at least she was breathing.

"Zhenya." I rolled her onto her side, so the blood would
flow out. "Are you all right?"

She had come back for me. She had faced him—fought
him—for *me*. She did not want me dead. She had lost her
brother, and her home, and still she came to save me. I bent
over her, letting the tears fall.

"I love you, Zhenya," I whispered.

She stirred, starting to sit up.

Another crate toppled. Then came the sound of more being shoved aside. I looked over to Commander Yurovsky.

He was no longer on the floor. He had only been dazed, not killed or knocked unconscious, and now he pushed the crates off him and staggered upright. Blood poured down his face, too, and he moved unsteadily, but he was still after me.

I sprang to my feet so quickly that my head swam and I stumbled, struggling for balance. I was losing too much blood. The bullet had passed through me, just beside my shoulder and above my chest, but I could not stop to treat it. Commander Yurovsky was running his hands over the floor.

He was searching for his gun.

My insides clenched. I dropped to my knees and swept my hands out, trying to find it first, even as my vision grew blurry.

I had to find it first.

My fingers brushed against something metallic beneath two leaning crates. Scrambling, I grasped the revolver and stood.

"Commander!"

He looked up. Then he rose to one knee and made to lean forward, ready to pounce on me.

I pulled the trigger. I nearly lost my grip of the gun as it recoiled.

But my aim was true. The shot landed in his stomach. He tripped over a crate and collapsed, his head hitting the floor. He clutched his stomach as blood spilled over his hands, and he lay there, twitching, like a dying animal.

I kept the gun trained on him. My breaths came out in short, panting, almost audible cries as the fear gushed out of me.

"Anya."

She touched my lower back. There was a world outside of the end of my gun and his body.

"Let's go," she said. "Leave him. You don't have to be the one to finish him."

But I stepped away from Evgenia, and closer to him. I weaved around the crates until I could stand directly over him. I slid my foot under his torso, and lifted, forcing him onto his back. Commander Yurovsky stared up at me. He breathed in short, loud gasps like mine. Blood dribbled out of his mouth and stomach.

And my head spun.

"We must remain quiet," he had said to us. "This is for your own safety. The fighting has reached the city. I will lead you downstairs, through the basement, and out back to where cars are waiting for you. Your family will be moved somewhere safer."

My parents, sisters, and little brother, Alexei, stood with me in the dark hallway of the Ipatiev house, all of us dressed for travel. Our nurse, Demidova, our doctor, and our cook were there, too. As were the armed Bolshevik guards. Commander Yurovsky stood at the head of the assembled group. His face, normally scrupulously unemotional, appeared tight with tension. His gaze was very sharp as he surveyed us.

The hallway was eerily quiet. Shadows from Olga's lamp slithered in the corners as we walked. My heart beat too fast, while dreams of what lay ahead danced across my mind. Perhaps White Army officers would fight their way through and rescue us. They could escort us by train to join Grandmother in Sevastopol. That night, I was certain that we were on the verge of something. Anything felt possible.

I had been walking with Masha, but as we descended two flights of stairs, I released her arm and sidled up to Papa. I was too old for it, but I slipped my hand into his anyway. He smiled down at me.

"Shvibzik," he mouthed, not making a sound. "I love you."

I stuck my tongue out at him and swallowed a giggle at the face he made in return.

The commander opened a wooden door when we reached the basement.

"Wait in here," he said.

The room was lit with a single light bulb that cast a feeble light on the arched ceilings. It was otherwise largely empty aside from two chairs in the middle of the room. Olga ushered Mama into one and Alexei into the other. Papa stood beside Mama, and I huddled close to his arm. Masha stood somewhere behind me.

The soldiers glared at us from the doorway. They did not follow us in.

"Explain this, Commander," Papa ordered angrily. "Why have you stopped us here?"

Commander Yurovsky was holding his revolver in one hand. He lifted a half sheet of paper in the other.

"'Nikolai Alexandrovich,'" he read, "'in view of the fact that your relatives are continuing their attack on

Soviet Russia, the Ural Executive Committee has decided to execute you and your family.'"

Commander Yurovsky's hateful eyes, now glaring up at me, were the last things my father had seen. They were the last glimpse of this world for all the people I had loved.

I leaned over Yurovsky and pressed the revolver to his forehead. Our eyes met; mine were the last thing *he* would see of this world. I pulled the trigger.

The bullet tore neatly through his skull. I had expected more blood. I waited for his face to cave in, the way Nurka Petrova's had. But it didn't. A large pool of blood spread out underneath him and seeped at the edges of the ashy, round hole in his forehead. His eyes were still staring at me. It was as though we were frozen that way, as though he would stare, hating me, damning me and my family, for the rest of my life.

Evgenia pulled at me. I swung into her and wrapped my arm around her neck, burying my eyes against her skin.

"It's over," she said. "Let's go to Ekaterinburg."

32

EVGENIA

WE RAN INTO A CZECH soldier on our way out of the basement. He had dark hair and was bleeding from his nose and arm. He jerked back in surprise when we rounded the corner.

"There you are," he said to Anna. "I heard gunshots."

She glanced at me. There was something dark in her eyes, like when we'd first met. She looked like a lost kid again. I'd tried to stop her. I would've killed Yurovsky for her if she'd let me. I didn't want her feeling this empty, cold thing that I'd cradled in the bottom of my chest since stabbing Nemov. But now it was one more thing we shared. We were both killers.

"Yurovsky's dead," I said, so she wouldn't have to. The man nodded. His mouth twisted a bit when he took me in, but he quickly turned back to Anna.

"Jiri is upstairs," he said. His face rippled with emotion. "A Red soldier stabbed him. I need help carrying him down."

Anna wobbled. Her grip on me weakened, and I caught her elbow and lowered her to the floor. She leaned against the wall and dropped her head back. Defeated.

If after all this, Valchar lost his life, too, I wasn't sure I wanted to keep going, either.

"He's dead?" I asked.

"No." The man shook his head. "But it's not good."

Anna closed her eyes. She shifted a little, and a smear of blood trailed on the wall behind her. Her face was even paler than usual, too.

"I'll help you," I told the man. "But give me a moment. She's hurt."

Together he and I bandaged Anna's shoulder with torn scraps of my apron. It was enough to stop the bleeding, at least. Then I followed the man, who was named Karol, upstairs.

There were too many dead bodies in this house. Too many ghosts. I remembered what it used to look like. I remembered the tall roof, the bright white walls, and the flowering garden outside. And I'd been inside once before. Batya brought me with him when he came to ask for more time on a debt he owed. A servant made us wait at the back door. I'd peeked in to see shining floors under a long red carpet, a sparkling chandelier, cloth wall coverings, and framed paintings, all of it prettier than a sunset.

The Gersky family had refused to talk to Batya. It didn't matter that we were distant relations. The servant sent us away like dogs. But for years I thought back on that trip like a treat. Until I got older, and Kostya came home talking about communism, and I started to understand just how unfair it all was.

We'd stormed this house and left behind a ruined shell. No one bothered to rebuild it. But that was the important work. You couldn't just tear things down. You had to do something good with what was left. I didn't trust the Bolsheviks to do that anymore. I'd never trust the Whites, either. If neither side was good, then what was left for me? What was left for Russia if we had to choose between a heartless tsar and a brutal Bolshevik Party?

"He's in here."

Karol led me into a dirty room with burned walls and broken windows. Valchar lay on his side in the middle of the room. He didn't move. Neither did the other body that was heaped into a bloody lump in the corner.

"Lieutenant Valchar saved me," Karol said grimly. "When he came up here, I was fighting with this *hajzl*." I didn't know the word but got his meaning clear enough when he kicked the corpse in the corner. "Thought I would die. But it was the lieutenant he got."

I knelt next to Valchar. So that was the noise that had drawn him up here. Karol had already wrapped his wound. I touched his side. The cloth was warm under my fingers and a little damp from either sweat or blood or both. I reached up and pushed his sticky blond hair off his forehead. His brows were furrowed together, and his mouth was pinched. He looked so serious. I always thought of him as cheerful, even when I was rude to him, and I hated to think he'd look this way forever.

His eyes slowly opened. My hand froze.

"Evgenia?" His voice was soft, like he was falling asleep.

I didn't pull my hand back. I stroked his hair again.

"You'd better not die, Valchar. I mean it."

And right then his dry lips quirked up, his face lightened, and there was a hint of the smile I couldn't forget.

"Call me Jiri, and I won't."

I huffed, caught between a laugh and a groan. My nose prickled, and my skin heated. I was blushing and crying, and it was all too much. Why was I such an ass to him? He was just a boy. A *nice* one. I could've gotten to know him instead of hating him for so long. That was what war did, though. It turned you against people who should've been friends.

I patted his face sharply and felt tingles in my palm. He blinked his eyes open wider.

"I'll call you that if you stand up on your own two feet," I said. "Not before."

"Fierce Zhenya," he whispered. He closed his eyes again. "I don't think I can."

I sat back on my heels. Karol watched us quietly, tears pouring down his cheeks. He loved his lieutenant. That didn't surprise me. With all Valchar did for me and Anna, he'd probably done a lot more for his men. He cared about people. No wonder Kostya had liked him.

"He needs a doctor," Karol said.

"Well." I sighed. "I know where to find one."

Getting Valchar downstairs was ugly. Karol and I were both injured, and we struggled to carry him smoothly. Valchar moaned in pain with every twist and bump. I did, too. My chest ached, my fingers bled, and by the time we got him to the porch I wanted to fall down next to him.

But there were more bodies. We couldn't leave them there.

Karol and I carried and dragged all the Czech bodies into the main parlor. Anna saw what we were doing and came in to close their eyes and cross their hands over their chests. We ended up with a long line of bodies, one lost soul after another.

So many dead boys. Kostya would have fit in here. And Lev. Agapov, too. The Czechs had just been fighting for their own people. They might have helped the Whites, and they didn't care about our revolution, but they wanted freedom just like we did. They wanted to protect the people they loved, too. I sniffed as I looked down at them. I tried not to cry. Anna slung her arm around my back, pulling me close.

We called people who died heroes. But it made no sense to send heroes off to die. We needed them. We needed leaders like Kostya to help us rebuild. We needed artists like Lev and Nurka Petrova to remind us what mattered. And we needed kind souls like Valchar and Agapov to make it all worthwhile.

Anna let go of me and knelt next to one of the soldiers, a light-haired man lying peacefully on damp cloths. She reached behind her neck and slipped off her necklace, the one that belonged to her sister. She tucked it into his folded hands, and then she clasped her own together.

"Holy God, Holy Mighty, Holy Immortal . . ."

I got down on my knees and listened as she prayed.

33

ANNA

IT WAS NOT UNTIL WE stepped outside the house, in the full light of day, that I had the opportunity to take a closer look at Evgenia. And my heart broke all over again for her.

The skin around her eyes was mottled and angrily red; her cheeks were swollen to twice their size and so misshapen that they almost completely covered her eyes. Dried blood smeared her face and clothing. I had seen wounded war veterans in better shape.

"Zhenya," I breathed. "What did he do?" I reached for her hand but she pulled it away quickly. Her fingers trembled, and when I looked again, I saw that the tips were red and caked with blood. *She was missing two fingernails.*

She restlessly knelt to fiddle with Jiri's uniform. I had been relieved to find him conscious, but he needed immediate medical attention, and we were now preparing to head for the doctor's. Karol was off searching for some way to transport Jiri.

"It doesn't matter," Evgenia said.

"It does," I said, my throat tight. "May I hug you?"

She shook her head, but I reached for her anyway, and she did not resist, rising into my arms. Her chin dipped onto my shoulder.

"I almost wish he were alive, so that I could kill him again."

"Well, you did shoot him twice," she said.

I laughed, the sound wet with my tears, and released her.

We made slow progress in returning to Iset. Karol had found a small, low wagon that he affixed to his horse. Jiri lay on his side in the wagon, his feet hanging over the back, as we made our way down the road. Evgenia preferred to walk, complaining of pains in her chest, while I rode atop Buyan and fought to stay awake.

It was a cool, overcast morning. The doctor lived in the center of Iset, on a large square with several houses, a couple of small, shuttered shops, and an onion-peaked church. It was disturbingly quiet. A few shadowed faces spied on us from inside the houses lining the square, likely waiting to see if any soldiers would follow us. The noise of the fighting at the jail must have frightened everyone into their homes.

The doctor's house was a one-story log cabin with a dark red door. It was humble, but I noticed flowers under the windows and a well-polished iron knocker, setting it apart from the surrounding houses. Karol and I waited as Evgenia knocked several times.

"Yes?" The man who answered was around Papa's age, with a thin mustache and spectacles. Despite appearing relatively prosperous he wore a plain kosovorotka and no shoes.

"Can you help us, Mikhail Petrovich?" Evgenia asked simply.

The doctor's stern face softened as his eyes trailed over our pathetic collection of bruises, wounds, and bloodstains. He nodded.

"Come inside."

The front room held only a long, wooden table with two benches, and an open-shelved medicine chest full of vials and supplies. For a second I imagined myself back in Petrograd, visiting a war hospital with Mama and my sisters. They had drawn from such chests to treat fevers and pain, to clean lesions, to comfort the men who fought for Russia. Mama, like Papa, perhaps hadn't understood the lives of peasants. She was satisfied with the status quo. But she and my sisters had been healers. They treated hundreds of men. They'd saved many.

The demon who took their lives was lying cold and alone in a dark basement now. He could hate me for all of eternity, if his soul so desired. I'd given him no more than he deserved.

Mikhail Petrovich called his wife into the room. She was a short, plump woman with a lively face, and between the two of them, they gently lifted Jiri onto the table. The rest of us stepped out to wait in a little inner courtyard, where a few chickens wandered and pecked at the grass. I leaned back against the rough wooden wall and slid all the way down to sit, undignified but too exhausted to care. My arm ached, the wound underneath Evgenia's makeshift bandages throbbed painfully, and all I wanted was to sleep. But I could not stop thinking about Jiri, and whether he would live.

"I'm going to bring the rest of the men here," Karol said. "Probably some of them can use a doctor's care."

"They need it," Evgenia agreed. She sat next to me.

After Karol left we sat quietly. Every so often we heard Jiri moaning inside the house, but there was surprisingly little noise. The hens clucked and shuffled in the grass. A few birds sang to one another from somewhere out of sight. Evgenia breathed heavily. For the first time since the Ipatiev house—since that June afternoon I sat out in the yard, smoking with my sisters—I was not afraid.

"Are we safe, at last?" I said.

Evgenia shrugged.

"Maybe. Stravsky's still around here somewhere. And there'll be soldiers on the road less friendly than Valchar." She rested her hand on the rifle beside her unconsciously.

"At least no one will be chasing us."

With her other hand, she took mine.

"No. We'll get you to your cousin, and your general. Don't worry."

The doctor called us inside. Jiri had fainted at some point during his treatment, but Mikhail Petrovich and his wife seemed satisfied with their work. They'd cleaned the blood off his face and chest and wrapped his torso with clean bandages. The piercing smell of antiseptic lingered in the clean room, tickling my nose.

"Will he be all right?" I asked.

"Yes—sit down," the doctor said urgently. He pulled me over to a bench beside the table. "You're next. The young man is going to be fine. The wound wasn't deep enough to need further operation, but he needs several days of rest. He's been moved around too much already."

I muttered a quick prayer of thanks under my breath. God

had spared Jiri's life, and I was so glad that I might have cried. He wouldn't die for me.

"Days?" Evgenia echoed.

"At least. You don't want his stitches to split open, do you? Let him rest."

Evgenia looked at me. I knew precisely what she was thinking—we could not afford such a long delay. General Leonov might leave before we reached Ekaterinburg, and where would I go then?

"We'll figure something out," I whispered to her.

Mikhail Petrovich bade me take off my shirt; I carefully maneuvered it out from underneath my sarafan so that my corset remained out of sight. He had me lie down on the bench and then set to work cleaning and sewing both entrance and exit wounds below my shoulder. I had refused the morphine he offered, as I noticed his low supply, but downed a glass of vodka that made me mercifully light-headed. The procedure was still excruciating. I cried out and squeezed Evgenia's good hand more than once. When it finally ended, I felt perfectly sober again.

"Drink plenty of water, eat some red meat, and sleep," the doctor said as I sat up. "You should be fine as long as you stay away from men with guns."

"Thank you." I peeked at the neat stitches. "You have a defter hand than many surgeons I have known."

He smiled—the first hint of friendliness we had yet seen. With his carefully groomed mustache and intelligent eyes, he reminded me of the overly serious doctors I had volunteered beside in Petrograd. It had always been Masha's and my job to cheer up the patients after the doctors passed through.

"What brought you to Iset?" I asked curiously. "Rather than setting up practice in a city, where you might have more patients?"

"I'm needed here," he said gruffly. "Maybe I'd make more money there, but I'd do less good."

Guilt flared inside me like a flame, prickling my neck and arms, likely turning me red. This accomplished doctor had dedicated his life to people who would otherwise have had no access to medical care whatsoever. My family and I always prided ourselves on doing good for our people, but we had never sacrificed for them. We'd never gone without so someone else could survive, though we'd had more power to do so than anyone.

It was true that I had lost more than most people. I had lost my family, and our homes, and everything we once owned. The property taken from us would benefit the people of Russia— but they'd had to take it. We never freely gave it.

I looked down, hiding my mortified face as Evgenia sat beside me on the bench. I felt transparent, as though if she caught my eyes she'd see straight into my selfish, uncaring soul. And was that not what she'd thought of me when we first met? Had she not been right after all?

"Who did this to you?" Mikhail Petrovich surveyed the horrifying extent of Evgenia's injuries and shook his head.

"It doesn't matter," she said.

I swallowed, my throat tight. She'd gone through all of this—lost so much—for me. Only to help me. And what had I done in return?

The doctor cleaned and applied ointments to her bruises, wrapped her fingers, and bandaged her under her chest.

Commander Yurovsky and his men had broken her ribs in that jail.

"Take this," he said when he'd finished with her, and shoved a half-full vial of aspirin tablets at her. "For the pain."

"Thanks," Evgenia said. "Sorry we can't pay you."

He actually winked at her.

"It doesn't matter." He disappeared into the next room to speak with his wife.

"Are you feeling any better?" I asked.

"Not really. I guess I should try one of these," she said as she gingerly plucked a tablet from the jar. "I just swallow it, right?"

Another lump formed in my throat.

"That's right," I said. "He's a good man, the doctor, isn't he?" She didn't answer at once. "Do you not agree?"

"I wish I'd just *asked* him to help Kostya," she said, her voice tight like she was fighting tears. "He might have done it for free. I think he's a communist. I saw him at a party meeting once, talking to Katia Morozova. I didn't know then that he was the doctor."

I pulled her head onto my shoulder, wanting to be closer and give her something other than grief.

"I'm sorry," I said.

"Me too."

We sat quietly for a few minutes, as Evgenia mourned and I came to a decision. I waited for her to stop sniffling before I spoke.

"I want to give him my jewels," I said.

She pulled away and looked at me askance.

"Who?"

"The doctor," I said. "You and your brother were right, Zhenya. They should not belong to me anymore. Mikhail Petrovich can use them to help the people who live here, or he can give it to the soviet, if he thinks that best. It shouldn't be *me*."

I wished my parents could have been there. I wished they'd had the chance to get to know Evgenia and her family, too. If they had, I knew they'd be proud of me. And perhaps they were even now.

Evgenia snickered.

"Do you find something funny?" I demanded.

She snickered again, then laughed, then held her side in pain because the movement clearly hurt, and soon we were both laughing.

"Are you turning revolutionary, Anya?"

I huffed, nudging her with my elbow.

"I simply want to do what's right. And you have made some good points over the past few days. *But*"—I narrowed my eyes at her—"I prefer a peaceful revolution."

She shook her head.

"There's no such thing."

"A humane one, then."

She went quiet at that, seeming to like the word.

"Take it off, then." She grinned.

She helped me unlace the corset and slide it onto the bench between us, its twinkling rainbow of colors shining through the thin layer of cloth. My family had taken such care to protect our future with this corset. It had protected me in more ways than they ever dreamed. Now it was time to share that with someone else.

"Keep a couple for yourself," Evgenia whispered.

I looked at her in surprise.

"I don't want it," I said. "After all, the more one has, the more one wants, no?"

"We still have to make it to Ekaterinburg. We don't know what we'll run into. You can fight for equality and still look out for yourself, all right? I don't need you to be a martyr."

I giggled, and seeing the sense in her argument, dropped a couple of the smallest gems into my pocket.

When Mikhail Petrovich and his wife returned, I lifted the corset to show them. The doctor stood utterly still. His wife sat down heavily on the other bench, her hand on her heart.

"Where did these come from?" she asked.

"They belonged to my family. Now they belong to Russia, as they always should have. I think I can trust you to use them to help people."

"You could give them to the soviet," Evgenia suggested, because God forbid anyone forget to mention the soviet.

I made a face at her, wagging my tongue teasingly. She tugged at my hair. It was almost like having a sister again.

34

EVGENIA

MIKHAIL AND HIS WIFE WERE happy to give us even more salves and pills after they got Anna's gems. And they gave us a bundle of food for the road, which was why they'd gone into the other room in the first place. We thanked them and went outside to check on Buyan.

The Czech soldiers came rumbling into the square right as we stepped out. They were mostly on horseback, with a couple of men lying in the bed of a wagon. Anna and I waved them over and sent the sick men inside. The rest of the soldiers stood in a group, shouting at one another.

We couldn't understand them, but it was obvious they were arguing. One of them kept pointing in our direction. I glanced at Anna.

"That doesn't look good," I said. She shook her head, pressing her lips together tightly.

"Noisy bunch, aren't they?"

I smiled as Anton walked over to us. He'd been hiding among the horses, but I was glad to see him now, just as dirty and lanky as I remembered. He patted my shoulder.

"It's good to see you again," he said. "And this must be Anna?"

I'd been dying to tell him. Now that we were all free, I didn't have to keep the secret anymore.

"It's Anastasia, actually," I said.

Anna narrowed her eyes. I smiled again.

"This is Anton Utkin," I said. "He's a journalist. He's all right. He was in jail with me. The Reds arrested him in Ekaterinburg."

"She's correct," he said cheerfully. "I used to write for *Delo Naroda*, a newspaper in Moscow and Petrograd. I came to Ekaterinburg a little while ago to cover the situation of the royal family. The Bolsheviks noticed me poking my nose in— and I guess it's pretty hard to miss." He patted his nose like an old pet. "If you have a story to share, I am all ears."

"Oh, she has a story. Don't you, Anya?"

She'd wanted to find a journalist to tell her story. Now one had landed in our laps. Her eyes lit with understanding; she took a breath and then turned to Anton.

"If Evgenia trusts you, then I will, too. My real name is Anastasia Nikolaevna Romanova," she said. "The soviet government here announced that they executed my father, Nikolai Alexandrovich Romanov, but in truth they murdered my entire family. I was the only person to escape."

She took the folded postcard from her pocket and handed it to him. I'd been so angry when I saw that postcard. Now it felt like I'd always known. She was still Anna, and I loved her, no matter whose daughter she was.

Anton's face got very serious. He glanced back and forth

between Anna and the photograph of the royal family on the postcard. Did he recognize her? She was younger and happier in the picture, and had longer hair. But it was obviously her.

"I have further evidence," she said, "but we will need to speak with the doctor to show it to you."

"I'm at your disposal," he said.

Karol walked over to us then. He watched the ground, like he didn't want to see our faces. The Czechs had stopped arguing and were now watering their horses, getting ready to go.

"I'm sorry," Karol said. "The men are upset that we lost so many men at the house. I told them that we all wanted to help you—but they're angry. They . . . Some of them blame you." He glanced at Anna.

"That's ridiculous!" I burst out. "It's not her fault."

"I tried to convince them," Karol said. "But Josef is in charge as long as Lieutenant Valchar is ill. He agreed to escort you two"—he gestured at me and Anton—"because the men we rescued from the jail insist. But they refuse to bring you, Anna. I'm so sorry."

"They can go to the devil," I snapped.

"Listen," Karol went on. "I can take you. I'm staying here with the injured men and Lieutenant Valchar. As soon as they're ready, we'll take the wagon and horses and we can go together. But that may not be for a week or more."

"Can the lieutenant not simply order them to bring the girls?" Anton suggested.

"No," Anna said.

She met my confused look by taking my hand.

"We'll be better off without Josef's *protection*, believe me," she said softly.

The roads were more dangerous than ever now. With the armies fighting their way out of Ekaterinburg, it could be rough going. But Anna knew the Czechs better than I did. I trusted her word as much as she trusted mine.

"It's up to you," I said.

"Evgenia and I will find our own way to Ekaterinburg. Thank you for all the help you've offered us, Karol. I will look for you once we're safe in the city."

"And I will accompany you, as well," Anton added.

I wouldn't have minded traveling with him, but Anna shook her head at that, too.

"No. The soldiers will move faster than the rest of us, and you need to be with them. Once I tell you my story, you must reach Ekaterinburg as quickly as possible to publish it. Find a telegraph, a telephone, *something* to relay your story to your newspaper. Whatever happens to me, the truth must be told."

"Absolutely not!" Anton said. "Whoever you are, I can't leave two young women alone. It's not safe."

Scrawny as he was, Anton didn't look like he'd offer any protection. I doubted he had much experience using a gun, either. Anna was right. The truth was more important.

"You have to listen to her," I said. "Or she won't tell you her story."

Anna smiled at me.

"You'll want Zhenya's part of the tale, too," she said.

Anton gave in. He made plans to catch up with the Czechs at the Gersky house, where they were going first to bury the bodies. Then the three of us sat down behind the doctor's house. Anna started, telling the story of her family being locked up in Ekaterinburg, all the way through meeting me. I picked it up from there, and we traded off, finishing with Yurovsky's body in the cellar of the Gersky house.

Anton scribbled notes on paper he'd borrowed from the doctor. We took him inside to show him the corset and then waved him off when it was all done.

"I hope we see him again," I said. "Him and Valchar, too."

Anna sighed.

"Let's go say our goodbyes."

Valchar was awake by then. He was still lying on the table, only now he had his men to keep him company. He stopped his Czech chattering when we entered.

"Anna, Evgenia," he said. "Please wait for us. I know I'm sick, but—"

"Jiri, I insist that you stop worrying," Anna said. She held up a finger to her lips, shushing him. "Zhenya and I will be quite all right. You've done all that you can for us, and we are so grateful."

"I thank you," he said. "The doctor says we can stay here to rest, because you pay them."

Anna's face lit up, and my heart warmed. Her gift was already starting to pay off.

"I am so glad to hear it. Make sure you follow his advice and get all the rest you need, Jiri, won't you? And when you come to Ekaterinburg, find General Leonov and ask for me. Zhenya and I both want to see you there."

His eyes shifted over to me. One side of his mouth lifted.

"Is that true, Zhenya?"

I pretty much stopped breathing. My cheeks heated. At

least he probably couldn't see me blush behind all the purple bruises on my face.

"Anya has a big mouth," I said.

"But an honest one, yes?" she teased, elbowing me.

"You should come find us," I muttered.

Jiri smiled, wide and bright.

"Good," he said.

"Good," Anna agreed. She bent over and kissed his forehead. "God bless you, Jiri. Please take care of yourself."

She rose and looked at me expectantly. So did Valchar. My face got even hotter. Now Anna was smirking as she watched to see what I'd do.

"Turn around." I pushed at her until she looked away. Then I leaned down and kissed Valchar's cheek. It was thick with stubble. I'd thought my lips were numb from the bruising, but they tingled as I stood.

He caught my arm.

"See you soon, Zhenya," he said.

"In Ekaterinburg," I agreed. "See you there, Valchar."

"Not Jiri?"

"You're not standing yet."

He laughed.

"I find you in Ekaterinburg, I stand, and you call me Jiri then, yes?"

"It's a deal."

I grabbed Anna's arm and hurried her out of the house, but I couldn't stop smiling. I felt like I'd won something.

The day was cloudy and perfect for working. I should have been in the fields with Mama and Kostya, not helping the tsar's daughter load up Buyan for another journey. Not thinking about how my brother could've lived if I'd just asked the doctor for help. Not touching my lips because I could still feel a Czech soldier's skin. Not seeing Nemov's fists every time something moved in the corner of my eye.

"Let's get moving," I said. "Before anyone notices us."

Anna glanced around the square nervously. We led Buyan to the road, back the way we came a few days ago. We were going to avoid Pavlovo and head straight south. But we'd make slow progress. I couldn't move fast with my broken ribs, and Anna wasn't that lively, either. Using the side roads to steer clear of armies would slow us down, too. It would take a couple of days to reach the city. We'd have to sleep in the woods, give Buyan a lot of breaks, and try not to get into any trouble.

At least Karol had loaded me up with bullets. If the worst happened, I'd go down fighting.

"Keep fighting."

I'd keep fighting even if we made it to Ekaterinburg. I'd fight for a revolution that brought everyone along, even the children of landlords. I'd go home and help Mama protect our land. I'd tell Dasha and Pyotr that we had to build something better than what the Bolsheviks wanted. You could seize the means of production without burning innocents or torturing prisoners. You could make change by doing the right thing.

Couldn't you?

While I figured that out, I'd have to put my trust in someone. For now that was Anna.

"I've never been to a city before," I said.

She smiled. "I always loved leaving the palace to visit my parents' friends in Petrograd. So much happens in cities—not only things like theater and shopping, but conversation, too. There are so many interesting people for you to meet. You ought to come with me to the Crimea. You and Alena Vasilyevna. My grandmother and aunt will welcome you both with open arms, I promise."

That sounded like the silly future I'd dreamed up when she first offered me a diamond. I couldn't imagine going that far. I couldn't picture us in Ekaterinburg, let alone Crimea. But it wasn't like I could bring Anna back to Mednyy. She'd never be safe under the Bolsheviks. That meant I'd either have to say goodbye to my old life, or to her.

I added that to the list of things I didn't want to think about.

"What'll we do in the Crimea? Drink tea and swim all day?"

"No. You know I cannot go back to those ways, Zhenya. That's why I gave up the corset. I know I need to change. *Russia* needs to change. And we will."

But who was going to change it? The Whites would take us backward if they won. People with power didn't share it just because you asked. You had to burn things down. And that was fine, if you remembered you were dealing with *people*. People like Anna were more than just landlords and kulaks.

The Bolsheviks didn't care about people. They didn't think the price of freedom mattered. Anyone who did what they did would never let us live free. I still wanted more power for peasants, and communism. But we had to get it without losing our souls. We had to act better than the tsars if we wanted to rule better.

"We will all be all right," Anna said. She looked at me sideways, then took my wrist in her soft fingers. "You believe me, don't you?"

"Sure."

She tugged at me.

"Don't you remember *Dead Souls?*" she pressed. "We are harder than anything the world can throw at us."

I nodded. In a way she was right. Nothing had stopped us yet. If Yurovsky and these wounds and our sorrows hadn't beat us, maybe we'd make it after all.

But it wasn't hardness that would get us through this world. It was each other.

AUTHOR'S NOTE

The legend of Anastasia is an old and beloved one. Until 2007 people believed she might have survived. There were many pretenders throughout the years who claimed to be the lost Romanov daughter.

Unfortunately, we now know that the entire Romanov family died in the Ipatiev House basement. The Ekaterinburg Soviet ordered Yakov Yurovsky to execute them. Very early in the dark morning of July 17, 1918, he and his guards brought the family down to the cellar and massacred them—along with their servants Anna Demidova, Alexei Trupp, and Ivan Kharitonov, and their doctor, Eugene Botkin. All four Romanov daughters wore jewel-lined corsets, which actually did repel the bullets. The girls were shot and bayoneted repeatedly until they died.

The civil war raged on for another three years. The White Army eventually lost, and the Bolsheviks controlled Russia for the next seventy years. They formed the Union of Soviet Socialist Republics (USSR), or the Soviet Union for short.

As Evgenia (an entirely fictional character) fears, the party that took power with brutal tactics went on to govern with brutal tactics. The first thirty years of communist rule in Russia were marked with mass starvation, terror, forced labor, and repression. While the country became safer and more prosperous after dictator Joseph Stalin died in 1953, the communist government began to decline, and collapsed in 1991.

The Czechoslovak Legion did find their way home, and

won independence after the end of World War I. The free country of Czechoslovakia was founded on October 28, 1918. My own grandfather, who shares a name with Anna's and Evgenia's favorite Czech officer, was born there seven years later.

The history of the Russian Revolution and civil war is fascinating, dramatic, and useful in understanding the shape of world events in the twentieth century. If you'd like to learn more, check out the bibliography on the next page.

BIBLIOGRAPHY

For an introduction to the Russian Revolution or the true story of the Romanovs, I encourage you to start with one of the following:

Figes, Orlando. *A People's Tragedy: The Russian Revolution 1891–1924*. New York: Penguin Books, 1998.

Fleming, Candace. *The Family Romanov: Murder, Rebellion & the Fall of Imperial Russia*. New York: Schwartz & Wade Books, 2014.

Massie, Robert, K. *Nicholas and Alexandra: The Classic Account of the Fall of the Romanov Dynasty*. New York: Random House, 2011.

Steinberg, Mark D., and Vladimir M. Khrustalëv. *The Fall of the Romanovs: Political Dreams and Personal Struggles in a Time of Revolution*. New Haven, CT: Yale University Press, 1995.

From Steinberg and Khrustalëv's volume I drew the original text of the Bolsheviks' announcement of Tsar Nicholas's execution, and the words sung by the people of Pavlovo in the opening chapter. In reality, those words were found in graffiti scrawled by guards on the walls of Ipatiev House and read as follows (as translated by Steinberg and Khrustalëv):

To all of the peoples Nicholas said
As for a Republic, go fuck yourselves instead
Our Russian Tsar called Nick
We dragged off the throne by his prick

For further reading on the revolutionary and civil war time period, see:

Azar, Helen. *The Diary of Olga Romanov: Royal Witness to the Russian Revolution.* Yardley, PA: Westholme, 2014.

Bainton, Roy. *A Brief History of 1917: Russia's Year of Revolution.* New York: Carroll & Graf, 2005.

Eagar, Margaret. *Six Years at the Russian Court.* London: Hurst & Blackett, 1906.

Figes, Orlando. *Peasant Russia, Civil War: The Volga Countryside in Revolution.* London: Phoenix Press, 2001.

Figes, Orlando. *Revolutionary Russia 1891–1991: A History.* New York: Metropolitan Books, 2014.

Gorky, Maxim. *My Childhood.* Translated by Ronald Wilks. New York: Penguin Classics, 1991.

Massie, Robert, K. *The Romanovs: The Final Chapter.* New York: Ballantine Books, 1995.

Mawdsley, Evan. *The Russian Civil War.* New York: Pegasus Books, 2009.

Pipes, Richard. *A Concise History of the Russian Revolution*. New York: Vintage, 1996.

Rappaport, Helen. *The Romanov Sisters: The Lost Lives of the Daughters of Nicholas and Alexandra*. New York: St. Martin's Griffin, 2015.

Reed, John. *Ten Days That Shook the World*. Urbana, IL: Project Gutenberg, 2012.

Semyonova Tian-Shanskaia, Olga. *Village Life in Late Tsarist Russia*. Edited by David Ransel. Bloomington: Indiana University Press, 1993.

ACKNOWLEDGMENTS

Andrea Somberg, my literary agent, is a true partner and over-achiever, with a strong editorial eye and infinite patience. Her knowledge and guidance kept me moving forward during the long journey of bringing this book to life.

My editor Mekisha Telfer's targeted and insightful edits brought this book so much closer to my vision than I thought possible, and her faith made my dream a reality. Thanks also to the entire team at Roaring Brook Press—Aurora Parlagreco, Avia Perez, Connie Hsu, Brittany Pearlman, cover artist Aitch, and everyone else who contributed to creating this wonderful book and getting it into the hands of readers.

My mentor, Jen Mann, believed in this book and made me believe, too. She was the first person to get it, and gave me courage and hope. It was through Alexa Donne's encouragement that I applied to Author Mentor Match and met Jen, and for that and more, she too has my gratitude.

Amateur and professional historians alike helped tether this story to reality even as it imagined a (slightly) better one. Many thanks to Mark Steinberg, Greg Ryzhak, and Anna Doumnova as well as keen-eyed readers Katia Raina, Anya Konstantinovsky, and Elizabeth Abosch! It was a joy to work with them all.

Early readers Heather Glick, Jessica Plummer, Graci Kim, and Emily Beck are hugely talented writers who shared their time, wisdom, and words with me. And enough cannot be said of my Lady Hook Revenge crew, the brilliant Jennifer Poe, Rosemary Melchior, Elishia Merricks, Gigi Rodriguez, Shannon C. F. Rogers, Theresa Park, Sara Lord, Randi Burdette, Phoebe Low, and Samantha Panepinto, who have read pages, kept me company, and cheered me on over the years.

Thanks and love also to AMM r3; to Shirin P. for reviewing the historical notes; to Becky Allen, whose debut novel inspired me to pick this one up again; to David L., who helped me find my soft side (and thereby my characters'); and to Orlando Figes, who doesn't know me but whose wonderful book *A People's Tragedy* ignited my love of history and this era in particular.

A special shout-out to English teachers I was so lucky to have: Fred Daly, who laughed when I stayed up all night to finish *Jane Eyre*; Paige Passis, who expected great things from me; Chris Burchfield, who made me memorize poetry I carry with me today (Nature's first green is [still] gold); and George Faison, who saw a strong writer in me and let me know it.

Thanks also to the Barnard and Columbia Butler Libraries, the New York Public Library's Schwarzmann Building, and Dear Mama Coffee in East Harlem for many useful resources and productive workdays. And to Advanced Copy Center, which offers the best manuscript printing rates in the city.

Eternal thanks, always, to: Kevin, Helen, and Crystal, because what would my stories be without siblings? To Mom for your constant support and good company; and to Dad, who would have loved nothing more than to add this book to his shelves. I love you all.